"Are you sure you know what you're saying?" she asked.

"I'm sure." He looked quite serious.

"Mick—"

"But it doesn't change anything." He stroked her hair. "I wish I could tell you I love you enough to do anything you say, but I can't."

"Or won't."

An expression of pain crossed his face. "Maggie, I didn't say that, and you shouldn't, either."

She reached up and caressed him tenderly. "Oh, dear. What are we going to do about all this?"

His grin was wry. "For the long run, damned if I know. For the short . . ." He leaned down and gave her a long, slow, deep kiss. After a moment she responded enthusiastically, and matters proceeded naturally from there. . . .

ABOUT THE AUTHOR

An avid traveler who recently journeyed to China with her college-age daughter, Sharon Brondos has used Colorado and Australia as backdrops in her sixth Superromance. Fans are sure to enjoy *Special Treasures*, which features Sharon's usual sure, lighthearted touch. Prepare to fall in love with the craggy hero from Down Under!

Books by Sharon Brondos

HARLEQUIN SUPERROMANCE

HARLEQUIN TEMPTATION

Don't miss any of our special offers. Write to us at the following address for information on our newest releases.

Harlequin Reader Service
901 Fuhrmann Blvd., P.O. Box 1397, Buffalo, NY 14240
Canadian address: P.O. Box 603,
Fort Erie, Ont. L2A 5X3

Sharon Brondos

SPECIAL TREASURES

Harlequin Books

TORONTO • NEW YORK • LONDON
AMSTERDAM • PARIS • SYDNEY • HAMBURG
STOCKHOLM • ATHENS • TOKYO • MILAN

Published April 1989

First printing February 1989

ISBN 0-373-70353-8

Dedicated, out of friendship,
to the real-life Maggie,
who makes jewels of thoughts:
Dr. Maggi Murdock,
political scientist and good buddy.

CHAPTER ONE

MAGGIE WELLINGTON FELT a sense of terror rising from a dark place deep within herself. The man who had just come into her jewelry shop was definitely going to rob her!

He had chosen an ideal time of day; early in the morning, just as she opened and before many people were out on the street and sidewalks of the small Colorado mountain resort town. Why hadn't she listened to the police chief when he had suggested that she operate at more normal hours and install an alarm connected to his office?

That was all hindsight, however. It was too late now. She was about to be deprived of everything she had worked so hard for. She would be lucky if her jewelry was all he took!

She hadn't looked up immediately when he had entered the shop, causing the little bell over the front door to chime. Since it was so early in the morning, she had figured it was only a delivery person, but when she had glanced at him, all of her instincts screamed danger. His back was turned, so she could only tell that he was a man of medium height with wide shoulders and short reddish-brown hair. He was wearing worn jeans, old work boots and a sheepskin jacket, but it was his hands that made her certain she was in trouble. They were big and scarred and they were turning her OPEN sign around so that it read CLOSED. Then they pulled down the fabric blind she used at night when working late in her back room. No one could see in to observe whatever he was going to do to her and her creations.

Maggie hunted around frantically with her wits as well as her eyes for something to use in defense.

"Miss Wellington?" The robber faced her and grinned. His features weren't as frightening as his hands, but they did her nerves little good. He was deeply tanned, and there were creases at the corners of his eyes and smile lines at his mouth. His teeth were white and a bit crooked. The edge of a front one was slightly chipped. His nose had obviously been broken at least once, and his green eyes as brilliantly cold as ice on the river in winter. "My name's Mick O'Shay."

"M-Mr. O'Shay?" Amazed she had the voice to repeat his name, Maggie was even more astonished he had given it. "W-what can I do for you?" *Cooperate*, she warned herself. *This might not be as bad as you think.*

"Oh." He held up an admonishing finger. "It's more what I can do for you, Miss Wellington." In his other hand he carried a battered gym bag, which he lifted up for her inspection. His grin widened and his motion made the edge of his jacket fall back from his left side, revealing the tip of a leather holster.

Maggie felt her knees weaken and she had to grasp the counter to keep from falling. He had a gun. "G-go ahead," she stammered. "Take whatever you want. Just please don't do anything. Don't hurt me."

"Hurt you?" Mick O'Shay stared at the pretty woman behind the counter. In contrast to her jet black hair, her face was as white as a sheet. Her big brown eyes were like those of a terrified kitten; her hands shook on top of the glass counter and her pale lips trembled as if she was about to start crying. Oh, for the love of Pete! She was probably thinking he was going to stage a stickup. The ridiculous notion hit him as extremely funny, and Mick started laughing.

The laughter shot a jolt of fury and courage through Maggie. It was one thing for a thug to enter her establishment and rob her. It was quite another for him to have fun doing it! She might be small, but he was going to find himself with a fight on his hands! With an inarticulate cry of rage, she launched herself from behind the counter in a gymnastics move she hadn't done in years and with another wild leap, she was on the robber, beating at him with her strong hands and kicking furiously with her feet.

"Hey. Hey!" Mick tried to adjust to the sudden onslaught, but he was fending off an agile, swearing demon of a woman. Short of decking her with a well-aimed fist, treatment he would never accord any female, he had no choice but to protect himself from her punishment until she ran out of steam. He raised one hand to guard his face and lowered the gym bag to shelter an even more tender region. "Miss, stop!" he yelled. "I'm only here to... Ow!" She connected with his nose and managed to kick the bag hard enough to pop the zipper open. A goodly part of Mick's fortune began to spill out onto the floor and under their feet.

That was it. The whole situation was now no longer funny or tolerable. One misstep and thousands of dollars worth of fine opals would be ground into useless dust. Mick dropped the bag and grabbed the woman, lifting her clear off the ground and trying to ignore the pounding of fists on his head and shoulders and the kicking of feet against his shins and knees. "Calm down, Miss," he bellowed. "I'm not a robber. I'm peddling opals I dug with my own hands, and I'm here to make you a very special...Oof!" A sharp knee rammed into his stomach. Mick wrapped his arms more tightly around her. It was like trying to contain a five-foot eel. "Will you listen to me!" he pleaded loudly. "I'm here to make you an offer of a treasure, the like of which you've never seen! Right now most of it's underfoot, just waiting to be smashed into nothing!''

Maggie hesitated. His accent was thick and nearly unintelligible, but she did hear the words *treasure* and *underfoot* and *smashed*. She quit hitting and kicking and swearing and looked down. It took but a moment for her to realize she had made a serious mistake.

The wooden floor gleamed with a veritable carpet of opals, each individually contained in a plastic bag. No robber brought jewels to a robbery, did he? She looked at the man who was carrying her as easily as if she were made of feathers.

''O'Shay, was it?'' she asked, unsure now how she ought to behave. She would try for casual. After all, she was still totally at the strange man's mercy, even if that strange man seemed to be bearing lavish gifts.

''Mick. Mick O'Shay.''

''And you're an opal dealer?''

''Miner and dealer. I sell my own goods.''

''Well, Mr. O'Shay, we seem to have had a slight misunderstanding here. Oh, my goodness! Your nose. Oh, I must have hit it hard.''

''Think nothing of it, lovey. It's been bonked by far bigger fists than yours. Although I've got to admit for such a tiny sheila, you do pack quite a wallop. Ready to call a truce and gab this thing out?'' His grin seemed genuine and was infectious. Maggie almost smiled herself. Almost.

''Why don't you start by putting me down.'' She rested her hands on his shoulders, feeling the iron muscles under his leather jacket. ''I'm not really comfortable talking business in this position.''

Mick was suddenly acutely aware of the burden he carried tightly against his body. She had relaxed and her softness molded itself naturally to him. Even through the baggy sweater she wore and the jacket he had on, he could feel her full breasts and the narrow waist his arms were wrapped around. And his right hand . . .

His right hand cupped the firm curve of a round buttock. It seemed formed for his touch, fitting so neatly into his palm. Furthermore, she was much prettier this close than she had seemed at first sight. "Uh, yeah," he said, feeling his face become warm. "Just let me step around these stones here. Now that we're friends, I'm not worried about you crunching 'em, but I'd like to be on the safe side." He moved gingerly to the far side of the room and deposited her carefully on her feet. Then he stepped back and tried smiling as winningly as possible.

Instead of smiling back, Maggie Wellington glared. She reached behind the counter, grabbed a box of Kleenex and shoved it toward him. Then, as he stanched his bloody nose, she started in, surprising him with the vigor of her venom.

"You've got some nerve, Mick O'Shay," she snapped. "Coming in here like a thief and scaring the daylights out of me! What if a policeman had walked by and heard me yelling? If one had burst in and seen us like that, we both might have ended up in the slammer. What did you do? Leave your common sense back in England?"

"Not England." Mick didn't know whether to be annoyed or amused. "Australia. And my venerable ancestors were Irish convicts. Not in the least well-intentioned towards the British Empire. Though the emotions have been watered down a bit with the passing generations." He pressed the tissue against his nose, then removed it, satisfied the bleeding had stopped.

"Australian." Maggie eyed the pile of opals. "Of course. Did you really mine those stones yourself, or are you looking for a fence?"

"Fence?"

"Someone to disguise the stones so the authorities won't recognize them. What I am asking is are they really yours and can you prove it?" She put her hands on her hips and continued to glare at him. "Or did you use your gun to take them from their real owner?"

Mick felt a cold flush of anger rising in his mind. "I'm no thief, Maggie Wellington," he said. "To my mind a thief is almost the lowest form of life—just one step above a murderer. I'll not tolerate you thinking I am one." He reached in his jacket pocket and took out a fat notebook. "Every one of those stones is registered in this book. I also have the customs sheet itemizing them. And I can tell you exactly where I dug or found each of them. So don't go insulting me by calling me a damned thief. I won't have it! As for the gun, it's simple good sense to carry protection with so many opals on me."

"Then why come sneaking in here, turning my sign around and pulling the blind if you wanted me to think you were an honest man?" She was not about to be intimidated by the brawny ape of a man who was acting insulted when he had asked for it.

He pointed at the small mountain of opals. "Was I just to top those out on your counter for all the world to see? Talk about inviting robbery. If the wrong person saw that, your little shop would be under siege before you could blink. I told you I brought a treasure. It's far more than that. It's a bloody fortune lying on your floor."

"Well, don't you think you ought to pick it up, then?"

He stared at her malevolently for a moment. "I guess I should. It's clear to me you aren't interested in anything I might have to show you." He turned his back on her and went over to the opals. Bending down, he started to scoop them up and put them back into the bag.

Maggie forced herself to count to ten and take a deep breath. She disliked the man intensely, but rarely did a jewel merchant of any kind come directly to her and offer to display his wares. She had always bought through middlemen, paying dearly, often for inferior stones, or she had sought out the merchants herself, spending valuable time traveling to them and then haggling over prices. Only a few times when she was still living in San Francisco had she been contacted personally. One of those times had yielded the finest stone she had ever been privileged to work with. Coincidently, it had been a large and unusually fiery opal, which she had bought under the strictest proviso that she would never reveal the identity of the man from whom she had purchased it. Also an Australian, he had seemed paranoid about thieves locating his mine through the jewelers he sold to.

"Just a minute," she said. "Don't be so hasty, Mr. O'Shay." She did know how to swallow her pride when necessary. It seemed that this was one of the times to do so.

He glanced at her over his shoulder and continued to put the opals away.

"Mr. O'Shay." Maggie walked carefully around to face him. She squatted down so she could look in his eyes. "I lost my temper, but I'm willing to apologize. You frightened me, and I lashed out. Not very adult of me, I suppose, but understandable, if you think about it. I'm alone here in the shop. Hardly anyone is out and about this early. I have enough valuable pieces to attract the attention of dishonest people, and you are a rather intimidating figure of a man. What was I to think?"

"You should have waited a few seconds to let me introduce myself and state my purpose clearly. I'm surprised that with such an immature and impulsive nature you've managed to stay in business at all."

Maggie held on to her temper by a fraying thread. "Mr. O'Shay. Did you or did you not come to Sullivan Springs to show me your opals? If you try telling me I was just one stop along the road, I won't believe you. We are a dead end with nothing beyond us. When you came to the Springs, it was because you wanted to. Am I right?'' She crooked her neck slightly, trying to read the expression on his averted face.

Mick had to keep from looking at her for a moment. She had managed to hit the nail square on the head. He *had* been seeking her out. Margaret Worth Wellington was the designer of the brooch with the telltale opal. She was his one and only lead to the bastard who had killed Ian and copped the stone. Much as he would have preferred to do his hunting by other means, he was stuck with this highly attractive, highly idiotic jewelry artisan. He could only hope he would be able to avoid the impulse to shake the stuffing out of her obviously cotton-filled brain before he got the lead he sought. Forcing himself to smile again, he raised his head.

''You've got my number, Maggie,'' he said, realizing that smiling at her didn't take such a terrible effort at that. Her full lips turned upward slightly and her brown eyes looked like the finest amber shot through with gold. ''I saw some pieces you made in San Francisco and decided I wanted you to work with the stones in my collection. The inferior ones I plan to sell to other jewelers. The finest, though, I'd like to be set under your hand.'' Actually, he thought, it wasn't as much of a lie as it might have been. It was obvious she wasn't just a hack worker; her treatment of the stolen stone had been nothing short of magical. The gold filigree she had used to set the opal in displayed the fiery gem so well, he would have assumed a far more experienced craftsman had worked on the brooch—certainly one older than the twenty-eight years he'd learned she was. If Ian's stone was any example, she might prove to be a true genius. A genius in disguise, he reminded himself. She really didn't look like anything but a cute little sheila. Not that that was so bad. No, it wasn't bad, at that.

"Oh." Maggie sat back on her heels. This was an odd development. She hadn't been in the business long enough to get much of a reputation. After graduating from college with a degree in art, she had apprenticed with a master jeweler long enough to understand what she wanted to do and had then branched out on her own. Her parents had aided her financially, but then tragedy had struck. For a time she'd had little energy or leisure for work. Only now that she and her father had moved to the Rocky Mountains, far away from the scene of sorrow and pain, had she really been able to let her creative juices flow. Her only work of note before the move had been an unusual opal brooch.

"I can't imagine," she said, "what pieces of mine you might have seen, Mr. O'Shay. Except for one opal brooch I made, my best works are still here on display in the shop. With Christmas coming I hope to sell some of them, but—"

"It was the opal." His tone betrayed his excitement. "I've never seen the fire in a stone displayed so brilliantly. Have you any idea where it was found? Or who found it?" he added, hoping she would spill the beans immediately and save him the trouble of having to deal with her further.

But she wasn't spilling. "Oh, Mr. O'Shay." She stood up, brushing off her jeans. "I'm afraid that is privileged information. It's a policy of mine not to reveal the identities of my suppliers. Many of them request silence. For their protection, of course. Many miner-dealers are extremely nervous about revealing the location of their claims for fear of claim-jumping or robberies. I know you'll understand that. I will accord the same courtesy to you, providing we reach an agreement, of course."

He closed the bag and stood. He hadn't figured she would be clever enough to keep her source confidential. This made matters much more difficult and complicated. He was going to have to win her trust, or at least her loyalty. Then, perhaps, she would give him the information he needed.

"Let's give it a go then," he said, finally. "Is there a place where I can show you these without half the population of your town getting an eyeful?"

"Right this way." She led him into the room at the rear of the store that served as a workroom.

Mick stifled the first comment that came to mind. He was bound and determined to be as pleasant as possible until he got what he had come for, but the workroom was a disaster. She had her tools set up on a wooden table that was thick and serviceable but gouged and filthy from stains and burns. Pieces of metal were scattered about haphazardly. They gleamed in the fluorescent light, and Mick would have been willing to bet there was a thousand bucks worth of silver and gold in scrap alone. The floor was just as littered, but with paper and the remains of fast-food restaurant bags and cups. On the walls hung sketches of designs. Here and there she had pasted a photograph of a famous stone up beside the drawings. Like posters of rock stars in a teenager's bedroom, they indicated the yearnings of the shop's occupant. Although she was in her late twenties, he thought, she was not much more mature than a sixteen-year-old, judging from her actions and surroundings. The sooner he was out of here, the better! The only sign of good judgment on her part was a large safe set against the back wall.

Maggie cleared an area on the worktable with a sweep of her arm. Then she bent down and took a velvet display board from a shelf under the table. "Why don't you put a few of the stones on this, Mr. O'Shay," she said. "Then I can see exactly what we're dealing with. But I'll warn you, I won't take a job I don't feel capable of giving my best to. Professional ethics, you understand."

Mick made no response. He stepped up to the table and opened his bag. After fishing around for a moment, he took out a handful of small bags and began to set the opals on the board. The silence in the room grew.

So did the tension.

Maggie kept herself from exclaiming aloud only by the strongest application of willpower. Never had she seen such consistent magnificence! He had said he carried a treasure in the bag. He was carrying a king's ransom! The stones were cut in a variety of shapes—oval, tear, round, oblong and even fascinating uneven configurations. She could tell that each piece had been cut specifically to show off its fire to the best advantage. To be asked to work such opals into jewelry was the chance of a professional lifetime. She simply could not refuse.

Besides, she knew in her heart she would do a first-rate job. "Mr. O'Shay," she said. "I have never seen anything like this. Anywhere. I'm honored you've even considered me to work on these."

"You'll do it?" He sounded so casual, she glanced at him in surprise. There wasn't a sign of what he was feeling in those green eyes.

"If you want me to, I'd be out of my mind to say no. I have a few rather ordinary pieces I want to finish for the holiday sales, but as soon as I'm done with them, I could start on—"

"No. I have a limited amount of time to spend here. You'll have to begin at once."

She bristled at his curt tone. "Your time isn't an issue, Mr. O'Shay. Just leave the stones, tell me when you want them and I'll have them ready. You needn't be inconvenienced."

"Sorry, but I can't leave the stones." He showed her a smile that didn't reach his eyes. "They're sort of my babies. I found them and I want to be with them all the way to the final sale. In fact, I insist on it. I won't enter into any deal unless you agree." It was the only way he could think of to stay near her long enough to get what he wanted.

Maggie couldn't think of a thing to say. She had never heard of a dealer insisting on being part of the artistic process. Suspicion about his motivation for bringing the stones to her rose.

"You see," he continued, not looking at her directly, "it's more than just a business deal for me. I've got a lot of emotion invested in these." He ran a fingertip caressingly over a particularly beautiful black opal. "I found this one the day my son turned seven. It's kind of my lucky stone."

"And you want to sell it?"

This time his smile seemed more genuine. "No. Actually, I'd like a ring made out of it—for myself. Can you handle men's jewelry?"

Maggie picked up the stone between her thumb and forefingers and examined it for fire and flaws. "Sure," she said, already picturing the heavy silver setting she would use. "Look." She replaced the opal on the velvet and took a sketch pad from the table. With a few swift strokes, she limned her idea. "What do you think of this?" She handed him the drawing.

Mick stared at the paper. He could never have imagined a more perfect setting for his favorite stone. It was as if she had dipped into his mind and taken out a design that perfectly suited him. It was ornate, but not too fancy; rough without being crude. Perfect. He had been uncannily right about her. She did possess an unusual talent. "Um," he said, "this is fairly good. Would it be possible to have at least a dozen sketches like this by, say, day after tomorrow?"

"How about week after next?"

"Miss Wellington, I don't think I've made myself clear. I don't intend to wait while you finish up your other work. And I'm willing to pay for your time." He picked up a pencil from the table and jotted down a figure on the paper beside the sketch of the ring setting. "Something like this per piece suit you?"

Maggie all but exclaimed aloud. His offer was more than generous. The robbery she had feared would take place with herself as the criminal, if she accepted such a lavish commission! "That's too much money," she said. "I'll be happy with half that. And call me Maggie. Miss Wellington makes me sound like some old maid. Here in the Springs most of us residents are on a first-name basis. It's a friendly, informal place. I've gotten used to being just plain Maggie."

"There's hardly anything plain about you, Maggie." The complimentary words slipped out before Mick could stop them. *Stupid!* he thought, starting to berate himself for letting his eyes and hormones get in the way of his real purpose. Then he forgot almost entirely about that purpose.

Maggie Wellington blushed. Pink color rose from the collar of her ratty gray sweater and slowly, sensuously stained the pale skin of her face, her cheeks taking on the deepest, purest rosiness. Mick was utterly enchanted.

"You look like a prize opal yourself," he said softly reaching out to touch her skin with the same fingertip he'd used to caress the cold stone. The living jewel he touched was warm, however—hot where the color was pulsing like elusive fire. Impulsively, he curved his palm so that her small chin was cupped in it.

Maggie held very, very still. His hand was big and the skin on his palm rough and calloused. But it was also warm, and his touch was gentle to the point of delicacy.

And there was a strange light in his eyes that made her wonder if she ought not to be more afraid now than she had been when she'd thought he was going to rob her.

However, she found she was far from afraid. The blush that had burned her face seemed to have turned inward and was heating the rest of her. Her heartbeat speeded up, and her breathing grew faster. She could not look away from Mick O'Shay's emerald eyes.

He was going to kiss her. She wasn't going to stop him.

Mick fought with himself as his male instincts took control of his mind and moved his mouth closer and closer to the soft, parted lips that lured him irresistibly. She wore no lipstick, no makeup of any kind and that natural moistness and pale color was turning his juices on faster than the skillfully painted faces he had admired of late. It was as if he'd been content with mannequins and was now being confronted with a real, live woman. His mouth made contact with hers.

It was a step into another world, a step into a gentle, erotic fantasy. They didn't so much kiss as just touch; his thinner, slightly chapped lips rested questioningly against her full, satiny ones. Mick remembered how her body had felt pressed up against his and he was barely able to keep from embracing her and pulling her close again. But some instinct deeper than sexual desire warned him not to try.

Maggie hadn't lost her wits, although she knew she was acting as if she had. The kiss was so careful and gentle that she felt no anxiety, no alarm; only a warmth that suffused her entire self, body and mind. It was like stepping into sunlight after being in damp, cold darkness. Like slipping back under down covers after getting up briefly before dawn on a chill winter's morning. Like that first spring day after eons of snow and ice. Like—

"Maggie!" The yell was muffled, muted and far away. The pounding sound was what really got through to her brain. She stepped away from the Australian. "Someone...someone's at the front door, Mr. O'Shay." She blinked and looked up at him. "I...I'd better answer it."

Mick took a deep breath. "Maggie, I'm...I guess I overstepped. If you're put out at me, I can't say I blame you. I came here to talk business, not to be kissing you." The corners of his mouth turned up in a lopsided grin. "Though it was mighty pleasant."

"Yes, it was." The hollering of her name and the pounding on her door increased in volume, but Maggie couldn't break her gaze away from his. "And don't apologize. If I hadn't wanted you touching me, I would have let you know."

"I'm not apologizing, Maggie. Hadn't you best answer that door. Sounds as if someone's trying to break it down."

His tone was brisk and spoiled the spell. Maggie turned away before he could see her blush again and hurried out of the workroom. She unlocked the front door and threw it open. "Oh, hi," she said, suddenly feeling childishly guilty for kissing a stranger in her back room.

Mick leaned against the doorjamb, studying the newcomer. He was an older man with graying black hair and a trim, lean frame marred only by a slight softening of his belly. The man looked angrily from him to Maggie and put his arm around the woman's shoulders. "Who the hell is this?" he asked, gesturing in Mick's direction. His abrupt tone grated.

"I'm Mick O'Shay," Mick said, standing straight. "And who might you be?"

"Patrick Wellington," the older man replied, sliding his lower jaw forward belligerently. "Maggie's father. And what the hell are you doing with my little girl?" His brown eyes glittered with the exact same fiery anger Mick had seen in his daughter's eyes when she had attacked him like some wild banshee. Mick braced himself for combat.

CHAPTER TWO

"COME ON INSIDE, Papa," Maggie said. "It's cold." She pulled her father the rest of the way into the store and shut the door behind him. "There's nothing wrong. Mr. O'Shay is from Australia. He has some opals he wants me to mount. And they're some of the finest stones I've ever—"

"Beth Sprinkle called me and said she saw some man go into your place and then pull the blind shut." Patrick was still staring hostilely at Mick. He lowered the furry hood of his parka. The garment wasn't zipped up in spite of what Mick considered mind-numbing cold weather. "When you didn't raise them again after a while, she got concerned. Called me. I came down to see what was going on."

Mick assessed the situation and decided he could avoid trouble if he said something to alleviate the father's fears. So, he had kissed the daughter. It didn't mean he had to take a beating over it. "I didn't think it wise to leave the shop open, Mr. Wellington," he said, walking toward the man. "The stones I'd like Miss Wellington to work with are extremely valuable. If the wrong people knew she had them, she could be in some danger. I was simply taking precautions for her safety." He held out his hand.

"Hmm." Wellington didn't reach for the hand. He looked at his daughter. "You look shaken up, Mag. Are you sure...?"

"Papa! Will you please shake hands with Mr. O'Shay. He has made me an incredibly generous and attractive offer. I think the least we can do is be pleasant to him. Of course, I'm shaken up. It isn't every day I get a chance to work on jewels the quality of Mr. O'Shay's opals. And he found them all himself."

His daughter's scolding seemed to have the effect of defusing Patrick Wellington's paternal suspicions. Mick thanked his lucky stars the blind had been pulled. If the man had seen him wrestling with his child and then kissing her, there was no telling what might have happened. As it was, Wellington did shake hands with him briefly, just long enough for Mick to know that the older man was not as soft as his belly made him look. His facial features were youthfully firm, and Mick realized the daughter got her looks, at least in part, from her father. Mick decided he was mildly interested in meeting the mother.

"If I came on a little strong," Wellington said, "I guess I have to apologize. But Maggie, well, sometimes she needs looking after. You understand."

Mick glanced at Maggie and saw an annoyed expression pass over her delicate features before they relaxed in a smile. Both of these people seemed to be strong of spirit, so why the obvious dependence? *Papa? Little girl? Needs looking after?* She was a grown woman. Her kiss testified to that, if nothing else did. "I have a son, Mr. Wellington," he said. "So I do understand the concerns of a father. I've raised the boy by myself, and I've had to be a mother to him, too. It hasn't always been easy." To his amazement Patrick Wellington's eyes filled with tears and he turned away abruptly.

"I'll be heading back to the house now, Mag," he said, not looking at his daughter. "If you need me, call." Then he was out the door before she could say a thing. She shut the door behind him carefully, as if she was afraid of slamming it.

"Whew." Mick scratched the back of his head. "What'd I say? I sure seemed to have pushed the wrong button."

"It isn't you." Maggie raised the blind and turned the OPEN sign to the front. Her tone was sad. "My mother died several years ago. Papa still hasn't gotten over it yet. He's still grieving, and I don't know what to do about it." She crossed her arms over her chest and hugged herself.

"Grief's a strange emotion." Mick chanced putting a hand on her shoulder. "Some men get sad, some get angry. It's got to be worked out in its own way by each person."

Maggie looked at him. "Your wife died?"

"No." His eyes were cold again. "No, she abandoned me and Tad not long after he was born. Not liking the life of a miner's lady, she ran off and found herself men more to her taste in Sydney. We were both only seventeen when we married, so I guess a lot was going against us. Last I heard, she was living in Hong Kong with some banker. I swear I never grieved a day over that woman."

"Then who? You sound like you know what you're talking about."

"You want to hash out our life stories or make a deal over the opals?" His face showed he was keeping a variety of negative emotions barely in check.

"I'd like to make a deal." She injected as much ice into her voice as possible. What an idiot she was for letting down her guard with a total stranger. Letting down her guard and even *kissing* him. "But I will not agree to drop everything immediately. I'll put in extra hours at night and finish my other projects as soon as possible, but that's as far as I'm willing to compromise."

"Would it be asking too much for you to have a few show pieces ready before Christmas? I have three import shops, two on the coast and one in Denver, that are already carrying jewelry made from my opals. I'd be pleased if your work could be included in the collections. Listen, it isn't that I need the money, Maggie. I've plenty, and to spare. Mining was good to me. But I'm proud of my stones. I'd really be pleased if they made a bit of a splash, if you understand me." This part Mick didn't have to lie about. He did have a lot of pride in what he had been able to lure by luck and hard work from the earth, and he wanted to be recognized beyond the confines of his old homeland, achieve some fame in return for his life's work.

"Well . . ." Maggie tried thinking clearly. It had all happened so quickly and was so . . . strange. His words touched her, despite her determination not to be pushed around. She felt as if she was hearing something coming from inside the real man, a man she might actually grow to like, given the opportunity. "I could try," she said at last. "I wish I knew someone I could hire to help, but in this town, at this time of year, everyone I can think of who might have the skill is also up to his or her eyeballs in the pre-Christmas scramble. The big weekend we have is the first of December—"

"I can help." Mick didn't want her to end on the negative note he saw coming. Volunteering to assist her served several purposes. Working with her would give him the opportunity to gain her trust and, thereby, her confidence. When he put his mind to it, he could get anyone to talk about himself. Maggie Wellington would prove no exception, he was sure. Sooner or later he'd get the information he was after. And he could keep tabs on how she was treating his precious opals. His respect for her abilities had grown since he had seen the drawing, but he would still feel better if he could watch her work. One false move with the fragile opals and it was all over.

Then there was Tad. It would be better for the boy to be settled down with him a while, rather than shifted around among friends any longer. Colorado was certainly different from what his son was used to, and he thought the lad would enjoy the change. They could plan on his starting school after the holidays, or whenever the next term in

American schools began. It was summer at home, any-how, so Tad wouldn't be out much Australian schooling. The experience would be good for him, even if he might fuss a bit at the extra work.

Plus, Mick missed him like the very dickens.

"I've had plenty of experience working the stones," he said. "And while I don't know much about metal, I can learn. My hands are tough and strong. How about it?"

"I...I don't know, Mr. O'Shay." Maggie regarded him. Now that he wasn't an overt threat, she could assess him more objectively. He wasn't a tall man, only about five feet eight inches. But he carried himself proudly and the breadth of his wide shoulders and chest made him look much bigger than he actually was. A miner. That explained the scarred hands that almost looked like shovels and the musculature on his torso and arms, as well as the broken nose and the chipped tooth. He was a man who had made it in a rough and individualistic world. She had read an article once about the Australian opal fields in *National Geographic* and remembered that it was a world that operated for the most part on community spirit and honor. Thieves were hated and despised. No wonder he had bridled so when she had suggested he might be one. "I suppose we could work something out."

"Then call me Mick, Maggie." His smile was sudden and completely charming. "And let's shake on our deal." He held out his hand.

Hers was engulfed. "Don't you want a written contract?" she asked. "For your protection as well as my own."

"Do you really feel we need one?" He kept her hand clasped in his. "Isn't our mutual word good enough?"

"Mick, you're trusting me with stones worth more money than I care to think about. Before he retired because of my mother's illness, my father was a lawyer." She smiled at the memories. "It was kind of a family firm. My uncle and cousin are still running it. *Wellington, Worth and Wright*. They kept my dad's name, even though he's retired. Anyhow, he could draw up an informal agreement for us."

"If it would make you happy." Mick told himself to release her hand. They weren't in the back room any more, and the glass on the front door gave an unobstructed view of the shop's interior. While he hardly minded being seen holding the hand of a pretty woman, he was aware that gossip in a small town could be vicious. They were going to be working together, probably alone most of the time. He ought to have some consideration for her reputation.

But her hand seemed to nestle in his palm; her fingers were curled invitingly against his skin.

"It's not just to make me happy," she said, starting to blush again. "It's the right thing to do. I know our customs are different here, but if you're planning on doing much business in the States, you should get used to putting everything down in writing and keeping good records."

"Bloody boring. But I suppose you're right. Personally, I've always found business details tedious. I'm afraid I don't have much patience for paperwork and bureaucratic nitpicking." But, he thought, he would have lots of patience when it came to studying how embarrassment or high emotion managed to cause her fair skin to turn such a rare shade of rose. Lots of patience, indeed.

"No." She was caught again by those eyes. When they shone warmly, it was like bathing in a tropical sea. But how, she wondered, could she possibly be attracted to him when he was so blunt and abrupt? She liked men with far more grace and subtleness. Didn't she? "I don't suppose a man used to a life of adventure and action would be able to tolerate such things easily. But my father—" She broke off as the door to the shop burst open. Mick grasped her hand more tightly and pulled her closer in a move that was protective and more than a little possessive. Maggie groaned silently as one of her best and most gossipy friends careened into the room.

"Whoa!" Charlie Jensen literally skidded to a stop inches from Maggie. The tall, blond ski instructor took in the hand-holding and leered. "Sorry if I'm interrupting anything, babe," he said, waggling his eyebrows.

Mick dropped her hand. "Miss Wellington and I were just finalizing a business deal," he said in a cool tone. Turning to Maggie, he said, "Go ahead with your suggestion. I'll get back to you this afternoon or tomorrow morning." He started to leave the shop, bracing himself for the cold so foreign to him and regretting the necessity of leaving, even though his mind screamed out with the wisdom of it. What the devil had gotten into him to act like that? Pulling her close, as if she was his woman and he had to protect her. *Mick*, he warned himself, *think with your brain and not your—*

"Hey, wait a minute, man." Charlie reached out and grabbed the Australian by the arm. "You're new in town, aren't you?" He stuck out his hand. "I'm Charlie. Charlie Jensen. Party animal extraordinaire."

Maggie moved quickly, imposing herself partway between the two men. O'Shay didn't look as though he cared for the way Charlie had grabbed him. "Charlie," she said. "This is Mick O'Shay. He's from Australia." She tried to signal to her effervescent friend that a little more decorum might be a good idea.

But Charlie wasn't much for decorum and tact on the best of days. This morning he seemed determined to splatter social convention all over the place. "Hey! An Aussie! Down Under! Yeah!" He took Mick's hand and pumped it for all it was worth. "Hey, man. You've got to come to the party tonight. We get Swiss, Austrians and Germans all the time, but never Australians. You gonna hang around the Springs long?''

Once Mick figured out that this guy wasn't a boyfriend who'd give him trouble for being familiar with Maggie, he started to relax. This kind of bumbling friendliness was closer to the kind of socialization he was used to than was the formal sort of dance he'd had to put up with in San Francisco, New York and Denver, where he had pieces of jewelry made from his opals for sale. He could tell Maggie was worried about his reaction, and that prodded a bit of the devil in him. ''I don't know how long I'll be here,'' he said, glancing at her meaningfully. ''That sort of depends on Miss Wellington. But I'd like to come to your party tonight. If you don't mind a single male. I'm not married, and all the women I know are either back in one of your cities or in Australia.''

''Maggie'll bring you,'' Charlie said, grinning. ''She usually comes by herself and leaves after a little while.'' He winked. ''Maybe you can talk her into staying past eleven. We got bets she turns into a pumpkin at midnight.''

''Charlie,'' Maggie said. ''I'm going to kill you.''

''*After* the party, babe. Eight o'clock. My place. You don't come, Mag, I'm sending out the dogs. And bring this guy. He looks like he could stand a good blast. You got worry lines on your face, man. Got to get rid of 'em. This is a party town. Meant for having fun. See you at eight.'' He waved and was out the door before either of them could say anything further. The arctic air that followed his departure seemed a shade less frigid to Mick than had the gust following Patrick Wellington's exit.

''That was Charlie.'' Maggie closed the door, this time making rather a bit more noise. ''He's quite an excellent ski instructor. If you or your son want to learn the sport, he's the one I'd recommend.''

"The party animal extraordinaire?" Mick pulled a horrified expression. "I should risk my life hurtling down a mountain under his fine hand? I think not." Actually, he thought Charlie Jensen seemed like he'd be a good cobber. Like to party, did he? Well, so did Mick. Only he wasn't going to let Maggie know how much just yet.

"Appearances can be deceiving. You are a perfect example. You look like, well, a rather rough customer. But you kiss like a gentleman." She resisted the urge to smile when he looked at her in astonishment and turned red under his tan.

"Perhaps we'd better forget about that," he said, mumbling the words. "It wasn't exactly a businesslike thing for me to have done." He glanced at her quickly and saw that she had a mischievous glint in her eye. Not bloody likely she was going to let him forget it. She liked to tease, he realized.

"About tonight," she said. "You certainly don't have to go. Charlie's a good sport. He won't mind—if he even manages to remember inviting you."

"Oh, I wouldn't miss this. What's your home address? I'll be by around eight. Meanwhile, I've got a lot to do. I hadn't planned on living here, and I need to find a place for me and Tad to hang our hats." He turned as the door opened and the bell tinkled, signaling customers.

Maggie grabbed a piece of notepaper and scribbled her address on it. After handing it to him, she hurried behind the counter, smiling at the two women who had come into the shop. They were unfamiliar, therefore tourists or visitors, hopefully willing to spend some money. Asking Mick with her eyes to hold on a moment, she spoke to the newcomers. "Is there something you were particularly interested in, ladies? I'd be happy to show you any of the items in the cases." One wanted to check out a garnet necklace and the other seemed intrigued by a silver bracelet with turquoise stones. Maggie heard the bell tinkle again as she bent behind the counter to get the items. When she straightened, she saw that Mick O'Shay had left the store.

"NO, PAPA." Maggie passed her father a plate of mashed potatoes. "I have no idea where he's staying, or if he's actually going to take me to Charlie's party, or even if he's sane. The man barged into my store this morning, offered me the chance of a lifetime—to work on the finest opals I've ever seen—and then disappeared, entrusting me with a literal treasure trove of stones. You'd better believe I locked those babies up in the safe, first chance I got."

"You'd probably be wise to store them in a deposit box down at the bank," Patrick said, spooning potatoes and then gravy onto his plate. "I don't mean to be negative, but what if this character is planning something funny? Like having his stuff stolen while it's in your care, then claiming an insurance payment."

"Why, Patrick Wellington, you sound like your old Machiavellian self. I get the feeling you don't much care for Mr. O'Shay." Her father's interest, even if it was negative, delighted her. His depression had worried her so much that she had continued to live with him though she yearned to have the privacy and freedom of a place of her own. But she was thrilled at the possibility that he might be recovering from his sorrow. It was a small sign, but a sign, nevertheless.

Her father's expression didn't change. "I don't know the man well enough to form an opinion about him. I just find it a bit odd that he would come here just to find you. And wanting to stay here? Doesn't that strike you as a little odd? How will he manage? You know as well as I do that rents are high as heaven during the ski season. He hardly looked like a man with cash to burn."

"He says he's wealthy, Papa. *You* know as well as I do that looks can be misleading. And he says he wants me to do the work because he saw the brooch I made for Mrs. Mason. Remember? It was the big one with so much fire it looked alive."

"You got that one in an unusual way, too, as I recall." Patrick started eating, shoveling food into his mouth with the same sort of desperation that had characterized his approach to meals since Maggie's mother had died. "Man calling you up in the middle of the night. Meeting him in that dive down by the waterfront." He shook his head. "I never did approve of the way all that went."

"I got the stone for half what I would have paid through a middleman. So he was a little creepy. He had the proper papers. It was a legitimate transaction. He was the nervous type, that's all. And I made a good profit when I sold the brooch. Mr. O'Shay says he's going to pay me a very generous amount for working on his stones, and I won't have to bother with trying to sell them myself. It looks like a good deal to me. Will you try to draft a contract for us tonight?"

"All right." Her father didn't look at her. His eyes had taken on the unfocused stare that they usually did when his thoughts wandered back to happier times. Maggie sighed to herself. Until he worked through the mood, he wouldn't be much good for conversation or anything else. She seriously doubted that he would even get around to the contract tonight. So much for signs of improvement, she thought.

MICK PAUSED before ringing the doorbell. Maggie's house hadn't been hard to find because of the excellent directions he had gotten from the real estate salesman, and he was running a few minutes early. So the thing to do was take a deep breath and reflect for a moment. He had managed to get in a lot of thinking since leaving the jewelry shop, and he was certain he finally had control of his feelings toward that shop's proprietor.

His single purpose in finding Maggie Wellington had been to get from her the name of the man who had sold her Ian's opal. But now he had to admit to himself that that purpose had sprouted shoots. She was talented. Her designs would do his stones proud, if the sketch she had done was any indication. By accident, he might have found the artisan who could immortalize the fruits of his labors. It wouldn't be too hard to get closer to Miss Wellington in ways not pertaining to business, either. She was a darling woman, a breath of feminine fresh air with her natural good looks and impulsive behavior. He grinned to himself when he thought about her attacking him. She was a game sheila, all right. And then when he had kissed her... And her adorable teasing of him...

He rang the bell. It didn't do to dwell overly long on folly.

Maggie answered the door almost immediately, smiling when she saw him. "Hi," she said. "You're early. I like that. Come on in and say hello to my father. He's going to try to get some work done on our contract this evening."

Mick entered the house. Warm and homey, the place seemed to reach out and enfold him. The entryway was only a few feet of tiled floor. To his right was a small living room with a fire blazing in a brick fireplace. He noted the solid, comfortable-looking sofa and chair and the pictures on the walls—mostly photographs of people. Family? To his left was an equally miniature dining room with some evidence of dinner still waiting to be put away. He noted the fine tablecloth and silver—something of a contrast to the humble dwelling. If her father had made money in his law practice, he had chosen not to reveal it by the size of the place he lived in. Interesting.

"Papa, Mr. O'Shay's here, and we're off to Charlie's for the evening." Maggie had shrugged into a parka while Mick had been gathering his impressions of her home. "I won't be out too late, but don't stay up for me, okay?"

Patrick Wellington came out of the kitchen, a dish towel in his left hand. "O'Shay," he said, nodding at Mick. To Maggie he said, "I'll leave a draft of the contract on your dresser. You and he can go over it in the morning."

"That'll be fine," Mick said. "I'll just come over early, and then we can get started right away on the work."

"Not so fast," Maggie said, her good humor suddenly evaporating. In her desire for her father to continue his interest in her business for his sake, she had forgotten just how pushy Mick O'Shay could be. "I still have to finish my other pieces. I didn't agree to drop everything for you."

He grinned. "Not yet, lovey. Not yet, but you will."

MAGGIE SIMMERED all the way to Charlie's place. She hadn't wanted to start an argument in front of her father, so she had kept silent about Mick's blatant challenge. Patrick had seemed to have come out of his blue mood—evidenced by his intention to work on the contract—and she hadn't wanted to do anything that would be likely to throw him back into depression. But when she had tried to discuss the issue after they had left the house, O'Shay had simply refused to cooperate.

"About doing your opals immediately," she began as they walked down the sidewalk toward Mick's rented Jeep.

"I don't think I'll ever get used to cold like this," the Australian said. "I'm a man of the Outback. My blood's too thin for this kind of weather. Brr." He gave an exaggerated shiver.

"Mick, don't ignore me." She was shivering a little herself in spite of her warm clothing. The night was clear and cloudless, and the frigid air of winter had full reign in the valley where the town nestled under the mountains. When they had settled in Sullivan Springs, she and her father had been advised that the air would always be warmer in homes up on the slopes, but the snow was also much deeper there. They had opted for cheaper, more convenient housing in town, even though it had meant higher heating bills. Unless it was really bitter like tonight, they usually depended on the fireplaces for warmth. Both their upstairs bedrooms had them. It wasn't that money was a problem; since her mother's death, Maggie and her father had worked on simplifying their lives, and economy had been an integral part of that process. "I warn you that I'm not going to be bullied into doing things your way," she told Mick in an insistent tone, hugging her parka closer to her.

"I'm not intending to bully anyone." He opened the passenger door of the Jeep and gestured for her to enter. "I just expect you'll see the sense of my plans. I'm certain that behind those pretty brown eyes is a brain that's able to see a good business deal when it stands up and hollers. You can make all the jewelry you want to put up for sale in store, but how many really important customers are going to drive all the way up here to see your work? If you finish my stones as soon as possible, on the other hand, you'll be exhibited in some big cities for the holidays. Think on it, Maggie. And for Pete's sake, quit calling me Mr. O'Shay. It makes us sound as if we aren't friends."

"I'm not sure we are." He laughed and she settled into the seat, annoyed.

Mick followed her directions to the party. In contrast to the traditional homes in Maggie's neighborhood, the area where Charlie Jensen and his ilk hung their ski toques was all slick, modern condominiums. When Mick parked in one of the few spaces left, next to a huge snowbank, he asked about this. "It's like another world," he said. "Lights blazing, music blaring. Don't the neighbors complain?"

"Most of the neighbors are at the party. Or are having one of their own. This is the swinging section of the Springs. Young singles live out here."

"But you don't."

"Well, of course not. Papa'd go crazy with all the noise and action. He likes things quiet. Peaceful."

They began walking up the snow-encrusted wooden staircase that led to Charlie's condominium door. "That must be rather dull for you," Mick commented. "Is it really necessary for you to give up the life-style you might want for what your father prefers?"

Maggie glanced at him, but saw only mild interest in his expression. He seemed to be concentrating on not slipping. "I'm not giving up anything," she said. "Sure, I'd rather have my own place, but Papa needs me. I like people, but I've never been much of what you might call a party animal, and by not living out here, I can come and go as I please. At times I work very late at night. All this noise would be a severe distraction. I'm serious about my art, Mick, and I dedicate most of my waking hours to it."

"Glad to hear that." He grabbed at the handrail and her elbow as his feet skidded on an icy patch. "Then we will certainly be able to structure your labors to include beginning on my opals immediately. All it takes is a little juggling of your schedule, Maggie. Isn't that right?" His arm went around her waist just as Charlie flung open the front door of his place and bellowed a hearty welcome to them both. Warm air and hot music billowed out and engulfed them, and they entered the room entwined like lovers.

CHAPTER THREE

"MAGGIE? Maggie, girl, are you all right?"

The sound of her father's voice pulled Maggie out of a gray, cotton-lined unconsciousness. It was not sleep. She tried sitting up in her bed, then lay gingerly back down, groaning at the dull ache behind her right eye. "I'm okay," she managed to call out. "Just feeling a little sluggish. I'll be down in a few minutes." Patrick seemed mollified by this and left. His footsteps sounded on the stairs.

She sat up, this time not allowing herself to indulge in self-pity. It had been no one's fault but her own that she had drunk twice the number of beers she usually had at a party. She had been flustered by the reaction of her friends to Mick—particularly to their entrance. There was no doubt in her mind that Charlie had set the scene by already blabbing to one and all about the friendly picture he had seen in the shop. When the crowd had been treated to the sight of Mick's arm around her, it had clenched the rumor. All evening, she had been congratulated on her new lover, and no amount of denial on her part had made any difference. As far as the young social set of Sullivan Springs was concerned, Mick and Maggie were a hot new item.

So, stupidly, she had tried to calm her nerves with beer. She got carefully out of bed and staggered over to the dresser. *Not bright, Mag,* she scolded herself as she stared at the miserable apparition staring back at her from the mirror. Her hair looked as if she'd kissed an electric socket,

her eyes were muddy brown marbles on bloodshot sur-
faces and her lips—

Say. What was the matter with her lips? She put up a
hand and touched the swollen tissue. Good grief. Her
mouth hadn't looked like that since high school days and
lengthy make-out sessions where deep kissing was the final
frontier. She rarely drank much, but she was certain a
hangover did not cause your lips to swell.

Just what had happened after she and Mick had left
Charlie's?

At first it had seemed that Mick was drinking more than
she was, but before her senses got fuzzy and her ability to
concentrate lessened and narrowed, she had finally realized that he'd been nursing the same can of beer for hours.
She had mistaken his party exuberance and energy for ine-
briation. When they had finally left in the early morning
hours, he was as sober as a judge and it was she who was
having trouble remembering her own name.

Amused at her tipsy state, he had treated her kindly,
helping her out of the condo, down the slippery stairs—
catching her once in his strong arms when she had lost her
footing. She blushed at the memory of how close their faces
had come. But they hadn't kissed then, even though she
remembered having wanted to very much. She recalled
wobbling with his help up the walkway to her house, but
nothing after that. Had they kissed at her front door?

She didn't remember.

A hot shower helped, followed by a few seconds of bone-
chilling cold water. By the time she emerged, gasping, she
felt more human. She tugged a comb through her shoul-
der-length hair, and pulled it back from her face with two
plastic barrettes. After throwing on jeans, socks and a fresh
sweater, she started toward the staircase and was halfway
down when the doorbell rang.

"Get that, will you, Mag," Patrick called. "I'm scrambling the eggs."

Knowing darn well who it was, Maggie reluctantly went to the door and opened it. Mick O'Shay grinned at her.

"Well," he said. "I'm pleasantly surprised to see you up and about this fine morning. Feeling all right, are you?"

She squinted at the painful sunlight. "I'm fine, thanks. And yourself?"

He hunched down in his sheepskin jacket. "I'll be a sight better when you ask me inside. It's no warmer this morning than it was last night."

She forced a smile and stepped outside in her stocking feet. "Nonsense. It's got to be at least twenty degrees. There's no wind and the sun is shining. It's practically a shirt-sleeve day." It was one-upmanship of the crassest kind, but today she was going to take anything she could get.

"For you, maybe." He shivered and jammed his hands in his pockets.

She relented. The fresh air had cleared away the remnants of her headache. "Come on inside, O'Shay. Papa's got breakfast ready."

Mick followed, feeling puzzled. He had been sure she would be laid up with one whale of a hangover, judging by the way she had behaved after just a few beers the night before. She wasn't an experienced drinker, at all, he had surmised. But here she was, bright as a cricket with just a trace of shadow under her eyes.

And she was being so brusque with him. *O'Shay?* What happened to the soft, seductive way she had cooed his first name last night after they had shared that initial searing goodnight kiss? Had she actually been so loaded she had forgotten how she'd melted in his arms? It was an experience *he* wasn't likely to forget for some time. She had been more woman than he had been close to for ages, although he had done nothing more than return those passionate, if clumsy, kisses. He wondered if she kept any beer at the shop. He definitely preferred her with a little suds in her system.

But over breakfast, she showed a capable, businesslike approach to their relationship that he had to admire in spite of himself. The contract her father had drafted was clear and concise, and totally fair as far as Mick could tell. "I see no problems with this document," he said as Maggie poured him another cup of coffee. "I'll be willing to sign a final draft just as soon as we work out an agreeable timetable for the completion of the work."

"You mean, as soon as I agree to do things the way you want." She put the pot back on the stove and sat down, regarding him steadily out of eyes that had slight traces of red at the edges.

"I told you I'd be willing to help. And at no charge for my services, either." His good mood was fading. She was hung over and was trying to hide it. He already knew she was stubborn, and her temper wasn't likely to be improved by her condition. Not for the first time he wished there had been some other way to get a lead on the man he hunted.

"Mick, I just cannot—"

"You could subcontract," Patrick said. He had sat through most of the meal without saying a word; just responding when asked a question. "That boy over in Three Pines. He's got talent."

"Davey Abrams?" Maggie was surprised at her father's suggestion, but it was a good one. Davey had been in an automobile accident when he was thirteen and was confined to a wheelchair. He had little skill in design, but she had seen some of the work he had copied, and Patrick was right. He could handle stones and metal well. Certainly he could do well enough to take on the job of finishing the less important pieces she wanted done before the Christmas shopping rush.

"I suppose I could talk to him," she said. "If he isn't too busy, he might be interested." She turned to Mick. "But it will cost you more to have me subcontract. Are you willing?"

"And able. Maggie, Mr. Wellington, I'm not one of your tycoons, but I'm more than comfortable. I don't live a fancy life. Never have, so my resources don't dwindle much even when I'm not mining. In fact, I don't intend to spend much of the rest of my time digging. It's a young man's game, and I saw thirty a few months ago. And there are risks. I have a son who has no one else but me. I owe it to him to be careful with myself, don't you think?"

Maggie listened to him spout this personal information. Something in his tone and in the expression deep in his eyes told her there was far more to his purpose in life than living quietly and raising his son, much as he might love the boy. Mick O'Shay was becoming as multifaceted and interesting as a fine diamond. She still didn't really like the guy, but he was compelling in a number of ways.

One of those ways, she had to admit, had to do with the growing physical attraction she was feeling. She only wished she could remember how the previous night had ended. Her body tingled as she searched vainly for the memory.

"If you're agreeable, then," she said, "we could drive over and talk to Davey this afternoon. I'd like him to look at my sketches before he makes up his mind, so a personal visit is in order, I think."

"I'll give his mother a call this morning," Patrick said, surprising Maggie again by joining the conversation. After he had made the suggestion about Davey, he had turned inward and broody and she hadn't expected any more of a response from him than a distracted grunt when she kissed him goodbye. "If she says Davey can see you, I'll tag along. Could use a little outing, if you don't mind."

"Not at all!" Maggie went over and hugged him, pleased by the sight of a rare smile. "You can tell Mick all about the legends of the gold rush in these mountains. I'm sure as a miner, he'll be fascinated."

Mick was already fascinated, but not by the prospect of hearing tales about precious metal. The relationship between Maggie and her father was far more precious than any inanimate object could be, and it made him yearn for Tad's presence. He cleared his throat, stood, then walked over to a window and stared out at the wintry scene while he gained control over his emotions.

Shortly after that, they drove to her shop. Usually, she walked, but in deference to his sensitivity to the cold, she agreed to ride in his rented Jeep. The tires scrunched over the packed snow on the road, and the air almost sang with the crystalline cold that hung suspended in the valley. Up on the slopes of the surrounding hills and mountains she could see the occasional lone skier—it was still too early for the regular lifts to be open. That would happen after Thanksgiving. But the hard-core types like Charlie either hiked their way up or hitched a ride with a willing snow-mobiler once the snow was deep enough for a run or two in the morning. "This really seems like paradise to me," she said, by way of conversation. He had been surprisingly quiet. "But I guess it's all in what you're used to."

"I grew up in a tiny town in the Outback," he said, squinting against the glare of the sun on snow. "In the winter you could get sunstroke most afternoons if you stayed exposed. Summers, well, summers were spent mostly staying in what shade you could find and panting for air. I'm a desert rat. This is as alien to me as Mars might be."

"Doesn't sound like much of a place to raise a family. What did your folks do?"

Mick pulled the Jeep to an abrupt stop in front of her store. "I'm told my Pa drove a lorry. He left when I was five. I don't remember a thing about him. Ma took in laundry and mending." He got out of the Jeep and slammed the door. He paced quickly to the shop and stood in front of it with his shoulders hunched and his hands jammed in his pockets. His head was bent and to Maggie he looked like a man guarding secrets.

Maggie got out, her mind brimming over with questions, but she knew that asking them would be blatant bad manners. Mick O'Shay would or would not satisfy her curiosity about himself. It was entirely up to him. She smiled at him as she opened the front door and led the way into her shop.

He waited all morning for her to spew out the questions he had seen in her eyes when he had let slip those bleak details of his childhood. But she never said a word about personal matters. All business, she reviewed the contract with him until they were both satisfied with the conditions—dependent upon the Abrams boy's willingness to take on her unfinished pieces.

Maggie seemed confident he would. "Davey is only fifteen," she told Mick, "but he has shown signs of being a highly skilled craftsman some day. As it is, he's already a good one, more than able to copy from my instructions. I don't know why I didn't think of him myself when you were having such a fit about my getting your stuff done quickly."

"Maybe you just wanted to fight." Mick was leaning against the frame of the door to the workroom. They had left the door open so that if a customer came in, she could move quickly forward to serve the person. It had been agreed that Mick would shut the door so that the opals wouldn't be seen by the casual observer. "We started off with a rather rousing encounter," he continued. "Perhaps you were just in the mood to be difficult.'' He paused a beat. ''Not like you were last night.''

Maggie looked up from where she had been sorting through the opals. ''What do you mean?'' she asked, alarmed.

''Well.'' He shrugged. Waiting around didn't sit easily on Mick, and he had been shifting about in his mind for something to say to liven up the situation. It looked as if he'd hit on a good topic. ''After you started on that third beer and I suggested it might be time to head for home, you took on a bit of a romantic attitude. Right lovey, you were.''

''You're lying!'' She bumped the velvet pad as she pointed an accusing finger at him. Several opals scattered onto the surface of the wooden table, clattering musically as they went.

''You remember, then?'' His grin was wicked.

''You really are a bastard! Forget whatever I said yesterday about your kissing like a gentleman. There's nothing of the gentleman about you, is there?''

''No.'' He stopped smiling, and crossed his arms over his chest. ''There isn't, Maggie. But I—'' The condition he was going to put on his statement was interrupted by the ringing of the front door bell. Maggie hurried from behind the worktable and dashed to the front of the store, slamming the inner door behind herself. Mick eased away from the door and moved the scattered opals back onto the pad with a careful finger, wondering why he had let his devils loose to tease and mock a woman who was so honest and whose feelings were so transparent.

He also wondered why he was allowing himself the luxury of feeling bad about it when, after all, he was only using her for the information she had and for the artistic genius with which she would bring his stones to life. Mick squared his shoulders and began to look around the work-room.

MAGGIE WAS STILL ANGRY when the couple left her shop. She had sold them a pendant made of gold with a small tourmaline as the centerpiece. It had brought enough profit to justify closing the shop for the rest of the day, though she didn't at all relish spending it in the company of Mick O'Shay. To make herself feel better, she vowed she would never again go anywhere socially with him and never, never drink more than one beer at a party, no matter what!

She called her father and learned that Mrs. Abrams had told him Davey was very excited about the possibility of working for her. Patrick had readied sandwiches, and as soon as she and Mick could come back to the house they would eat and be on their way to Three Pines. Maggie's temper was improved by the enthusiasm she heard in her father's voice, and she went back into the workroom intent on being pleasant.

But when she saw him rifling through papers in the file she kept for business correspondence, she lost that resolve. "That's private!" she cried, rushing over and slamming the drawer shut, almost catching his fingers. "What the devil are you doing, looking in there?"

His smile didn't reach his eyes. "Just bored," he said. "Messing around. Sorry."

"That's no excuse," she said, fuming. "I'm taking you on as a customer, not a partner. That gives you no right to my files." She grabbed her parka from the back of a chair and rummaged in a pocket until she found her key chain. Taking a small key from the ring, she locked the file cabinet. "Since I can't trust you, I'll have to lock up with you around. For a man who claims to be so damn honest, you really stretch your limits, O'Shay. Come on. Papa's waiting with lunch." She put on her coat and brushed past him.

"Papa can wait a few minutes." He grabbed her arm and spun her around gently so that she had to look at him. "You're right to be mad. We aren't partners. I had no business looking in your papers. I'm sorry." The fire she saw in his eyes said he was nothing of the kind, but behind the blaze, she saw a vast range of emotions that surprised and confused her. He was angry, but full of sorrow. Tough, but hurt, vulnerable. She put together what little she knew about him. As a child he'd been deserted by his father, and later, as a young man, his wife had left him. What other wounds and pains did this man carry, she wondered.

And why did she care?

"All right," she said, freeing her arm. "I accept your apology. Maybe you just don't know how things are done here. But I'm going to keep my stuff locked up, anyhow. Once bitten, twice shy."

He looked puzzled.

"It's a saying that refers to the attitudes and actions of a person who has had an unfortunate encounter with a nasty snake," she explained, giving him a smug smile, knowing she had won this round. But why did every encounter with him seem like a contest?

There was little conversation between them during the ride back to her house.

ON THE WAY to Three Pines that afternoon, however, the conversation between the Australian and her father was surprisingly animated. Patrick sat in the front of Maggie's Bronco with his daughter, but his attention was on the man in the rear seat. Maggie watched the road for slick spots and listened to the men talk mining tales. For every legend about the Colorado digs Patrick had, Mick O'Shay had one concerning the rich deposits in his homeland. By the time she turned into the village of Three Pines, legends had clearly turned into lies and both men seemed much more at ease with each other.

"Mrs. Abrams said Davey has been doing much better with his physical therapy lately," Patrick informed them, as Maggie drove along the residential street where the young metalsmith lived with his widowed mother. "This opportunity for work, she thinks, comes at a fortuitous time for him."

"For both of us," Maggie said, not looking back at Mick.

Soon, Nell Abrams, a tall and dignified woman whose blond hair still had the shine of younger days, was leading them through her home to the back of the house where Davey had set up shop. Neatness was not the order of the day here as it seemed to be elsewhere in the house. Mick marveled that anyone could work in conditions worse than the ones he had seen in Maggie's back room, but it was obvious Davey Abrams had the same character defect. What was also obvious was that the kid could work metal. Examples of his craft hung on fishline from the ceiling, sat on shelves along the walls and were scattered over a worktable twice the size and half the height of Maggie's wooden bench.

Maggie smiled as she saw Mick's interest click. "Davey," she said to the thin, wheelchair-bound boy, "I'd like you to meet Mr. O'Shay, an opal miner from Australia. He's the reason I need your help."

Davey attempted a pleased-to-meet-you smile, but it bordered on painful shyness. Mick held out his hand.

"This is great stuff, Abrams," he said, waving his left hand at the collection of metal airplanes, cars, dinosaurs, horses and abstract designs littering the room. With his right he gave the boy a firm, man's handshake. "Maybe I took my opals to the wrong metalsmith." His glance at Maggie took any sting out of his words.

"Oh, no, Mr. O'Shay," Davey protested. "Maggie...
Miss Wellington is the best there is around here with jewelry. My own stuff's too crude. But I can copy. Anything
she can draw, I can copy, sir."

"Mick," Mick said. "I haven't been a sir ever in my life.
All right. You take the backlog off her hands and free her
up to work my stones, and I can guarantee you it'll be
worth your time and effort." He walked over to a particularly unusual abstract design propped up against the wall.
"Tell me about this one. Looks like a barmaid I knew once.
Same..." He looked pointedly at the women. "Well, it just
reminds me of her," he said with a grin at Davey. With
those words, an easy rapport was struck.

Maggie lingered in the workroom long enough to ac-
quaint Davey with the sketches of the pieces she would be
asking him to do. Then she and Patrick and Nell departed
for the front of the house. Nell had generously offered afternoon tea. Mick and Davey had been invited, but both
had answered abstractly that they'd be along directly. It was
obvious they wanted time alone to talk.

"Your Mr. O'Shay seems to have quite a way with the
boy," Nell commented, as she brought the tea service into
the front room. "I've never seen Davey take to an adult so
quickly. What's his secret?"

"He has a son a few years younger than Davey," Maggie replied. "Maybe Davey reminds him of the boy and so
he feels comfortable with him. I suppose that's his secret."

"Well, he certainly seems like a nice man. And how
wonderful that he wants you to do up his opals. Patrick was
telling me about your good fortune."

Maggie glanced at her father who was concentrating on
sipping his tea. It was unusual for him to be so gossipy.
"It's good fortune," she said to Nell. "But I'd really appreciate it if you'd keep it to yourself—and Davey, of

course. I'd be nervous if too many folks knew I had that kind of loot in my shop."

"You need to get over to the police station and talk with Sam Glover about some security, Mag." Patrick set his cup down on the coffee table. "You've put it off long enough in my opinion."

Maggie had to agree that he was right. For the next while, she said little. Patrick and Nell carried the conversation between the two of them, amazing her with their knowledge of local news and gossip. The two communities weren't so far apart or so large that most events of note weren't privy to citizens of both towns. However, this was the first time Maggie had seen her father come out of his personal despondency long enough to be interested. It was quite a revelation and cheered her immensely. After a while, she told herself that no matter what aggravating things Mick O'Shay said or did during the afternoon, he would not be able to shake her good mood.

Mick and Davey didn't show until it was almost time to leave. From the look on the youngster's face it was apparent the Australian had made a friend. Mick's words confirmed it. "I was telling Davey about my boy, Tad," he said. "When he gets here, Davey's going to show him the ropes. Tad's never been out of Australia before."

"He's welcome here anytime," Nell assured him, putting her hands on her son's shoulders. "Davey's friends get so busy this time of year, and he does get a bit lonely."

"Oh, Mom." Davey looked embarrassed. He also looked happy.

"You won't be bored when you start working," Maggie said. "But, Nell, if this interferes at all with his schoolwork, he's to put the jewelry aside. Your grades are more important than making a little extra cash, Davey."

Davey made a face, but he nodded. "I guess you're right, Miss Wellington. I get *really* bored with homework, though. I'm not so sure going to college is all that important."

Maggie started to reply, as did Nell and Patrick, but Mick beat them all to it. "College *is* important," he said angrily. "Tad's going, if I have to drag him kicking and screaming. I never went to school and it's taken me most of my adult life to get to the point where I could carry on a conversation without making a fool of myself. At least in decent company, that is."

"You didn't go to school?" Davey seemed awestruck. "Ever? How'd you manage that?"

Mick's expression darkened. "It's a long story and not worth telling. Just take my word for it—going to school's one of the best things you can do for yourself in life." Maggie looked on, surprised, as he seemed to deliberately change his attitude and tell a joke that had the group laughing in moments.

They left the Abramses' house soon after that. Maggie promised to stop by the next day or so, once she had collected all the drawings and materials Davey would need. While Davey was saying goodbye to Mick and Patrick, Nell whispered to her how grateful she was. "This has taken him completely out of the depression he usually gets this time of year," she said. "It's when his accident happened, you know. It was just wonderful of you to ask him to help you."

"Actually, it was my father's idea," Maggie told her. "I'm afraid I can't take the credit."

"Patrick's idea?" Nell's face glowed, and she said goodbye to the older man with extra warmth.

ON THE WAY BACK HOME Patrick asked the question that had been burning in Maggie's head since Mick had mentioned his lack of schooling. "What the devil were your people doing that you didn't go to school, O'Shay? Don't they have laws about that sort of thing in your country?''

Mick was slouched in the back seat. "Laws don't reach every place, Mr. Wellington. My Ma had too much to do, taking care of my brothers and sister, to worry about what I was up to. I pretty much ran wild until I was twelve. Then I ran away. After that I kind of lived wherever someone would take me in for a day, a week, a month. I did plenty of work, but no school. It wasn't until a very special man took me under his wing that I learned what an ignoramus I was. I guess you could say Ian was the only real parent I ever knew.'' In the rearview mirror Maggie saw him put his hand up to his face and turn so that he was looking out of the window. A deep furrow had formed between his eyebrows. He looked like a man in pain. Patrick didn't pursue the matter further.

After Patrick was dropped off at home, Mick moved to the front seat. Maggie suggested it might be in both their best interests to pay a visit to the police station and get some advice on security from the chief. "Sam Glover's a sharp guy," she told Mick. "I'll feel better just with him knowing we'll be working with more valuable material than I usually have around. And it would be a good idea for him to see your face, in case you have to go to the shop alone. I wouldn't want you busted just because the cops thought you were a real burglar.''

He grinned for the first time in a while. "I look disreputable enough to worry the local constables?''

"I didn't mean that. I just—''

"Last night you were saying I was good-looking, in a rugged sort of way." His eyes shone with mischief. "Let's see. I think your exact words were 'diamond in the rough.'"

Maggie pulled up in front of the station and jammed on the brakes. She turned and glared at him. "All right, O'Shay. I don't remember any of that. Would you do me a big favor and admit you're lying, or go ahead and tell me precisely what happened after we left Charlie's. The suspense of not knowing is killing me.''

"You really want to know?''

"I asked, didn't I?''

"All right. The honest truth.'' He unbuckled his seat belt. Before Maggie could say another word, he released her belt and gathered her in his arms. His green gaze blazed into her eyes for a moment.

Then his mouth covered hers.

CHAPTER FOUR

MAGGIE TIGHTENED HER LIPS and balled her fist. That he would dare kiss her right on the main street of town and in the middle of the day infuriated her beyond measure. Fabulous opals or no fabulous opals, as soon as she got her face away from this rat's she was going to knock him right into the next county!

The only problem was that getting away was proving not only impossible, but less and less desirable by the moment. He held her securely, but gently. While her lips remained locked tight, he made no effort to force them open; he only caressed them with his own. His were warm and persuasive, and his breath was sweet and hot on her cheek. She had never before been embraced by a man who felt so solid, so strong. A delightful weakness rushed into her muscles. She unclenched her fist and moved to stroke his hair and neck. After that, she opened her lips and began to remember just how magical last night had been.

When he felt her relax, Mick folded her more closely to him. She was warm and willing, and it was wonderful to hold her this way. His senses swam with the sensations she caused in his body, although his mind kept warning him that this was not the real Maggie Wellington. Delicious as she might be, he had to remember that she was stubborn and argumentative and had no interest in him beyond her own selfish needs and ambitions.

But oh, my, was the sheila lovely and lovable right now!

Maggie tried to wrest herself out of the wonderful web Mick O'Shay's kiss and embrace had woven around her. She was enjoying herself far too much, and the last thing in the world she needed was to let passion trick her into thinking she liked him. She had gone that route before and knew how foolishly it could make her act. She turned her head slightly and he broke the kiss.

"That," he said, smiling and staring into her eyes, "was the honest truth. Exactly what happened last night. Except that you tended to fade in and out. Or maybe I should say pass out and come to. I've never seen a person get so loaded on three measly brews. You'd best steer clear of the hard stuff, woman. You've no tolerance at all."

She squirmed to free herself from his arms. "You could mess up a sunny day with that nasty mouth of yours, Mick O'Shay. I was actually enjoying kissing you, but now I'm sorry I ever set eyes on you, much less your lips. Let me go!"

"You didn't think my mouth was so nasty a minute ago." His grin turned wicked. "Aren't you protesting just a bit too much?"

"I'm warning you—"

"What?" He frowned and released her so suddenly she bumped against the door. "What is it, Miss Wellington? Hot or cold? In for a penny, out for a pound? Just what am I supposed to make of the signals you keep sending me?"

"I'm not sending any signals, damn it!"

"No signals? Well, excuse me, miss, but I've never gotten a clearer signal than your kisses are giving me. If we weren't business partners, I'd have—"

"We are *not* partners! You have hired me on a piecework basis to set those stones. You insist on hanging around while I do it, but that in no way makes you my partner. Or anything else for that matter. And my kissing you does not imply anything, at all. Certainly not that I want to go to bed with you. I just—"

"Maggie." His voice was quieter, his tone kinder. "Don't you have a lover or at least a boyfriend around here? I keep waiting for some six-foot Swede to come out of the woodwork and pound me into the ground. I watched very carefully last night, but not one guy made me think I might be poaching. What's the story with you?"

"There's no story." She looked away. His eyes had a fathomless quality, and she felt he could see all the way into her mind and heart.

"The hell there isn't." His hand touched her shoulder. "If you don't really care to romp with me, then why do you kiss as if you're starving for it? Maggie, you're a good-looking woman. There ought to be at least a half dozen men in this town ready to knock my block off for pushing my way into your life."

"I have plenty of friends. They just know I can take care of myself."

"I'm not talking about friends, and you know it." His hand left her shoulder. "All right, it isn't any of my business when you get right down to it."

"That's right."

"But I want you to know that if you're going to keep kissing me like that, you're liable to get more than what you bargained for." There was a cold glint in his eyes.

"Oh, mercy." She placed a hand over her heart. "Oh, I am trembling in my maidenly boots. Listen, O'Shay. Forget about the kisses. They meant nothing, especially not that I want to get into the sack with the likes of you. As for my not having a boyfriend, well, I've just been too darn busy to accommodate one, if it's any of your concern. And believe me when I say that I am not starving for anything, least of all sex. If you were the last man on earth, I wouldn't—"

"Ah." He placed his big hand over her mouth. "Don't say it, Maggie Wellington. Vows like that have an interesting way of being broken. Wouldn't you feel silly then?" The glint was gone and the humor back.

It made her even madder.

After a few more minutes of sparring verbally, they patched together a kind of truce and got out of the car. As they approached the police station, Maggie said, "I sure as hell hope no one saw that little display."

"Which display?" Mick had his back hunched against the cold and his hands buried deep in his pockets. "The kissing or the fighting?"

Maggie ignored the question.

She could not, however, ignore the quizzical, amused smile on Chief Sam Glover's face when she and Mick entered the station. The chief was alone in the front office, but she could hear a dispatcher using the radio in one of the small side rooms. Sullivan Springs had four officers besides Sam, and they were usually out on patrol, keeping the chief posted via the radio, which was operated by two women, one during the day and the other at night.

"Afternoon, Maggie," Sam said, leaning back in his chair. She nearly groaned aloud in embarrassment. From the placement of the window and the chief's chair, it was clear he'd had a ringside seat for the "display." "How're things with you, gal?"

"Things are interesting." Maggie cut her eyes around to Mick, warning him not to make a crack. "Sam, this is Mick O'Shay. He's from—"

"I know. Australia." The chief stood and extended a hand. "Welcome to Sullivan Springs, Mr. O'Shay. The local gossip squad's already filled me in. So you're settling here to work with Maggie?"

Mick took the man's hand and shook it. The chief was a lean man, with the leathery skin of one who had spent much of his life in the sunshine. Graying black hair framed an intelligent face set off by steel-rimmed glasses. "I don't know if I'm exactly setting up permanent housekeeping," he told the older man. "But Maggie and I have a lot to do. I expect to be here a few months, at least." The chief's grip was firm, as Mick had expected. He was regarded for a moment by light blue eyes. Then Sam Glover smiled.

"A few months in the Springs," he said, "can lead to some pretty pleasant habits that might be hard to break. I came here ten years ago just to visit an old buddy from the Chicago force. I'm still here."

"Habits?" Mick looked at Maggie. "What kind of habits?"

She said nothing, only smiled.

"Oh…" Sam settled back in his chair and indicated that they were to take the two in front of his desk. "There's breathing, for one. After the city air, this stuff's like the finest perfume." He waved a hand. "Had one fellow up from Denver looking for a job. Said he thought he might be suffocating 'cause he couldn't see the air he was breathing." He chuckled. "Been here near five years now."

"Sam's sort of a one-man advertising campaign for Sullivan Springs," Maggie said. "But he is particular as to who he encourages to stay."

"No bad guys, eh?" Mick grinned.

"Yep. I tend to make it real unpleasant for undesirables. Though being a tourist town, you can't pick and choose all the people who come through. With the skiing season starting, my officers and I are gonna be busy. So what can I do for you today? We ain't too busy yet."

"Has the gossip squad explained why Maggie and I are setting up shop together?" Mick asked, ignoring the sound of protest from his right.

"No." Sam drew his long fingers together in a steeple. "But you being from Down Under and Maggie here being a jeweler, I'd have to figure it had something to do with opals. Am I right?"

"You are right," Maggie said, shooting an angry glance at Mick. "But we aren't setting up shop together. I've agreed to set Mr. O'Shay's stones. He wants to watch. That's all."

"What kind of cash value are we talking about?" Sam asked, looking carefully from one person to the other. It didn't take any Sherlock Holmes to figure something other than jewelry business was going on between these two. Maggie Wellington had surprised him when she hadn't latched on to any fellow after she and her dad had bought the old Smith house. Maybe it was because she already had something going with this Aussie. From what he had seen of the clench between them in the car, it was obvious that if she didn't have something going before she sure did now. But it was also clear not all was smooth sailing. Sparks were flying off her like off a cat on a nylon blanket in January.

"Cash value?" Mick pulled out his notebook and extended the customs statement to the chief. "There's that. Then when you add what precious metals and other stones Maggie might choose to use for settings... Well, it'll be hard to set an exact figure. You probably ought to add half that sum again."

Sam whistled. "I think at the very least, Maggie, you ought to get down to Denver and hire some security. I'd like to see a twenty-four-hour guard on your place with this much at stake."

"It's going to take months to do the work." She pushed some stray hairs off of her cheek, feeling a growing nervousness. "I can't afford to keep guards around that long."

"The Chief's suggesting the most extreme line of defense," Mick said, his voice oddly soothing to her nerves. "As long as we keep quiet about what we're doing, chances are no one's going to tip off any big-time thieves. And in our case, those are the ones we need to worry about least. The minute a pro showed his face around here, I'm willing to bet Chief Glover would be on him like a snake on a rat.''

Glover smothered a smile. "I'm not real sure about the comparison, but you got the right idea, son. Okay, guards are out. How about some electronic devices? You sure want a connection with the station. Ought to have put in one a long time ago, if you ask me."

"I've been cutting corners," she admitted. "Until now, I didn't have anything resembling the kind of work where I could justify the expense."

"I'm paying for it." Mick sounded determined, and his expression showed he wouldn't stand for an argument. Maggie noted how his jawline seemed to harden and his eyes turn a lighter shade of green. "It's because of me she's even at risk. They're my goods, not hers."

"It's my place, though. We should share the cost. Who would you recommend, Sam?"

They discussed the details of setting up a system that would alert the department in the evenings if there was an intruder in the shop. Maggie's safe, all agreed, was proof against all but the most professional and determined of burglars, but it was always possible one might get wind of their project.

"What about during the day?" she asked, looking to Sam for advice.

"This'll do during the day." Mick reached inside his jacket and pulled out an enormous revolver. "I've guarded my stones ever since I've been a miner. No reason to plan on stopping now."

The chief eyed the weapon. "Got a permit?"

"An international gem merchant's permit. I can carry this almost everywhere in the world, no questions asked."

Maggie stared at him. Something new and very dangerous showed in his face, even though his features seemed carved from stone. She would not, she decided, ever want to try taking something from Mick O'Shay he didn't want to give up.

"You can use this thing?" Sam prodded the weapon gently with the end of a pencil. "Last thing I need is some kangaroo cowboy shooting up my town because he's seen the wrong kind of shadow. And whether you got an international permit or not, this is still my town and is likely to be when you're long gone."

Mick grinned. "Good. I'm glad to see I can turn up the heat on you and get a strong reaction, Chief. Have a place I can show you my style? If you don't approve, we'll make other arrangements and you can take my gun while I'm here."

Glover raised his eyebrows. "Pretty darn confident, ain't you?"

"Yeah," Mick said, holstering the gun. "That I am."

AN HOUR LATER, Maggie had to admit he had reason for his cockiness. She, Mick and Sam had driven out to a quarry about five miles beyond town and the Australian had proceeded to demonstrate an awesome talent with his revolver.

"I've handled firearms since I was big enough to lift one," he explained from the back seat as they rode out to the makeshift range. Sam, settled in the front next to Maggie, looked over his shoulder.

"They let little kids shoot in Australia?" he asked, a worried expression on his face.

"I was never a little kid."

That put a damper on conversation until their destination was reached. Maggie stopped the car, stamped on the brake and stepped out into the late afternoon sunshine. The air smelled like clear crystal looked, and a gentle wind in the trees made a soft melody that rested her jangling nerves.

Dark shadows bisected the light gray rocks in the quarry in intriguing patterns. Snow lay in cottony patches around the bases of trees and in crevices where the wind didn't reach. It was an altogether peaceful scene.

At least it was until Mick O'Shay drew his gun and started blasting away. Maggie covered her ears quickly, but they still rang from the sounds of the first two shots. She squinted her eyes and wasn't able to see what he was shooting at, but a glance at Sam Glover's expression told her everything.

The chief was awed. He slowly removed his glasses while still looking off into the distance where, apparently, Mick's shots were having an effect on something. His mouth opened and a smile turned his thin lips upward. Maggie turned her attention to Mick.

Her heart seemed to leap into her throat. He stood casually at an angle to his target, the gun held in his right hand and his hand on his hip. His coat was open and the thin sweater he wore served to show off his broad chest. She felt as if she were seeing him for the first time, and she thought she had never seen a sexier, more compelling male.

Mick shot once more at the tree stump he had chosen as a target. It had been a while, but he hadn't lost his touch. The branch he'd been chipping away at flew into the air and fell into the quarry. Satisfied, he lowered his gun and turned back to his audience.

Maggie's face was all he saw. She was staring at him with an expression he recognized but didn't believe.

It was desire.

"That's pretty darn fancy shooting," Sam Glover said, his voice breaking the spell. "I guess you do know what you're doing with that weapon, but just don't give me any cause to regret letting you hang on to it."

"I won't." Mick holstered the revolver and looked intently at Maggie, but he saw that now her features were arranged in a neutral, almost bored expression. Had he only imagined what he had seen on her face? If, indeed, he had been correct, what were the implications? A rush of heat traveled along his body. Maggie *wanted* him!

Meanwhile, Maggie was struggling for self-control. So he had looked sexy while he was shooting. He was still the same man: just as annoying and pushy, and just as hung up on himself and his stones. As alien to what she sought in a man as an extraterrestrial might have been.

So why, then, was her heart still beating so quickly? And why were her palms sweaty on a cold, dry afternoon? She got angry at herself, and that helped.

But not enough. No matter how many times she might blink her eyes or pinch herself, she couldn't get away from the fact that he rang her chimes.

She drove back into town while the two men swapped stories in exactly the same manner Mick and her father had earlier. This time, however, the accounts and lies were about law enforcement, official and unofficial. Maggie tried not to listen, but Mick's voice tuned her ears irresistibly to his words. For the first time in her life she understood what it was to be mesmerized by another human being.

Impossible that she had actually fallen for a man she didn't even like! Impossible.

After they dropped Sam off at the police station, they went back to the shop. Maggie unlocked the door and turned the sign around to indicate she was open for business. She hadn't said a word to Mick. Hadn't been able to. His mere presence now had her in such a state she didn't trust herself to speak. She shrugged out of her coat and hung it on the rack behind the counter. Then she looked at him.

"Okay." Mick grinned and rubbed his palms together. "Let's get on with it."

"Wha...what?" Her heartbeat accelerated.

"The opals." He took off his coat and hung it over hers. "We've got hours yet. Let's get going on the jewelry."

"Oh. The jewelry. I...I didn't know what you meant."

"What did you think I meant?" He moved closer, close enough for her to smell cordite from the gun and musk on him. His eyes narrowed and the green irises seemed to glow.

Maggie swallowed hard, but she couldn't look away. Her heart was definitely going to jump out of her chest. She was also completely unable to utter a word.

Mick stared at her for a moment that stretched into an eternity. His hand touched her cheek. "That's what I thought you thought I meant," he said softly, a strange expression in his eyes.

Maggie held her breath. He was going to kiss her again, and this time she couldn't wait. To feel his lips on hers, his strong arms going around her, to be pressed to his body... She trembled in sensual anticipation.

But he didn't kiss her. Didn't embrace her. He turned his back on her and spoke to the wall. "Don't do it, Maggie," he said, jamming his hands in his pockets. "Don't fall for me. I'm a real stinker when it comes to women. I'll only hurt you in the long term."

His words were like a face full of ice water. "Don't flatter yourself, O'Shay," she snapped. "I don't know where you get your delusions, but I guarantee you not now or ever will I fall for you. I don't even like you!"

He turned back around. His expression was unreadable. "That doesn't always matter when a woman wants a man. In fact, sometimes dislike can fuel passion. But I suppose you're too inexperienced to understand that."

"*Inexperienced?* Listen, buster. I'm so experienced I could teach classes. Until we moved here, I had a love life so active it would have killed most women."

"I don't believe you."

"Believe! I even had an affair with a married man." No sooner were the words out of her mouth than Maggie clapped her hand over her lips. How could she tell him about the most humiliating experience of her life! How *could* she?

But he didn't smile or mock her. "A married man? Did you know it at the time?"

Tears filled her eyes. "No. I would never have deliberately hurt another woman like that. I thought he was really in love with me. That he wanted to marry me. Pretty dumb, huh? Pretty naive."

"Aw, Maggie." His arms went around her, pressing her to his chest. One big hand stroked her hair gently. "Don't cry. Men like that are not worth the tears. You're a fine woman and you deserve the best."

"Oh, sure."

"No." His hand continued stroking. "I mean it. Not many a young woman would willingly give up an independent life to look after her father. That takes a special kind of unselfishness. I admire that in you. I could never adjust my life to suit another person's needs."

Maggie sniffed. "Not even for your son?"

Mick was silent for a moment. "I guess I've been an all-right dad until recently. But Tad's needs never ran counter to mine. When I had to come here, though, I had to leave him."

She pulled back so that she could look up at his face. "What do you mean *had* to come here? Didn't you want to?"

He frowned and stopped touching her hair. "No, I didn't. I could have run my opal sales from Australia, although it does work out better to meet buyers face-to-face. No, I came here for another reason altogether." As soon as he had spoken, he could have kicked himself. The last thing in the world he ought to do, he thought, was tell her the truth.

Maggie waited.

He released her and stepped back. "You have any makings for tea around here? I could surely use a cup." And time to recover from that potentially disastrous burst of honesty, he added to himself.

"In the back room." She walked over to the door and turned the sign around, then locked the door. "I think we have some talking to do."

"Right." He followed her into the workroom without further comment.

While she prepared tea, using a small hot plate and water drawn from the sink in the tiny cubicle of a bathroom, Mick sat silently, thinking furiously. If he broke down and told her the whole truth right now as he wanted to do, he would very likely blow everything. She would know he had been using her, and her pride would undoubtedly force her to kick him out of her life. Maggie was a prideful woman, he cautioned himself. Could he risk it?

No, he couldn't. Lies came hard for him, but he was going to have to keep up the deceit. His need for revenge was greater than his need to get close to this woman. No matter how much he wanted to drown in her brown eyes. No matter how vulnerable she made herself to him.

And, damn it all, it was her own honesty and openness that made him feel like such a snake. He did his best to shut down his emotions while he watched her complete the small, homey task of making tea. It was not easy.

"I don't have any cream or sugar," she said, as she set the mugs on the worktable. Her slender fingers seemed to be shaking slightly, but that might have only been his guilty imagination.

"It's all right. I take it straight. My partner used to make a billy tea that'd curl your teeth." He wrapped his hands around the mug, savoring the aroma and warmth.

"Billy tea?" Her eyes were fixed on him.

"You make it outside over a fire."

"About your partner—"

"Ian's dead." Mick stared down at the tea. Ian would have knocked him into next week for lying like this. "I promised him I'd find some of his old mates and let them know what happened to him. That's why I came to the States. To look them up. I think one of them was the man who sold you the opal I admired in San Francisco." He tried to meet her eyes, but couldn't.

"Oh, dear."

"If I could know his name—"

"I don't—"

"Let me tell you about Ian Richards, Maggie." He took a sip of the tea. There was no need to lie about Ian. Just about the manner of his death and the reason Mick wanted to find his killer.

Maggie settled back in her chair. He was so tense she thought she could almost hear the air around him zing. His knuckles tightened and whitened on the mug, and he tossed down the last of his tea. "Can I get you some more?" she asked gently.

He shook his head. "I was fifteen when Ian found me driving a lorry out in the middle of nowhere, lugging crud from noplace to noplace, just like my old man. I was young and tough and cocky. And stupid beyond measure. But he must have seen something in me he liked, because he made me his special project." He smiled and looked years younger. "By the end of two years he had me reading and writing like I'd done it all my life. He also gave me a home with him in Coober Pedy until I up and married." He paused. "You know how that deal went."

Maggie nodded. The harshness of the life he had led struck her once more. And yet...

And yet there was something familiar about the look on his face when he talked about Ian Richards or about his son. Something that warmed her inside.

"Anyhow, after the marriage went bust, Tad and I got on with life, and Ian was a part of it all. We had a good partnership. Made more money than I'd ever dreamed of." He looked directly at her for the first time since starting his recitation. "I'm a lucky miner. Did I tell you that? It's no virtue, but I can find stones where a dozen men only see dust and rock."

"Proof of that's in my safe, isn't it?"

"Right. So Ian and I dug and got rich. Tad had good schooling in the town. It's a rough place, but not like you might think. Living's hard because of the climate. The town's usually peaceful. I started to get some schooling Ian couldn't give me. Learned about business so I wouldn't have to rat in the rocks the rest of my life. Did I mention how old he was?"

"Ian? No."

"Day he died he was over seventy. A man ought to die peacefully when he's that age." He said the last part as if he was speaking only to himself. His expression had darkened, and Maggie felt a shiver go through her.

"How did he die?" she asked.

"Huh?"

"Mick, how did Ian die?" She reached out and took his hand. He pulled away almost immediately.

"He had a heart attack." Mick stood and walked over to the hot plate. His back was to her. "He died out in the open, under the sun."

"That's terrible!" She resisted the urge to get up and put her arms around him. It was clear he wanted no comforting from her. "And you found him?"

"I did."

"And now you want to tell his friends about it. Mick, why didn't you just say so in the very beginning? I would have given you whatever information you needed."

Mick turned and stared at her. Was it actually going to be this easy, after all? Her face reflected understanding and sympathy, and her kindness brought an immediate lump to his throat.

And he was a damned liar!

"Here," she said, getting up and going over to her file cabinet. "I've got the name of the guy who sold me that special opal. I expect you can trace the others through him." She riffled through papers.

"Yeah. I expect I can." His emotions were now wildly out of control. On the one hand, he felt triumph. His enemy—Ian's killer—would soon be in his hands. On the other, he felt like slime. She smiled and handed him a sheet of paper. Mick stared at the name on it.

CHAPTER FIVE

OPALS. They ran through his hand like beautifully colored drops of water; just as cool, just as smooth.

Just as dead as Ian. Just as dead as the dead end Maggie's files had turned out to be. Mick took another long drink out of the bottle.

Getting drunk wasn't going to help. In any case, he couldn't seem to be able to get much more than slightly loaded. He twisted the top back on the booze and got up from the table.

The bastard had been clever—Mick had to give him that—using the name of a past prime minister, a name most Yanks wouldn't recognize or think twice about if they did. After all, it was a fairly common Aussie name. What it did was render Maggie useless to him in finding the killer.

And now that he was partly oiled, he had to admit to himself that that bothered him almost as much as not knowing the man's real identity. If he hadn't signed the work contract with her, he would have no reason at all to stay.

Would he?

Mick went into the kitchen, barely noticing his surroundings. They had insisted he stay with them, the Wellingtons had. He guessed Maggie had seen something in his face when the name had turned up a dud. She had dropped all indications that she was interested in him sexually and had changed before his eyes into a nursemaid. Pressing another cup of tea on him, she had called home to inform

her father that they would be having an overnight guest and
to plan dinner accordingly. Then she had filed the offend-
ing paper and started to bundle him out of the shop. He had
insisted on taking a few handfuls of stones with him, and
she had put up no argument, although he was certain he'd
seen one brewing in her brown eyes.

After they had collected his bag from the motel he'd been
staying in and he had shown an equal determination to stop
at a liquor store, the storm had simmered even closer to the
surface.

But she had said nothing. She had stopped as he'd requested and had only glanced with disapproval once at the
bottle. Out of deference to her tolerant attitude, he hadn't
started drinking until after both Wellingtons had gone to
bed. The woman was one in a million, he thought blearily,
setting the whiskey on the kitchen counter. He stared at the
amber liquid for a moment, then unscrewed the cap and
tipped the remainder into the sink.

Slow applause sounded behind him.

"That's the first sensible thing I've seen you do since I
showed you the sales sheet." Maggie's voice was soft and
not at all sarcastic. Mick turned.

His heart jumped into his throat and stuck there. She was
framed in the doorway, her hair all soft and loose. She wore
no makeup and her feet were bare. A girlish flannel granny
gown covered her from chin to ankles.

Mick had never seen a woman so appealing in his life.

"It's a crime to throw out good whiskey," he said, hearing the slurred huskiness in his voice. "But I didn't see any
need to keep it around. I'm not really a drinking man."

"I know." Her arms were folded across her chest, making the rounded globes of her breasts jut out enticingly.
When she strolled into the kitchen, he could see her nipples pressing against the fabric.

"Aren't you cold?" he asked, amazed the words could get past that damn lump in his throat. "Your feet must be freezing."

"Yeah. They are. But I wanted to see if you were all right." She came closer, and Mick backed up against the sink. "Are you sure you're okay?"

"I'm fine."

She took his chin in her hand, turning his face this way and that, examining him. "Your eyes are bloodshot. Want some coffee?"

"In the morning." She smelled so fresh—no perfume; just clean woman. "In the morning will be fine, Maggie. Don't trouble yourself about me."

"It's no trouble." She moved away, and he breathed a little easier. His defenses were down, and the temptation to take advantage of the situation was almost overwhelming. If he had just a few less scruples...

"If you're sure you're all right, I'll get back to bed," she added.

He nodded. "I'm all right. See you in the morning, then."

"Okay." She turned and looked back over her shoulder. "I'm sorry you had such a disappointment. I know how I would have felt if I hadn't been able to contact my mother's friends and relatives when she died. How much worse it must be for you. Not to even know the names you need."

He nodded again, looking away, not trusting himself. He was far too near an emotional explosion, and he wasn't even sure if lust or sorrow would be the fueling force.

When she finally left and disappeared upstairs, he found he was sweating. Tomorrow he was definitely going to have to move out, using the excuse of having to hurry and set up housekeeping for Tad. After all, the boy was due to arrive at the end of the week, and it would be better all the way around to not have to bunk him in a motel. Thinking about his son, Mick felt better, more in control of himself. He walked back into the dining room to collect the opals he'd been playing with.

But looking at their gleam and fire as they nestled in his palm, he wondered just how long that feeling of control would last when he was working with a woman who could move him as Maggie Wellington apparently could. He had to take stringent measures to ensure that neither one of them got overly involved emotionally. It was the only honorable thing to do, and he was far too bankrupt honor-wise to ignore any way to regain his self-esteem in that area. His unpaid debt to Ian, lying to Maggie and her father, people who had only shown him consideration and kindness—it all weighed heavily on Mick O'Shay's heart, and he was determined not to compromise himself any further.

OVER THE NEXT few days neither one gave way to their feelings—although the emotional atmosphere between them remained volatile—and they were able to accomplish a great deal. Maggie got hold of the security system people Sam Glover had recommended, and was amazed when they drove right up from Denver and installed the system she wanted. If it hadn't been for the presence of the now-dour Australian, she would have felt as happy as pie.

Mick had seemed to lose his sense of humor. He didn't joke, he didn't tease. He didn't come within two feet of her if he could possibly help it. Maggie put it down to disappointment over the fake name.

She wasn't entirely wrong. Mick was suffering from an emotional flu brought on by the apparent collapse of his plans. He was also suffering terribly from a refusal to see that Maggie had come to be much more to him than a source of information. Every time the notion surfaced in his consciousness, he deliberately blacked it out. He kept telling himself he would only stay long enough to find another way to get Ian's killers; that his time in Sullivan Springs with Maggie was going to be very limited.

But he had sent for his son. And he had set up housekeeping.

THREE DAYS BEFORE Mick's son arrived Maggie was ready to kill the boy's father, cheerfully. After spending that one night on the hideabed in the den, he had moved out without much more than a curt thanks. He had rented a place down the street. She had offered to help fix it up, but he made it quite clear he wanted no interference from her. Insult was added to injury when he hired a woman to clean and cook without consulting her for local gossip about the lady.

"Rumor has it that she spent quite a few years operating a 'business' in Las Vegas," she said one afternoon while they were working on designs. The shop was stuffy in spite of the cold weather, and Maggie's temper had gradually frayed over the course of the day. Mick's taciturnity didn't help. "I'm not sure that's the sort of woman you want around your boy."

"She's cheerful, strong and has a great sense of humor." Mick set two designs in the discard pile. "She's exactly who I want around Tad. He's sure seen far worse. Celia Hawthorne wants and needs the work. And I'll thank you not to embarrass any of us by further small-minded remarks." Another design went the way of the trash can.

Maggie bit her lip to keep back a sharp reply and tried to control the burning in her cheeks. He was right to reprimand her. Stooping to gossip was not her style, and she knew she had only done it because her temper was so short. Celia Hawthorne did have a reputation in town for giving an honest day's work for an honest day's wages, and she had no business slandering the woman, ex-hooker or not.

But it grated terribly to have the Australian calling her on it, as if she were a small child.

Then there was the matter of her designs. He was as picky as any customer she had ever had, finding small flaws in the best of her work. She was ready to tear her hair out.

"Nothing I do satisfies you," she shrieked the morning before Tad was due to arrive. Mick had cavalierly tossed out a half dozen designs she had worked on long hours the night before. "If your kid wasn't coming, I'd tear up our contract in your face and dare you to sue."

"What's Tad got to do with it?" He shoved his lower jaw forward slightly—a movement she had come to learn foreshadowed a loss of temper on his part.

"You've rented a house, made arrangements for his schooling, bought him all kinds of winter clothes and probably got his expectations up when you talked or wrote to him. It's not right for you to take out your disappointment and general bad temper on me or to ruin what could be a wonderful experience for your son."

"That's what I'm doing?" His eyes could have sent emerald laser beams right through her. "Taking out my frustrations on a woman?"

"It sure looks that way to me, O'Shay." She retrieved one of the sketches from the can. "Now, honestly. Tell me what's so wrong with this?"

Mick took a deep breath and settled back on his stool. He hadn't really looked at the sketches before discarding them. This morning, simmering with frustration about his thwarted quest for revenge and anxious about how Tad would cope with life in this cold land, nothing was going to suit him. He rubbed a hand over his eyes and looked again.

There wasn't a thing wrong with the design. A pencil sketch of a gold necklace utilizing five of the larger opals, it was the first step to what would be an outstanding piece of jewelry. He grunted softly.

"You know," Maggie said in an equally gentle tone, "I've been doing some thinking. I may be able to help you find Ian's friends, after all."

Mick froze in place. She could see all of his muscles tense, and suddenly she wasn't sure of his reasons for wanting to find the man who had sold her the opal. It struck her that his not knowing the names of his partner's friends was odd.

"What do you mean?" he asked, his eyes and tone as cold as the snow piling up day by day on the mountain. "Exactly what do you mean?"

"Well." She drawled the word, playing for time to think. "I did see him. It's entirely likely I'd recognize him again if—"

"That's it!" He stood, his expression exultant. Grabbing her by the arms, he pulled her close until their faces were barely inches apart. "We'll figure out where the bas . . . where he might be. Then you can—"

"Mick, you're upsetting me." She tried pulling away, but his grip was too strong. She wasn't upset. She was frightened. It wasn't grief she saw reflected in his eyes, but hate. She had lived with grief long enough to know the difference. "Let me go!"

He released her immediately. "Sorry." He turned his back, and wiped his hand over his face as if to erase the look there. "I just got excited."

"Mick, tell me what's going on. You don't want to just relate the news of Ian's death. It's much, much more than that. I can tell."

When he turned back, he was smiling. It was not a warm smile. "They do need to know he died. That's the truth."

Pry and fuss as she would, Maggie could get no further information on the subject from him. His demeanor made her too nervous to really pull out the stops. However, she was sure he'd lied to her. They ended the day with an icy truce between them, and another dozen designs approved by the man of mystery. Maggie considered their progress only a minor success and was not happy. Mick O'Shay, she feared, was a dangerous man, and it was highly unfortunate that she had linked her professional life with his.

The next day, however, he astonished her by showing up at the crack of dawn and inviting himself in for breakfast. He seemed an entirely different man, more like the one she had responded to earlier: vulnerable and not quite sure of himself.

"I know it's a real imposition," he said after settling down to a massive serving of eggs, sausages and hash browns dished up by Patrick. "But I was wondering if the two of you would mind driving me down to Denver to pick up Tad. It's not as if I can't do it myself, of course. But I'm so excited to see him that I don't know if I can trust myself driving in the city. Wrong side of the road and all that, you understand." He paused. "And it might make things go smoother if there were other people to talk some. You know teenaged kids. Either it's a mile a minute or total silence."

"Tad's a teenager?" Maggie asked, still digesting the implications of this change in Mick.

"Well, twelve. But he's a big kid. Most people take him for fourteen or fifteen."

"But he is just twelve." Patrick entered the conversation for the first time.

Mick sighed and looked unhappy. "He's older than his years, although he's not nearly as old as I was when I was twelve."

Patrick and Maggie looked at each other, and Patrick smiled. "We'd be happy to go along, Mick. And I think the next time you run stuff over to Davey, Mag, you ought to take Tad along. Davey's had some hard knocks himself and might relate to a kid whose life's been a bit rough."

Mick's enthusiasm and gratitude was so plain it almost made Maggie cry. How could this loving, concerned father be the same man whose eyes had spoken with such hatred?

She must have misjudged him and overreacted, she decided, and was glad she hadn't confided her fears to her father.

TAD O'SHAY was a youthful, skinny copy of his father. His tanned, freckled face showed future development of the same strong features. His eyes were as green as Mick's and his grin as infectious. Only did his sandy hair and height offer evidence that he'd had another parent. Already he was almost as tall as his father, and judging by the length of wrists and ankles emerging from clothes he'd plainly outgrown, he was nowhere near stopping his climb. Maggie smiled at the thought that Mick would be looking up to his son in a very few years.

But for now, the boy was engulfed in a vigorous bear hug with his dad, and the two spent minutes laughing and pummeling one another. When Mick finally calmed down long enough to introduce Tad, Maggie saw that his eyes glistened with tears.

"This is my boy, Tad," he said, his arm around the lad's shoulders and his voice filled with pride. "He's grown at least half a foot since I last saw him."

Tad blushed and grinned, but responded to the introductions in a surprisingly mature manner, justifying his father's claims of his precociousness. By the time they collected his luggage and trunk of possessions, Maggie was thoroughly charmed.

On the way home she realized how much her father was taken with Tad. This surprised her, since he had never shown much interest in children, really only including her directly in his life when she herself had become an adult. Was this some kind of odd, belated longing for a son? Or even a grandson? Or some strange new manifestation of his grief?

"This sure looks different from home," Tad said as they pulled out of the city traffic and headed up toward the mountains. He hadn't paid much attention as they had driven through Denver, but now, as the scenery began unfolding, Maggie could see from glances in the rearview mirror that he was starting to take notice. He still wore a light jacket, in spite of Mick's suggestion that he change into one of the warmer ones he had brought along. The kid, she decided, had a bit to learn about life in Colorado.

"You aren't going to believe how different it is," Mick commented dryly. "At home, your bones bake. Here, they just ache." Both O'Shays laughed, and Patrick joined them.

"You'll both get to like it," he said. "When I first moved from the coast, I thought I'd dry out and blow away. No humidity, you see. But now if I go back to sea level, I feel like I'm swimming in the air. Mountains are good for the human spirit."

Maggie listened with interest. Moving to Sullivan Springs had been her idea. She had hoped that the change would bring her father out of his depression. Apparently, she had done something right.

"There ain't any mountains like this back home," Tad announced. He was craning his neck to see out now.

"No, there aren't." Mick's tactful grammar correction brought a smile to Maggie's face.

"I bet in no time you're going to be a heck of a skier." Patrick smiled at the boy. "Makes me kind of wish I was younger, so I could join you."

"You ain't so old, Mr. Wellington."

Mick's pride in the boy increased, if that was possible. The boy had learned something of the social graces while living with their friends in Adelaide. He listened while Patrick bantered with Tad, and reflected on the delight being a father always brought him. He wondered how he could have gone off and left him, even for a good cause. Looking at the back of Maggie's head, he also began to wonder if what he was planning for her in that regard was as foolish and wrong. The idea had come to him during the night and the more he thought about it, the better it seemed.

Her dark hair gleamed in the sunlight, and he remembered how soft and silky it had felt on his hands. He had treated her badly all week, hoping that he could keep his warmer emotions at bay by doing so. Then yesterday, when she had announced that she could identify the opal thief, he had lost control again—only this time he had shown her his dark side. His delight at being reunited with Tad faded a little as he remembered.

Tad poked his father in the ribs. "You got that look, Dad," he said, his expression grave. "Didn't find him yet, did you? You acted so happy to see me, I figured you had."

"We'll talk about that later," Mick snapped. Tad jerked as if he'd been hit. Maggie's head turned for a second, and Mick realized she hadn't missed a thing. Tad could give away the whole truth if he kept blabbing!

He didn't. For the rest of the ride to Sullivan Springs, he maintained a sullen silence. Not even Patrick's joking could arouse a smile. The older man finally stopped and lapsed into a silence of his own. Maggie didn't say a word, but her shoulders stiffened and stayed that way for the rest of the trip.

Mick felt about a sixteenth of an inch high.

"YOUR MR. O'SHAY certainly has a strange way of dealing with a son he says he loves so much." Patrick finally commented after they had dropped the other two off at their new home.

"He is not *my* Mr. O'Shay, but I agree." Maggie debated giving her father a rundown on her suspicions about Mick, then decided he didn't need the extra burden. If Tad's presence in Sullivan Springs was going to help his mental attitude, so much the better. She wasn't about to interfere negatively. "I expect they'll work things out once they're alone, though," she added.

"I hope so." Patrick was quiet until after they arrived home and had entered the house. Then he said, "But tomorrow I'm going to go over and see. Maybe I'll take the boy around town while you and O'Shay are working—help him get used to his new home."

"I'm sure both of them would appreciate that." Maggie unzipped her coat, but didn't take it off. The house was chilly, and she could see that the stack of firewood by the hearth was low. "I'll go get more wood. Why don't you start a fire?"

"All right."

Maggie went through the kitchen to the backyard and started piling logs in the leather carrier. The sun was starting to set behind the mountains, and the sky was turning gold-red. She stopped working and straightened, pausing to enjoy the fleeting beauty. The outstretched branches of the big tree toward the rear of the yard made a black lace pattern over the sky, creating a natural piece of jewelry for her. She stared, willing her mind to retain the image.

Mick would absolutely flip tomorrow when he saw the sketch!

Mick would flip...

Mick would...

Maggie suddenly knew. The only reason he had come to her in the first place was for the name of the man who had sold her that opal. The only reason he had commissioned her to set his stones was so that he could get the information he needed. Undoubtedly the only reason he had played with her romantically was to get past her defenses. He had not even so much as touched her in passing since the name in her files had turned out to be a fake. Her eyes filled with tears as she realized how she had been lied to and used. The beautiful scene faded, and the sun set....

"HOW MANY TIMES do I have to tell you I'm sorry I yelled at you?" Mick faced his son, seeing in the hard set of the boy's jaw and the coldness of his eyes a reflection of himself. "I couldn't let you spill the story with Maggie and her father right there. Don't you understand?"

"Sure, I understand. You're gonna get her to help you find the guy, then you're gonna leave me again and go hunt him, just like you did at home. Why'd you bother bringing me here at all?"

Mick felt close to tears because of his frustration. "I brought you here because you're my son and I love you. Don't you know you're more important to me than anything else?"

"Sure I am."

"Tad—"

"Excuse me, Mr. O'Shay." Celia Hawthorne's voice interrupted him. "Dinner is ready."

"Just a minute, Celia." Mick held out his arms. "Tad, please. Don't you want Ian's killer found?"

The coldness in the boy's eyes wavered. "Yeah."

"Then will you just trust me? I haven't been such a bad old man before this, have I?"

"I guess not."

"Well?"

Tad hesitated for a moment, then flung himself into his father's arms. Relief and love flooded through Mick and now he did cry.

LATE THAT NIGHT he wandered through the quiet house, trying to put his emotions and thoughts in order. Tad had seemed his normal, cheerful self during dinner and throughout the evening. Celia's cooking was excellent, and the boy had stuffed himself on pork roast, potatoes, applesauce and gravy. He had even eaten his green beans without the usual fuss over colored vegetables. Mick's appetite hadn't been up to scratch, but he had enjoyed the meal as well. Celia had been a great choice for housekeeper and cook. With that one meal she had made a friend for life in Tad.

Tad had also found the house to his liking, once he'd taken the time to explore. Built in the twenties, the place had the kind of small rooms, nooks and crannies that would delight any child, but especially one who had spent most of his young life in a cave.

Mick smiled as he remembered the home he had carved right out of the rock. Like many other miners, he lived underground to protect himself and his family from the scorching heat of the Australian desert. It was a large, comfortable place, more than adequate for Tad and him, but not nearly as interesting as this house.

Which was a good thing. Tad would be stuck indoors just as surely as he had been during the many hundred degree-plus days back in Coober Pedy. The kid was an avid reader, and the American television programs would likely keep him occupied as well. But having a house like this would make all the difference. And once Christmas was over and he went to school, he would find friends. Tad would be happy. He wouldn't be able to stand it if Tad became unhappy....

Mick sat down on the couch and stared into the coals of the dying fire. He'd had no idea the boy had been so miserable away from him. He had seemed enthusiastic about moving in with Jack Taylor and his family. But then again,

Tad had never been away from the two adults in his life at the same time. When Mick had had to travel in the past, Ian had always been there. He'd loved the kid as if he'd been his own grandson, and Tad had returned the affection. Mick knew he'd never forget the look on his son's face when he'd told him about Ian's death.

Pain went through Mick like a knife. Ian would never be there again.

But Tad plainly resented Mick's quest for revenge. He rubbed his forehead, trying to get his thoughts straight. Hadn't he explained it to the boy over and over? How the authorities had given the murder such short shrift; how the only way retribution was to happen was for him to make it happen.

Wasn't he right in this?

Mick rose and stirred the coals. A flame flared and he saw Maggie's face in it. Wasn't he right in this, either? When he faced his feelings about her, he had to admit she was getting further and further under his skin. He'd done pretty well this week, keeping her at a distance by his behavior. But so many times he had wanted to silence her arguments with a kiss. So many times he had wanted to apologize for his actions and words. So many times—

Oh, hell, he thought with a grimace. It was going from bad to worse. He wasn't going to get any sleep if he kept on worrying about his problems. Thinking things through wasn't exactly his strong point, anyhow. Action was.

The problem was, if he took the kind of action he wanted to he'd end up taking the lady to bed. Wouldn't that throw a nice monkey wrench into his already messed-up life? Boy, oh boy, would it ever! Mick adjusted the screen in front of the fireplace and went to bed.

He didn't sleep worth a darn.

The next morning dawned bright, without a hint of the snow clouds usually hanging around the summit of the mountains. Tad ran outside in his pajamas and started flinging snowballs at all targets, including Mick when he went out to drag his son in for breakfast and adequate clothing. After eating and changing, they spent a happy, wild time together in front of the house, only stopping the horseplay when Patrick Wellington ambled up the sidewalk.

"I thought I'd stop by and see if I could show Tad around town," he said. "Maggie took off for the shop right after breakfast, so I know she's waiting for you, Mick."

"I hadn't really planned on working today," Mick said, looking at his son. "This is the first day we've been together in a long time."

"It's okay, Dad." Tad was grinning. "The more you work, the quicker you'll be done. Right?"

"You sure?"

The grin remained. "Sure. I bet Mr. Wellington knows lots more about this place than you, anyway."

Feeling a little confused, Mick agreed to the situation. It wasn't until he was almost at the store that it occurred to him how similar Tad probably found Patrick to Ian. Although the American was younger, they did bear a resemblance to one another. That was great, he decided. Patrick had sought out the boy, and Tad had responded. Maybe a friendship would grow, he mused, making adjustment to life in Colorado easier for the boy.

Of course, they weren't going to be here forever, he added mentally. Only long enough for Mick to bring his plan about. Only long enough for him to find the murderer.

And he knew exactly how he was going to get Maggie to help.

He pulled up to the curb and got out, feeling that maybe he was finally on top of things. If he could just keep his glands from getting him into trouble, he would be all right.

Tad was fine, it was a beautiful day, he seemed to be getting used to the cold, finally, and he had his plan. Yeah, things were going well.

He opened the door. A stinging shower of opals and curses hit him right in the face. Maggie Wellington stood in the middle of the shop, looking madder than he had ever seen a woman look before.

"You *bastard*, Mick O'Shay!" she screamed. "Take your damn opals and get out of my life. I never want to set eyes on you again!"

CHAPTER SIX

MAGGIE KNEW she was hysterical, but she couldn't help herself. All night long, since her epiphany, she had simmered in rage and humiliation. She'd been used! Lied to! Tricked! Deceived! Oh, wasn't it all just an old record playing? Wasn't it just like what had happened to her in San Francisco? "Get out!" she screamed again. "I *hate* you!"

Mick stood his ground, although Maggie looked as if she could easily kill him. "I'm not going anywhere until you tell me what's set you off," he declared. "Or have you just lost your mind, tossing those stones around as though they were jelly beans." He knelt down, keeping his attention on the enraged woman, and started picking up the opals.

She took a deep breath, struggling for control. "I'll tell you what's set me off, Mr. O'Shay. I suddenly realized exactly why you came to me with your lousy collection of stones. It should not have taken me so long but, then, I didn't have my eyes completely open, thanks to your deliberate manipulation of my emotions, did I?"

"Deliberate manipulations? Maggie, what the hell are you talking about?" He had most of the stones now. A few were outside in the snow. They would wait. He rose.

"You didn't come here because of me." She pointed a trembling finger at him. "You came because of the opal. The one I bought from that man. The one that belonged to Ian. He was no friend of Ian's. He *stole* it. That's what happened, didn't it. Didn't it!"

She couldn't know. Couldn't have pieced it together. But Mick knew she did know. "Oh, God," he said softly.

Maggie watched him for a moment, saw the truth on his face, didn't see the anguish, and thought she understood. Her anger was washed away in the worst hurt she had ever known. Her muscles seemed to collapse and the tears gushed, but she managed to stumble into the workroom and close the door behind her. Almost without her knowing it, her hand turned the lock.

Mick tossed the opals on a countertop. "Maggie," he called. "Maggie, open the door. We have to talk." He hit the door with his fist and tested the lock. It was solid. "Maggie!"

Her voice came faintly through the door. "The only talking you'll hear from me will be through a lawyer. You got me to sign a contract under false pretenses."

"You can't prove that!"

"I don't need to. I know it!"

"You and I know that's not enough. Now, will you please quit acting hysterical and open this door? I don't want to break it down, but I will."

"Just try it, you snake. Sam Glover and his people will be here so fast, your head will spin!"

Mick hesitated. Although the system they had installed was geared for alerting the police to nighttime action, if he did damage the door, it would indeed trigger an alarm. This was not an argument he wanted strangers drawn into. No, sir!

"All right," he said in what he hoped was a reasonable tone. "No door-shattering. But you aren't going anywhere, are you? Not unless you've some talent as a miner, and I doubt very much if you do. So you've got to listen to what I have to say. There's nothing else for it, Maggie."

He waited.

Silence.

Then the raucous sounds of a rock station blared from the workroom. Mick cursed long and loud, but it did him no good. She had effectively garnered this round. Damn her.

He turned around to face the shop. It was early, but a few people were strolling the street, checking out the windows. *Okay,* he thought. It would be his round next time.

MAGGIE DRAGGED the sleeve of her shirt over her eyes, drying them. At least the silly contest of wits had allowed her to master the overwhelming emotion that had reduced her to doing something as unoriginal as locking herself in the room. She smiled, wishing she could have seen his face when she turned on the radio. It must have been a sight!

She must have been a sight, and not a pretty one. Where in the world had that anger come from? she wondered. Why, if she'd had a weapon other than her tongue, there was no telling what shape O'Shay would be in right now. Maggie shuddered.

She wrapped her arms around herself and wandered over to the safe. Earlier, she had opened it, reached in and taken a handful of opals out to fling in Mick's face, but now she looked in carefully.

She had managed to grab the best, the ones set off for special treatment. Special little treasures, he had called them affectionately. She shuddered again. Some of them might have been damaged by the violence, and that filled her with regret. She had intended to hurt him, not his opals.

Going back to the workbench, she sat down and tried to think rationally. He hadn't denied her accusation, so he was guilty as charged. All right. This wasn't pleasant, but it was over. He'd be out of her life in no time, since he couldn't count on her infatuated cooperation any more, or any kind of cooperation, for that matter.

Tears stung her eyes again. Why did she have to get this terrible, empty feeling whenever she thought about never seeing him again, never working by his side, never arguing, never—

Stop it! she ordered herself.

Learning about that crud, Dr. Jerry Linder, had hurt, and she had felt humiliated, but there had never been this kind of pain. She hadn't even cried; she'd simply gone into the creep's office in the hospital where her mother had lain dying and had told him calmly what she thought of him. It had been a highly satisfactory experience, and she'd felt no regrets.

So why, with this man, was betrayal so agonizing? Maggie bowed her head in her hands.

MICK CONSIDERED his options. None of them looked promising. However she had managed it, Maggie had him pegged and had blown him right out of the water. How to get back in was the question.

Finally, he decided honesty was the only answer. The question was, could he afford to be honest? Baring his soul was going to make him vulnerable, expose his heart. And this to a woman who had a hold on him he didn't yet understand.

It was a thoroughly frightening situation, when one thought about it.

He spent a few minutes on his hands and knees by the front door, rooting in the snow for the rest of the opals. Satisfied that he had found them all, he returned inside and went behind the counter, where he arranged the stones in a haphazard fashion on the black velvet bed Maggie used to display her finished pieces. The unset stones made the jewelry display more interesting, he decided—rather like a promise of things to come.

Things to come.

He stared at the door to the workroom in an attempt to will its occupant to give up her stubbornness and come out. It didn't matter who was right and who was wrong; they had to talk. No matter how things ended—if she finally threw him out on his ear—he had to explain, make her see, make her understand. It was like an itch inside him that couldn't be scratched.

And why in hell was that?

Mick ran a hand through his hair and let out his breath slowly. He sensed that the answer to his question was just around the corner somewhere in his mind but he could not, for the life of him, get to that place. All he could do was see Maggie's face the moment she realized her suspicions were true, the moment he couldn't think of another lie quickly enough . . . the moment his own heart had given him away by his expression.

What a fool I am, he thought. *What a bloody fool.* To have believed that he could carry off a deception over a period of time. Hell, he couldn't even play poker without losing his shirt. Ian used to say his cards were written on his forehead for all the world to see. And he had expected to play a far more serious game with a woman whose profession required an eye for truth, for details hidden to others; whose own feelings were completely visible to anyone caring to look.

He had seen them in her face and in her eyes, when she had gazed at him the day he'd demonstrated his shooting ability for Chief Glover.... She had made them clear when she had yearned for a kiss and embrace that time they'd been alone in the store. Then there was her concern for him that night, and the intensity of her rage over his lies and deceptions....

It was more than lust for him she'd been feeling.

She was in love with him!

Mick felt light-headed and a little sick. What had he done? The poor little sheila! Remembering her tearful confession about the affair with the married man, his sense of guilt increased dramatically. He was about to get up and go knock on the workroom door again, this time pleadingly, when the shop door opened. At exactly the same moment, the rock music went off.

"Hi," the newcomer said. "Maggie around?"

Mick studied him. The man was no local. He was young, but unlike most of the young men Mick had observed in the town his skin wasn't deeply tanned and already creased from exposure to the high-altitude sunlight and bitterly cold winds. He was dressed like a city boy, too: fur-collared topcoat over a three piece suit . . .

He began to suspect this was the guy from San Francisco she'd told him about.

"Who wants to know?" he asked, coming out from behind the counter.

"Who're you?"

"Someone looking after her best interests. Now, I asked you politely, who wants to know?" Mick readied himself for a fight. Anyone who had hurt her for whatever reason was definitely deserving of a beating.

"Where's Maggie? I went by the house and her dad was gone. I don't have time to fool around—"

"She's busy and ain't able to see just any—"

"Jeff!" The workroom door opened with a bang and Maggie flew out, wrapping her arms around the newcomer. Mick felt an unaccustomed wave of jealousy. "What in the world are you doing here?" she asked.

"Tryin' to relight an old bonfire," Mick said dryly, not sure he cared if anyone else heard him. He was just about ready to punch the man in the face. Remembering how she had looked when she had told him about the affair made him actually see red.

"What're you talking about?" Maggie let go of the other man and turned on him. "What bonfire?"

"Well." Mick gestured toward the stranger. "It's pretty clear you two have some kind of interesting history. Maybe I ought to just leave and let you—"

"Who is this guy?" Three-piece-suit looked worried, Mick noted. "Maggie, are you all right?"

"No." Maggie glared at Mick. "In fact, Jeff, you are just what the doctor ordered. I want to break a contract with this man. I need a good lawyer. One who's objective, which Dad is not."

Mick looked from one to the other, realized he had made a mistake and said, "This isn't your old boyfriend? The one who was married?"

"This is my cousin, Jeff Wright," Maggie explained belligerently. "Jeff, Mick O'Shay." She completed the introduction. The men shook hands.

"Cousin?" Mick felt nothing but relief.

"He's a lawyer, like my dad." Maggie put her hands on her hips. "And he's as good as they come. Jeff, you've got to get me out of this!"

Much to Maggie's annoyance, Jeff couldn't get her out of it. When he looked at the contract she and Mick had signed, he declared the document watertight. "Uncle Pat always did know how to draw up a document," he said, smiling. "Looks to me as though you two had better start negotiating."

"Negotiating?" She looked at Jeff, then at Mick. The Australian was showing absolutely no expression.

Under Jeff's direction, they ended up at Mick's house in two separate rooms. The young lawyer had been in Denver on business and had driven up to Sullivan Springs for a surprise visit to his relatives. Challenged, however, by the situation between Mick and Maggie, he had agreed to stay overnight. "Nothing is so serious that it can't be worked out between two reasonable human beings," he had stated optimistically back at the store.

But Mick and Maggie were not reasonable human beings.

"He lied to me!" she protested when Jeff told her that every conflict had two sides. "How could anyone believe he has the right to lie?"

"Put it on paper, Mag." Jeff had said after listening to their garbled explanations for only a moment. Hoping to spare Patrick the sight of their conflict, Maggie had agreed to go to Mick's place, not realizing until it was too late how much of a psychological disadvantage this would put her at. The room she was in was Tad's, and it was clear the boy had already made himself at home. His belongings were strewed all over the place. If she was successful in getting Mick to agree to ending their relationship, Tad would be uprooted once more.

So...?

What difference did that make to her? Why should she care about the feelings of his kid, when it was quite plain that Mick cared not one whit for hers? Why?

Because she couldn't help it. That was why. She was more angry with Mick O'Shay than she had ever been with another human being, but that didn't make her a witch. Her indignation didn't include the innocent child. She cleared some space on the boy's desk, sat down and started to write as Jeff had instructed her.

MICK CHEWED at the eraser end of his pencil. Hell, he couldn't put his motivations down on paper, could he? She'd never understand. So why bother? He balled up his piece of paper and tossed it in a corner. A few minutes later, Jeff knocked on the door.

Mick let him in. "I couldn't write anything," he said. "I didn't tell her the whole truth, but I had my reasons."

"And they were...?" Wright sat down on the edge of the bed. His expression was one of concern. He had dark hair and brown eyes, just like Maggie, but the resemblance ended there. The young San Francisco lawyer had strongly carved, masculine features and a build that attested to physical strength and fitness. Maggie, while not weak, was definitely delicate and feminine. So feminine that even now, Mick ached to touch her, to hold her...

"Why the hell should you care?" he exploded. "I'm a stranger to you. Maggie's your relative. You ought to be working for her best interests, not mine."

Wright was unperturbed. "Could be they are one and the same." He laced his fingers together and hooked one knee. "Sure, I don't know you, but I do know Mag and when I see her looking at you, I get a very clear signal. She cares about you, O'Shay."

Mick sat back down on his chair. "I know."

"Maggie's not one to give out her affections easily. While her mother was in the hospital, there was a guy who—"

"I know about that. When you came in, I thought you might be him." Mick grinned. "I was going to punch your lights out."

"Why?"

"For hurting Maggie. Why else?"

"It bothers you that much? Enough to run the risk of an assault charge?"

The younger man's gaze was beginning to make Mick uncomfortable. "Leave it to a damn lawyer to think that way. I just think a guy who's married and runs around with an unsuspecting girl ought to be taught a lesson. He deceived her."

"And that's what she says you've done."

"I'm not married!" Mick stood and ran a hand through his hair. "I never lied to her about myself."

Jeff Wright just looked at him.

"Well, I didn't! I just wanted some information, which it turns out she doesn't have."

"How long have you known that?"

"Days. Why?"

"And you're still here? Why?"

"I... She does know something that might help me. She's seen the face of the man I'm looking for. She could identify him if she saw him again."

"That's why you're staying."

"Yes. I—" Mick broke off. Maggie was standing in the doorway, a piece of paper clutched in her hand. Her jaw was set, her mouth firm, but her eyes were soft with tears.

"I can't help you, Mick," she said. "The chances I'll ever see him again are one in a million. Here's my list of grievances." She thrust the paper at him. "I hope it amuses you." Then she turned and was gone.

Mick looked helplessly at Jeff. "She won't even talk to me. How am I going to explain myself to her?"

"You could write—"

"Oh, bloody hell, man! I can't write my way out of a paper sack. I need to speak, to face her."

"Why? Just so you can get what you want from her? So you can use her to chase after someone who—" The sound of a slamming door interrupted him.

"Goddamn! Maggie!" Mick brushed past the other man. Not bothering with his coat, he rushed out the front door and caught up with her at the end of the walk. Grabbing her arm, he pulled her around to face him.

"Let me go!" She punched him on the chest. The impact of her little fist stung.

"Ow! I won't let you go until you give me a chance to explain. To tell you why—"

"I don't need any explanations from you. I heard you tell Jeff why you're staying. I'll tell you what, I'll draw a picture of the guy for you, then you can spend the rest of your life—and your son's—traipsing all over the world trying to find him. How will that be? You won't have to be bothered with me ever—"

Mick cut off the angry flow of words with an intense kiss. And as he kissed her, a part of him that had been locked up by the experiences of his younger days began to sense light and freedom. He didn't understand the feelings rushing through him, but he liked them and didn't want to do anything to lose them.

Maggie didn't try to struggle free. She knew it would be futile and, besides, her body had no intention of letting her take it away from Mick O'Shay. Her body loved being held and caressed by him. It didn't know what a rat he was; didn't know all he really wanted was an identification . . . didn't know he was using her just as she had been used in the past. Tears began rolling down her cheeks.

"Maggie, Maggie." Mick spoke softly and tenderly. "When I first came to you, all I did want was the name of the guy with the opal. I set you up, hoping you'd learn to trust me enough to tell me. But nothing has worked the way I thought it would."

"W-will you p-please just tell me the truth. I don't think I can stand any more l-lies." She squeezed her eyes closed, trying to stop the tears.

"The truth is, I need you, Maggie. I need you to help me find Ian's killer, to set my opals, to—"

"K-killer? I thought he died of a heart attack. That's what you told me."

Mick shook his head. "I lied. I worried that if you knew how much violence was involved in the situation, you'd back out for good. I know now I should have been completely honest with you. But hindsight is always clearer. Maggie, a man, probably the one who sold you the opal, robbed and shot my dearest friend and left him to bleed to death out on the plain where the temperatures can go well over one hundred degrees." Pain twisted his face. "It had to have been an agonizing death. He was dead when I found him. I couldn't even wish him godspeed."

"Oh, Mick." Maggie reached out and touched his cheek. "You should have told me this sooner. I understand now."

He stared at her.

"You want justice, don't you? If I can help in any way, I will. That's a promise."

His eyes turned to green ice. "You don't understand at all. I don't want justice. I want revenge! If I get my sights on that bastard, he's as good as—"

"That's a wonderful idea, you idiot! You blow him away and end up in prison. What's going to happen to Tad? Who's going to look after your boy? Really terrific thinking, O'Shay. Kind of a code-of-the-west deal. An eye for an eye. That sort of thing."

"You don't understand. A woman can't."

"Women aren't into revenge? Oh, be serious, Mick. What about Medea? Wasn't Elizabeth the First motivated several times by revenge? Both of them killed people they loved. How bright! History and literature are full of sterling examples of women who have allowed the satisfaction of revenge-taking to screw up their lives. It is not gender-particular, buster. Just stupid-particular."

"What am I supposed to do? Forget the whole thing? Maybe he'll kill someone else for money or gold or stones. Won't I be partly responsible, then?"

Maggie put her hands to her face. "Okay, okay. So you can't just walk away from this. But I will not help unless you promise to turn him over to the authorities if we find him."

Jeff appeared at the open front door of the house. "I'll go one better than that, O'Shay. If you don't do as she says, *I'll* inform the police of your intentions. I won't have Maggie mixed up in anything violent or illegal." He raised a hand. "I didn't intend to eavesdrop, but with the two of you shouting it was impossible not to overhear."

Mick looked at Maggie and then at her cousin. "You can threaten me all you want, both of you. I won't change my mind. The law isn't strong enough. I am." He ran a hand through his hair. "It's cold out here. Let's go back inside."

"Mick!" She thought she saw a slight hint of self-doubt in his eyes. "Please. Think of Tad. If you can't promise outright, at least promise that you won't act hastily—that you will consider options and consequences. Jeff, talk to him."

"Listen to her, O'Shay. I won't threaten you, but I am an officer of the court. If I become aware that you intend to commit a crime, I'm obligated—"

"Unless you have a professional relationship with him," Maggie interjected. "Jeff?" she added pleadingly.

"Maggie, don't compromise your cousin." Mick took hold of her shoulders. "I'm not worth that."

She just glared at him, defiantly.

"All right. But this isn't easy for me, you know. I've lived with the idea of revenge for a long time. I can't just give it up."

"You can learn to change your attitude. Come on, let's go back in. I'm getting chilly, and you must be freezing." She was smiling as if she had won a great victory.

Inside, Mick put on some water for tea and invited the cousins to sit down at his kitchen table. "I've got an idea," he said, "that might just solve the problem of locating the man. Since it fits in with other things we're doing, I don't think you'll have any objections."

"Let's hear it." Maggie turned her chair so she could watch him.

"The San Francisco Jewelry Exposition." He grinned and spread out his hands.

Maggie and Jeff looked at one another, then back to the Australian.

"Don't you see? A show like that is bound to draw jewel thieves. It's like a gourmet menu for them. Spot the stones you want, target the owners and—"

"Mick, no one displays stones he owns at that Exposition. It's strictly a jewelers' competition. And it's juried. I don't know if I could even get in."

"Maggie, you're one of the best," Jeff protested. "Why you insist on being so modest about your talents is beyond me."

"Well. I have learned a lot in the time we've lived here. My technique's improved just by practice. But my designs—"

"Your designs are great." Mick set the teapot and three mugs on the table. Then he pulled up a chair for himself. "I admit I've been kind of hard on you about them, but—"

"*Kind* of hard? You've torn apart almost everything I've shown you. You're harder to please than . . . than . . ."

"Could you two possibly get along without arguing for five minutes?" Jeff asked. "Maggie, I think Mick's idea is a good one. Even if you don't spot the guy there, it would do wonders for you professionally to show at the Exposition. And don't tell me your stuff's not good enough," he added when she opened her mouth to protest again.

"Listen to the man," Mick said. "You might not trust my judgment, but surely you do his. He's right. Don't even think about my problem. Think only about what it'll mean for you."

She looked from one man to the other. Both faces showed only encouragement. "What can I say? With such loyal fans, how can I lose? Okay, I'll try to get something in the show. If, that is, Mr. Particular lets me get a design off the launch pad."

"Done." Mick put out his hand. She shook it and was not surprised when he continued to hold hers.

"Well." Jeff stood. "You two have a lot to talk about, I can tell. Have any idea where I can find Patrick? I did come up here to see both of my relatives."

"Oh, he's—"

"He's out with my boy," Mick said. "They went out about nine-thirty to explore. Hit it right off, they did."

"How old's your kid?"

"Almost thirteen."

Jeff's eyebrows went up.

"I know." Maggie said. "It's not like Papa to take up with a child, but he seems to be coming out of his depression at last and I am delighted."

"That is good news." Jeff leaned down and kissed his cousin's cheek. Then he shook hands with Mick. "Tell you what, O'Shay. We'll call this an unofficial agreement between gentlemen. If you need any legal assistance with your problem, I'll be glad to help out. Just promise you'll talk to me before you go flying off on some vendetta."

"I appreciate that," Mick said sincerely. "I can at least promise that much. And you've already helped out. Maggie would probably still be locked up in her workroom if you hadn't come along."

Jeff said he had been glad to be of service and left.

When they were alone, Maggie turned to Mick with tears in her eyes. "I want a promise, too, Mick. I want you to think so hard about this thing your head will hurt. I don't know anything about your beliefs, but I want you praying about it, as well."

"I'm a God-fearing man," he protested, amazed at her vehemence. "I pray."

"Then, mister, you get down on your knees and do it! Because, I swear I—"

He never did learn what she was about to swear. The love in her eyes was just too much for him, and Mick succumbed.

They were kissing and embracing with such emotional intensity that Tad was able to get close enough to slap his father on the arm before they even knew he was in the room. "Cut the clench, Da," the boy said, cheerfully. "We gotta go down to the sports shop. A friend of Maggie's called Charlie Jensen's gonna teach me how to ski!"

CHAPTER SEVEN

SHE DIDN'T GET an answer to her demand for a promise, but soon Maggie was much too busy to press the issue—much too busy and much too confused.

Jeff had stayed over that night and had said some things that surprised and shocked her. After Patrick had gone to bed, he poured them both a snifter of brandy and sat down on the couch with her. "I'm probably the last guy in the world who ought to be giving out advice on matters of the heart, Mag," he said. She nodded understandingly. Jeff had recently survived a messy divorce.

"But," he went on, "it's not hard to see you've fallen for O'Shay."

She nodded again and stared at her brandy. "I don't like him one little bit," she confessed. "But I *care* about him. About what happens to him. And I can't resist him when we kiss. It's crazy."

"Yeah." Jeff took a swallow. "He probably feels the same way about you."

"Oh, come on. He doesn't give a darn about me. I've been a means to an end from the very start. That's why it's so stupid that I'm even willing to continue helping him."

Jeff frowned. "You may not know the whole truth yet. He was all ready to beat the crap out of me just because he thought I was Linder. Said anyone who hurt you ought to be taught a serious lesson. Does that sound like a man whose emotions aren't involved, to you?"

"He seems to have an odd sense of honor—he obviously thinks that because I'm female I need protecting."

"Well, there's also the fact that chances are slim you can actually help him find the guy he's after. Yet he's still here, settled in as though he plans to stay."

"His kid—"

"I met his kid, Mag. Tad O'Shay strikes me as the kind of boy who can roll with the punches. He's tough, and in the long run he's liable to be as tough or tougher than his old man. No, Mick's here because Mick *wants* to be here. You ought to be giving some serious thought to what that means, especially if you're going to get yourself into another—"

"Forget it! I learned my lesson. I might enjoy kissing him, but Mick O'Shay won't get any farther than that. We argue all the time. Passion can't make it through that kind of fighting, believe me. At least, not my passion."

Jeff did not look convinced, but he did change the subject, switching to his mother, Mildred, Maggie's aunt. She was being a big pain over his divorce, and Jeff asked for some advice on how to get her off his case. Maggie did the best she could, knowing how vulnerable Jeff was and how Mildred, lovingly, would unwittingly ride right over his feelings without so much as a backward glance. By midnight, they had exhausted several topics.

Neither cousin slept well that night, and when Jeff left in the morning, he wished her the best of luck. She thanked him and wished him the same in return. They would both need it, she decided. She also decided that she was going to concentrate on controlling her feelings—that her attraction to Mick was totally unhealthy and ultimately self-defeating. She was dealing with a man whose values lay back somewhere in the dark ages, whose future was extremely uncertain and whose present was shaky at best. She would do his stones, as she had stated in their contract but she wouldn't be a part of any revenge trip, wouldn't help him with his search.

Then Mick threw her a curve.

He did it that morning. She had decided to keep the day free for designing instead of selling and had put the closed sign on the front door. When he arrived, she told him to lock up and come on in the back. He seemed to be in a gentle, pensive state of mind. If he hadn't had the same face and body, she wouldn't have recognized the man. He spoke softly and politely, mostly in short phrases or monosyllables. He approved everything she showed him. Finally, it got to be too much for her.

"All right, Mick. Spit it out. What's bothering you?" she asked in frustration.

"I'm thinking. That's all." His green eyes looked fathomless and cold, like the sea. But the coldness wasn't directed at her. It was an inward kind of chill.

She couldn't help it. A warm wave of tenderness washed over her. Tears filled her eyes, and her chest felt tight. *Oh, no!* she thought. *I really do love him!* She didn't even like him, but here she was, having to confront the fact that somehow, some way, this man had gotten into her heart. There was no other explanation for the way she was feeling. None.

If she let him know it, however, she would be entirely in his power. She had no intention of ever letting *that* happen. None!

But words tumbled out of her. "Mick, I don't understand much about the forces that drive you, but I—I want to help you."

"You shouldn't." His expression was grim, his eyes empty.

"Maybe not." She reached out and took his hand. "But if I help, maybe I can help you find another way. Maybe I—"

"Maggie." He pulled her hand close to his chest. "You have no idea what it's like to be me, no idea what I've done in my life. You were raised by decent parents in an environment that kept you safe, kept you innocent."

"I'm not—"

"Shut up and listen." Mick's grip on her hand tightened to the point of pain. His face was harsh, feral. "A man hits me, I hit him back. He kicks me, and I'll draw a knife. Now, you may not believe me when I tell you this, but I haven't killed anyone. Yet. But don't doubt that I've put my share of bully boys in the hospital or so out of commission they won't ever bother anyone again. And I *can* kill if need be. I'm a rough man, Maggie. Not the kind—"

"Mick, I . . ." Tears were now flowing down her cheeks, making it difficult to get the words out. "I lo—"

"Don't say it, Maggie! For God's sake!"

"But I lo—"

"Oh, bloody hell!" He jerked her to him and crushed his mouth down on hers.

PATRICK SMILED at Tad O'Shay. "Maggie's going to be very happy," he said as they reached the shop. "For Davey to have finished so much work in such a short period of time will really set her up for the Christmas season."

"I guess I oughta meet this kid." Tad sounded only mildly enthusiastic. "I mean, he is helping my old man out."

"You will meet him. Tonight at dinner. We're all invited." Patrick noted the CLOSED sign and frowned. "That's funny. They should be here."

"Maybe they're in back." Tad tried the door. When it opened, they heard the door to the workroom suddenly crash shut. "Yeah," the boy said. "They're in back." He went around the counter and reached for the doorknob.

"Tad, wait," Patrick called. But it was too late. The sight that met his eyes caused him to bellow in outrage and the boy to giggle in embarrassment. Maggie was on the work-table, not naked, but well on her way to being in that state. Mick loomed over her, his intentions quite clear. On the floor were scattered tools and fragments of precious metal. Maggie's face was flushed and her cheeks wet with tears. O'Shay's face was just flushed. Patrick yelled again and went for the man.

Mick saw it coming and didn't defend himself. He was in the wrong and he knew it down to his bones. Patrick landed one first on his jaw and then his belly. Mick said, "Ow!" and "Oof!" and sat down hard on the floor.

"Get up, you bastard," Patrick rasped, his fists balled tightly. "We take you in, befriend you, and this is how you repay us? I'm gonna beat the living—"

"Dad! No! Noooo!" Maggie pulled down her shirt. "No! It's not his fault! It's mine! He didn't start it, I did. I said—" Her hands flew to her face. "Oh, my God." The room suddenly closed around her, and the three others stared. She had to get out or she'd go insane! Gasping for air, she turned and ran from the room, grabbing her coat on the way out the front door. She took off toward the woods behind the shop without once looking behind.

Meanwhile Tad had run to his father, and had thrown his arms around Mick's neck defensively. "Don't hurt my Pa, Patrick," he cried. "If she says he didn't mean no harm, he didn't. He wouldn't hurt a girl. It ain't right." The boy's voice quivered, and he was clearly near tears himself.

Patrick unclenched his fists. Mick sat on the floor, one arm around his boy, the other bent so that he could rub his jaw. "I want to hear it from you, O'Shay," he said. "Were you about to"—he glanced down at the boy—"was Maggie going to be hurt?"

"Probably." Mick held up a hand as the older man again took a fighting stance. "But not like you think. It's pretty complicated. Is it safe for me to get up? We need to talk." Patrick didn't hold out his hand, but he did step back. Mick rose carefully. "It's all right," he said to Tad. "It's all right, son. We're going to work things out."

MAGGIE STOMPED through the snow under the pine trees, growing more angry with herself every step of the way. She was a complete idiot, and now she had been humiliated in front of her father, whom she loved and respected inordinately. What would he think of her? Throwing herself at a man she scarcely knew. Practically seducing the guy right there on her worktable. My God! She turned and started up a depression in the snow caused by the erosion of spring runoff. The wind was blowing gently, and occasionally a clump of snow would fall off a tree branch to land with a plop near her feet. She dug in, wanting to punish herself to make up for her foolishness. The uphill climb soon started her thighs aching.

It was bad enough that she'd been ready to forgo her principles of right and wrong and aid O'Shay in gaining his revenge. It was worse that she had been primed and ready to blurt out how she felt—how she *thought* she felt, anyway. She wasn't at all sure now that she really was in love.

How could she be? She remembered how dangerous he had looked when he had confessed to beating up other men, to putting them in the hospital, for heaven's sake! She could never love a man like that—a violent man. For all the immorality Jerry Linder practiced, he was at least a healer by profession; a gentle man, if not a gentleman. Maggie shuddered. O'Shay was a potential killer.

She couldn't love a man like that!

The woods began to thicken, and she considered the wisdom of turning around and heading back to the house.

Sooner or later, she was going to have to face her father and try to explain.

She wasn't ready. She still hadn't explained anything to herself. She raised the hood of her ski jacket and tied a knot in the cord under her chin. Her pockets yielded mittens, which she put on. No problem. She'd walk and think a while longer, then go back and face the music. It was deathly quiet in the trees. She could hear no sounds from town or the ski area. This was the kind of place she needed to be in order to really get in touch with herself. Maggie trudged on, heading uphill.

"IF YOU ASK me, it's pretty damn arrogant of you to think my daughter's in love with you, O'Shay." Patrick set down his mug of coffee. The two men were seated in the Wellington kitchen. Tad had been relegated to the den, from where the sounds of MTV now blared. He had clearly wanted to hang around and get the juicy details, but a scowl from his father had sent him dutifully, if not willingly, away.

"I can't help that, sir," Mick said, his tone belligerent. "It's true. If that makes me arrogant, I—"

"I'm still mad, and I'm going to say some hard things. If you can't handle it, we might as well end the discussion right now. I'll go find Maggie and see what charges ought to be brought against you."

"I didn't attack her." Mick held out his hands. "We were talking about . . . about some things we disagreed about. I didn't try to make her feel the way she does. It just happened. We were talking, then—"

"Yes?" Patrick's eyes were hard, and Mick decided he must have been a trial lawyer and a damned good one. He felt as uneasy as if he were actually on a witness stand.

"Then we were kissing. Look, sir, it isn't easy talking to a father about his daughter like this. She's a grown woman, and there was this feeling between us. What more can I say?"

"Do you love her?"

"Well..." Mick stood and turned toward the window, nervously brushing his hand through his hair. "That is, I...I'm strongly attracted to her. She's a very appealing woman. Look, it's starting to get dark. Don't you think—"

"Maggie can take care of herself. She's probably over at a friend's house talking her heart out. What makes you so damn sure she loves you? That it's not just physical?"

Mick grew more uncomfortable. "It's hard to explain. She tried to tell me, but I wouldn't let her. That's when I kissed her and—"

"She said she started it, but *you* kissed *her*?"

"To shut her up." He tried a grin. "It's worked before."

Patrick Wellington was clearly not amused.

Finally Mick seemed to convince the older man that he had not been assaulting his daughter. An uneasy truce grew between them, and their thoughts turned to Maggie. "I need to start calling around," Patrick said. "We're supposed to have dinner at the Abramses. Embarrassed or not, she is going to come. Nell Abrams is a fine woman, and I won't have Maggie disappointing her."

Mick said nothing, but he wondered just how that kind of attitude was going to go over with Maggie. It sounded suspiciously like parental bullying, and the woman he'd very nearly bedded on the worktable was not about to take that. Not unless he had misread her badly. And he did not think he had done that.

No, he hadn't done that at all.

MAGGIE SAT with her back against a rock and cried. After hours of walking and arguing with herself, she had come to

one inescapable conclusion: if they had not been rudely interrupted, she would have passionately, desperately demanded the finale of the rough lovemaking they had
started. She had wanted Mick O'Shay so badly it hurt. She
cried harder.

What had happened to her? After the San Francisco
folly, she had been in complete control of herself where romantic matters were concerned. Now and then she met a
man who was fun and exciting, but never all-consuming;
never someone she'd literally tear her clothes off for...never
someone she'd give up her beliefs for.

Never someone like Mick O'Shay.

When he had grabbed her and kissed her to keep her
from saying she loved him, something wild and uncontrol-
lable had erupted inside her. She had been gripped by a
primitive desire unlike anything she had ever felt before.
She had *needed* that man.

She still needed that man.

Maggie stood up. It was time to go home and face the
music, and very possibly the scorn her father felt for her
now. She expected Mick had wasted no time explaining how
she had behaved. Shame made her skin tingle hotly. But she
did love the man. It made no sense at all, but she loved him.
Jamming her hands in her pockets, she started downhill,
ducking her head against the stinging snow whipped up by
the rising wind.

"YOU'VE CALLED every one of her friends?" Mick was almost shouting. "Are you sure?"

Patrick looked a little worried. "Hmm. Yes. I believe
that's the last of them. I can't think of anyone else she'd go
to. Charlie said no one's seen her over at the ski area, either.
I'd better call Nell and explain why we won't make dinner." He almost sounded more concerned about that than
his daughter's disappearance, Mick noted.

He swore viciously under his breath and went to get Tad. The boy looked up, startled, when he came into the den and shut off the television.

"What's the matter, Da?" he asked, standing. "You look like something's dead wrong."

"Maggie's missing. And her Pa isn't doing a damn thing about it. Come on, let's get your coat."

"If he won't, why don't you?" Tad stood his ground and regarded his father steadily. "You're the best tracker in South Australia. Not countin' Davis 'n' his brothers."

"This ain't the bush. It's snow country."

"So, what's the diff? Snow. Sand. Wouldn't it all track alike?"

Mick stared at his son, then slapped the boy on the shoulder. "Too right, lad. Come along. You get an extra treat for thinking clear when your Da can't. Let's go talk to the sheila's Pa."

PATRICK HUNG UP the phone. His hand was trembling slightly. When Nell had heard about Maggie—not the whole story, mind, but just that she was missing—she had declared she'd be right over. He wasn't going to go through this alone. Up to now, he hadn't been worried. Perhaps he should have been.

O'Shay burst into the kitchen, Tad in tow. The two of them were talking ninety miles an hour, but in an Australian accent so incredibly thick, Patrick could only make out a word here and there. "Slow down, slow down," he said, rising from his chair. "What are you two jabbering about?"

"Who's yer best snow man?" Mick asked. "I mean" —he took a deep breath—"Patrick, if you were lost out in the wilderness around here, who would you want lookin' for you?"

Patrick brightened in understanding. "Why, Charlie Jensen, of course. He's in charge of Search and Rescue. He works in coordination with Sam Glover's people when—"

Mick grabbed the other man's shoulders, a wild look in his eyes. "Stop jawin' and *call* 'im. *Now!*"

MAGGIE AMBLED down a slope, kicking at clumps of snow and trying to let her thoughts wander, hoping that as they tumbled, she'd see some kind of solution to her situation. *Think creatively,* she told herself. If she pretended this was just another project she needed to understand in her mind before going to work on it, she might make some progress.

She wandered on a bit and paused again, her attention distracted by the sight of a small herd of deer moving through the trees. They moved delicately, picking their way over the snow on thin, lithe legs. What beauty, she thought. It was the kind that could never really be caught in art. It had to be experienced directly. Moonlight gave her a clear view, and she waited, still as a mouse, until the lead deer, a big female, caught her scent on the cold air and the group bounded away. She felt a strange sense of loneliness then, and turned back to her path.

The lights of town weren't visible yet, but she was certain of her direction and wasn't worried, even though it was growing steadily darker and colder. The sky was clear, and there was no cloud cover to hold in the warmth of day. The stars were jeweled points on the velvety sky. She paused, looked upward and sighed.

Wouldn't it be nice if answers really were written in the stars, she mused. But they weren't. She bent down and picked up a pine cone. Answers could only come from within yourself. If they were helped to the surface by a Higher Power, so much the better, but...

Maggie tossed the pine cone up and down and smiled as a thought occurred to her. Maybe her relationship with

Mick was like the process of casting gold and silver. First she made a model of the setting out of plain old wax—cheap, ugly material. But that was only the beginning. The wax piece was set in a special clay cast, then fired in a kiln at a thousand degrees. The wax melted out through special vents, leaving just the hollow impression of the setting. Then the cast and a cylinder of gold were placed in a special centrifuge. The force of the centrifuge drove the molten gold down through the same vents by which the wax had left, filling the hollow with an exact replica of the first model.

The cast was then broken and discarded, and what remained was a unique piece of art formed out of precious metal. Would her strange relationship with Mick turn out like that? Would fire and pain and stress eventually produce something beautiful and wonderful? Was it too much to hope for? Just a dream that would never come true? Was love always going to be like that for her?

She stuck the pine cone in her pocket. *Those are some pretty heavy ideas,* she thought, mocking herself slightly.

But was she really so far out? The casting process involved pressure, heat, breaking. Pain? She needed to pursue this, she decided. Trudging on, she pondered, her body feeling a gradual relief of stress as she meditated and exercised at the same time. The ache of erotic unfulfillment faded as she let her mind deal with more abstract problems.

"SHOW ME HOW to work the bloody things, mate." Mick finished strapping on the snowshoes according to Charlie's instructions. "I feel like a duck!"

"Keep feeling that way, and you'll be fine. You just keep your legs pretty far apart and get an even rhythm to your glide. The rhythm's important. Watch me a bit, and you'll have it." Charlie's voice was tight and his words terse. He seemed an entirely different man from the "party animal" or the cheerful ski instructor who had taken Tad under his wing. He was dead serious and businesslike, and that helped Mick's anxieties.

Somewhat.

Charlie had come over immediately after Patrick had called and briefly explained the situation. He had brought an extra pair of snowshoes for Mick and hadn't questioned his competence as a tracker. Mick had wondered at this acceptance of his ability until he remembered the length of time the skier had spent with Tad. Tad had never been reticent about his life—with people he liked—and Mick knew he liked Jensen. It had been evident in the broad smile with which he'd greeted the man.

A niggling thought about how quickly his son had made two adult friends in this place ran through his mind, but he dismissed it and concentrated on the current crisis. Charlie ran him through the finer points of walking with snowshoes, and soon he was confident, if awkward. *Bloody fish out of bloody water,* he thought unhappily. The clean heat of the desert seared at his memory.

"Let's get one thing straight before we start out, O'Shay," Charlie Jensen said as he made some last minute adjustments in his gear.

"What's that?" Mick already figured he knew.

"If I find out Maggie's hurt because of you, you might as well bend over and kiss your—"

"Hey, mate. Queue up."

"What?"

"Let's see." Mick worked the heavy mittens on his hands. They had been hard put to find ones big enough to fit. "I think the Yank term for it is 'take a number.' There are other people ahead of you. I guess you get to stomp the leftover pieces once they're done."

"So you did—"

"Listen, Jensen. I didn't do anything any other red-blooded man wouldn't have. If I have to answer up for that, well and good. But I ain't some kind of monster. Ask her yourself." He let anger override the uncertain emotions roiling in his brain.

"When we find her."

"We'll find her," Mick replied. They took off into the woods, following the furrowed snow where Maggie had run that afternoon. With the powerful flashlights they carried, it wasn't difficult to follow the easy trail. Mick concentrated on not being distracted by animal tracks and forced himself not to think about what they might find at the end of the trail. She was all right.

She had to be.

NELL ABRAMS HANDED Patrick a cup of hot tea. "Mick and Charlie will find her," she assured him, sitting down on the sofa next to him. "And when they do, we'll all sit down to that casserole I brought and have a good laugh over all this."

"God, Nell. I hope so." Patrick set the cup down. His hands were shaking so hard it rattled. "I don't think I could stand to lose . . . to lose . . ."

"Patrick, think." Her tone was kind, but firm. "Maggie is a strong young woman. She was dressed for the weather. You told me she frequently takes long walks. Do you know where she is every minute of the day and night? *Should* you?"

"Of course not. But she was . . . so upset."

Nell picked up the cup and handed it to him again. "And unless she came to you about it, was it really any of your business?" Her tone was still kind.

Patrick looked at her sharply. "Nell, she is my daughter!"

"Yes, she is. She's also a grown woman who has spent quite a few of her best years on you, dear man. Please forgive me, but I think it might be time for both of you to start trying to live for yourselves instead of each other."

Patrick stared. From the den came the voices of Tad and Davey underscored by the television. They sounded quite cheerful in contrast to the adults in the living room. Nell's words hung in the air like an admonition.

"I know it's forward of me to speak this way," Nell went on. "But I wish you would consider me a friend who has only your and Maggie's best interests at heart. That young Mick O'Shay loves her very much, you know."

He slammed the teacup down. "The hell he does. The man's a roué who's only going to cause her—"

She laughed. "Patrick, Mick O'Shay doesn't even know what the word roué means, mark me. He's as transparent as glass. You can't see it?"

"No."

"Your love and concern for Maggie blinds you. I understand." She reached for his hand and held it between hers.

Tears stung his eyes, and Patrick blinked to clear them away. "I don't know if you're right," he said thickly. "But thank you for being friend enough to say your mind. It's been a long time since someone's . . . cared enough to do that. Not even Maggie—"

"Maggie is being oh, so tender with you because that's the kind of love you need from her. Patrick, I understand your pain. My husband was very dear to me, and I will always miss him. But I have so much more to live for that I could not remain wrapped up inside my pain forever. I am not afraid to call things as I see them, even in myself."

He stared at her again. Compared to his loss, hers was so much greater. She had no husband and a son who was crippled. How could he have remained locked in his self-pity when there was this gracious, honest, dynamic woman to learn from? He straightened his back and wrapped his other hand around hers. "Tell you what," he said. "Why don't we go ahead and heat up that food. I have faith she'll be found in good condition. But I bet if we don't feed those two boys, they won't be." Nell laughed, and his heart felt lighter than it had in a long, long time.

CHAPTER EIGHT

MAGGIE'S MOOD WAS almost mellow by the time she reached the gate to the backyard of her house. The walk had cleared her mind and soul, she decided. She might still love Mick, but she knew she didn't love what he stood for and planned to do. She was able to separate the two aspects, she was certain, and would thus be able to deal with them. Her loving him didn't mean she could or would have him. Certainly, she would never have him for long. Not that kind of man! She didn't want or need him *that* badly.

The sweet, homey smell of wood smoke tickled her nose. As she neared the house, the savory aroma of stew, warm bread and coffee added itself to the air, and she was suddenly ravenous. Her flight had caused her to skip lunch, something she didn't usually do if she could help it. Her mouth started to water, and her tummy growled. She looked around the yard. Snow lay piled in corners where flower and vegetable beds flourished in summer. Her lace tree reached hopefully for warmer skies to come. Maggie's eyes teared, but this time with happiness. She loved this town, this house, this land. She could never leave it now. Not for anyone. Secure in her control of her feelings, she reached for the back doorknob. It was time to face the music with courage. With dignity. She put a brave, though contrite, expression on her face and opened the door.

And all hell broke loose!

It began with two unidentifiable male figures rushing from the forest she had just left. Yelling and waving their arms, they terrified her, and she shrieked and yanked the door open, darting in to safety.

Darting in to chaos! No sooner had she slammed the door and turned her back on it than she was swept into her father's arms. Nell Abrams was attempting to embrace her, as well. Both older people astonished her by crying and flinging a seemingly unending series of questions at her, none of which she fully comprehended. Then the door behind her burst open, and the two crazy men tramped into the kitchen. They were still yelling, but now she recognized them as Mick and Charlie. Out of the corner of her eye, she saw Davey Abrams and Tad watching from the other doorway, clearly delighted with the spectacle of five adults all going nuts at once.

"Shut up, shut up, shut up!" she shrieked, conscious of being disrespectful towards the older people, but determined to bring some kind of order to the situation. "One at a time, now. What *is* the matter with all of you?"

They all spoke at once. Maggie clapped her hands over her ears at the din. She shouted again for quiet, but this time to no avail.

Mick went still. The sight of her, surrounded by confusion she couldn't control, did something deep inside him. Suddenly, he wanted to whisk her away to some place private and quiet and tell her all the things he had been feeling while tracking after her in the cold and snow and dark; how the dark and cold had seemed to symbolize what it would be like not to find her safe. How Charlie's reassurances had fallen on ears unwilling to hear. How he had seen the strength and purpose in her tracks, but how his heart had feared it was only a reflection of her desperation over her feelings for him. How he had wanted only to find her, wrap himself around her and keep her protected for all time.

Unfortunately, he couldn't put all that into words. Hell, he didn't even understand it himself yet. So he did the only thing he could, given the circumstances.

"You scared the bloody hell out of all of us," he yelled, drowning out everyone else. Complete silence followed his outburst. He grabbed her wrists and dragged her hands away from her ears. Ignoring the shocked looks on the faces of the others, he continued to berate her, his accent getting thicker and thicker. "... and yer poor father, and this nice lady, and Charlie and Davey and Tad... You had us all beside ourselves wi' worry. Whad'd you think you were doing?"

Maggie waited, watching, until he ran out of things to say. She made no attempt to free her wrists or to reply, due to the genuine, naked concern she saw in his eyes—and something else hidden so deep she wasn't even sure she saw it. But concerned or not, he had gone well beyond the limit! *Well* beyond it.

Something was driving him, she realized. Her heart did a giant flip when she realized what that might be. If *he* had fallen in love with *her*, things would be infinitely more complex and potentially painful!

Patrick watched and listened and realized that what Nell had said was true. If Maggie was in love with Mick, he was equally in love with her. Only a blind, deaf man would deny it now. He thought of the times his love for Evelyn had caused him to react in much the same way—his fear for his beloved causing anger. Anger had disguised the anguish and helplessness he'd felt when... Emotion choked him, and he felt Nell's hand slide into his.

When Mick finally sputtered to the end of his tirade, he released Maggie's wrists and took a step backward. Looking around, he saw that everyone was staring at him as if he had two heads. He had, he realized too late, really done it now. But it had all come from his gut and heart, and he felt so strongly that there was far more to say and do that he was actually shaking. "I...I oughtn't to have yelled, Mag, but you had me scared. Scared clear to the bone." He brushed a hand over his hair. "Now that I know you're all right, I guess we'll be leaving. Tad, get your coat."

"No, Mick." Her hand touched his arm. "One of us running away per day is enough." Her gaze searched his face—and his soul.

"Tad's in the middle of a great dinner," Patrick announced. "As are the rest of us. I insist the three of you join us. After tramping through the woods, you must all be starved."

"Hey, yeah," Charlie piped up, clearly relieved to have the atmosphere lightened. "I could use some of what I'm smelling. Let me just get the snowshoes. We kinda kicked 'em off in the yard on the way in." He grinned and disappeared back outside.

"Okay, boys," Patrick said brusquely. "Back in the dining room. Excitement's over for the night, I hope." Tad and Davey laughed nervously and gave each other meaningful glances that spoke volumes about the eccentricities of grown-ups. But they followed Nell and Patrick without argument.

Mick and Maggie were left alone in the kitchen.

"I..." Mick began, the words sticking in his throat.

"Save it." Her tone was soft, her eyes kind. "We've both behaved like idiots. Let's apologize to the rest of them and wait before trying to work out what's going on. I have a feeling this is something that can't be rushed. As much as I understand about it, that is."

"If you understand anything, you're way ahead of me." His grin was tentative and wry. "I kind of lost control. I—" He broke off as Charlie came back inside, the snowshoes neatly tied together under his arm. The skier smiled uncertainly at them and hurried into the dining room. They could hear the others talking and the clank of plate and silverware.

"Maggie." Mick had lowered his voice almost to a whisper. His hand clamped hard on her arm. "You made me frightened. I was imagining things . . . happening to you. I felt responsible . . ." A vein worked along his temple, and in spite of the cold a trace of sweat appeared on his forehead.

"Mick, I know the woods. I was as safe as . . . as you would be in your own wilderness. I might be city born and raised, but I have always sought out the country. It nourishes me, refreshes me. Heals me."

The honesty of her gaze was almost painful to him. "And why do you need healing?" he asked softly, releasing her arm. "What's hurting you so?"

Her smile was gentle. "Loving you, Mick O'Shay." She turned and walked into the dining room, leaving him staring at her back, his ears ringing with her words.

THE DINNER WAS one of the most uncomfortable meals Mick had ever sat through. Everyone, Tad included, was making an obvious effort to act as if nothing unusual had happened. Charlie teased Tad about his skiing lesson. Davey announced that he and Tad were planning to design a low sledlike contraption for him to ride on so the two of them could at least go cross-countrying together. That brought raised eyebrows, but a smile from Nell. She was clearly delighted to see her son enjoying the company of another boy, even if he was younger and had some wild ideas. Then Patrick asked Maggie what she had done in the forest, and she told them. Mick listened, entranced, his food forgotten.

She explained nothing of why she had stormed out of her store and into the trees. She described the speed with which she had taken the slope and how the fire that had set her off had gradually burned out. She spoke softly of sitting by a rock and thinking and crying for hours. Mick couldn't meet the eyes of a single soul at the table, although he certainly felt them boring into his.

But she didn't make it seem as though it were his fault. In fact, in her description of the events that took place in the afternoon and evening, he was only incidental—only one part of the whole experience.

This made him more unhappy than anything else.

But when she got to the part about watching the deer in the snow, he was compelled by something in her voice to look at her closely. Her warm amber eyes shone, and her skin glowed, tinged pink by the exposure to the cold. Her hair was full of static electricity and stood away from her face and neck more than usual.

She was the most beautiful woman he'd ever seen in his life. And he was completely terrified of her. The rest of the evening was a nightmare.

He managed to get out of there without letting on how far his emotions had swung. He had shaken hands around with the men, thanking Charlie once again for putting up with him and receiving a generous compliment from the skier on his physical ability and tracking skills.

"Once we get you out of that shop and onto the slopes," Charlie promised, "you're gonna be hell on wheels. He's a natural athlete," he informed the group. Mick actually blushed, to his consternation.

Clearly, any lingering doubts Charlie might have had about Mick's motivations and relationship with his friend had been cast to the wind.

Nell treated him a bit more cautiously, but she didn't seem hostile, at all. Just careful. Davey was plainly taken with Tad and she asked pointedly when the other boy would be free to visit. Patrick assured them both he would manage any carpooling necessary. Mick sensed that something was going on between the two older people, but he was too preoccupied with his own personal problem to pay more than scant attention. Patrick's attitude seemed guarded, as well. Mick wasn't the least surprised about that.

Then, there was Maggie herself.

As the evening drew to a close, she acted as serene as a madonna, driving him insane with her beauty and her quiet spirit. He had feared she would insist on an emotional confrontation once the party broke up—a thing he was far from ready to face. To his relief, she only smiled at him and wished him good night. Only after he and Tad were inside their own place did he experience a sharp pang of regret that she had been able to dismiss him so lightly.

"Da?" Tad had been unusually silent on the way home. "What's going on?"

"If I knew, son," Mick replied, "I'd tell you."

"You're actin' crazy. Like when Ian was killed, only different."

"This is different." He put an arm around the boy's thin shoulders and hugged him hard. "You'll get to understanding in a few years, believe me."

"You like her a lot?"

"I don't know, lad. I don't know."

Much later, long after Tad had gone to bed, Mick sat in the kitchen, staring at a cooling cup of tea. The room was illuminated by a single dim light and that suited his mood just fine. Up to now, his life had been either brightly lit or plunged into blackness. It was the damned *grayness* he had to deal with now that was driving him out of his head. Sure he wanted Maggie, but in the gray area was the question: was it more? Sure he wanted Ian's killer punished, but should he really do it himself? It was sure he did love Tad. But was he living the kind of life that would best serve the boy, or was he just like his old man, selfishly doing what suited him, his family be damned? Mick groaned and rubbed his aching head. He opened his eyes and looked at his watch. 3:00 a.m. Time to go lie down, even if he couldn't sleep. Charlie may have been impressed with the way he forged over the snow, but he hadn't exercised much lately, and his body was tired. If only his mind and heart would let it sleep! he lamented. He rose from the table, tossed the tea into the sink and rinsed out the mug.

The phone rang.

Mick froze. This time of night, it couldn't be anything but bad news. Real bad news. Maggie! His hands started shaking again as he picked up the receiver. "O'Shay here," he said softly, not wanting to wake Tad. Not wanting to hear what the party on the other end had to say.

"Mick? Are you all right?" Maggie's voice sounded sweeter than any angels' chorus.

"Yeah. What's the matter? What's wrong?"

A pause. "Nothing more than what's already wrong, Mick. I knew you didn't want to talk this evening, but I also didn't think it would be smart to wait until we were back in the shop. I couldn't sleep, and I assume from the speed with which you answered, you were awake, too." Another pause.

"Yeah. That I was." Thousands of thoughts and phrases tumbled in his mind, but he couldn't say anything else.

"I want you to know I meant what I said about the way I feel, but I want you to file it and forget it."

"Huh?"

"You've got enough to deal with. You don't need to mess up your mind with anything else, including me. Let's just assume business as usual in the morning and get the work done. It's getting too close to Christmas to allow our feelings to interfere. Maybe you don't need the money, but I do. I depend on this season—"

"Hold on, hold on. Y'mean just forget we almost—"

"Well, I don't suppose we can exactly forget it." She gave a long sigh. "Oh, this is so much easier over the phone. I thought it would be. If we were face-to-face..."

Mick thought about what would happen if they were face-to-face. His heart started pounding and his palms became sweaty.

"Mick, I do love you, but I realized this afternoon that that doesn't mean I have to be more than a friend to you. And if I'm to be a good friend, I ought to act in your best interests when I can. You know what I think of your plans. You know I believe you're wrong. But I do believe in your opals. I believe I'm going to create a display that will make you the most famous opal miner in all the world. What happens after that is up to you."

"That's damned decent—"

"No, it really isn't. I probably should refuse to help, in order to save you from your own misguided judgment. But I won't. That's your problem, not mine. Now, are we agreed to go on with the opal project and put our emotions under wraps for the time?"

"Yeah. No problem."

There was another pause, and this time he thought he sensed a little steam coming over the wire. Maybe he should have indicated that it wasn't going to be all that easy for him.

But she had offered this truce. He'd be a fool to turn it down. It seemed the solution to all his worries.

"Good," she said finally, firmly. "Then in the morning you go to the shop, open and run it and make a final decision on the designs I'll drop off."

"And you'll be where?" He felt a moment of panic.

"I'll be with Davey. He needs some help finishing the more intricate projects I gave him. We have only a week and a half more before the big Christmas crafts weekend. I have to have my stuff ready if I'm going to make enough money to—"

"I've told you not to worry about cash, Maggie. I've enough to—"

"To pay your lawyers? To support Tad while you're in prison? Mick, I can't count on you. I've given in. You have to give in. If you want me to do my best work on your stones, you're going to have to trust me and let me do it my way from now on."

He felt she had woven a rug and then pulled it out from under him. "All right. You're a tough little sheila. We do it your way now. Anything else?"

"Tell Tad Papa will pick him up in the afternoon. They're going to the movies, if that's all right with you. Davey too, if he can."

"That's fine."

"Good night, Mick."

"G'night, Maggie."

Mick didn't sleep a wink that night.

Neither did Maggie.

THE NEXT DAY Maggie steeled herself to carrying out her plans and promises. Her call to Mick in the middle of the night had cost her more than she had imagined it would, and she prayed she'd have the strength to follow through. It would be so easy to be selfish, she realized; to use what she believed she had seen in his eyes—to tempt him until he admitted he shared her affection, and to force him to do as she wished on that basis. She knew the moves and could probably do it.

But that wasn't what she wanted. If anything was to ultimately come of her feelings for him, it would have to be because he had changed. Because he really understood what a destructive path he was walking. She couldn't do it for him and make it matter.

That was the hardest part.

So she went about her business, heartsick, but sure of her choice. This was far more than a difficult romance. It was a situation that was going to affect many people. She couldn't afford to do anything other than what she had decided during her walk and the night.

Mick was waiting for her at the shop. He looked positively ill, his face drawn and his color pasty under the permanent tan. She ignored the symptoms of inner turmoil.

"Here is the rest of the portfolio," she said brusquely, giving him a pleasant smile and slapping the drawings down on the counter. "Take your time. You know the stones. Go through them and decide which ones you want used with which pieces of jewelry. If I find we have some real artistic conflict, I will ask you to consider my opinion, but at this point, you are the judge. I'll be back—"

"In time for lunch?" He sounded eager, although his expression was deadpan. "Celia can bring down sandwiches."

"If I'm not back, have her bring them for you. If I am, we can close up for half an hour and go over to Beth Sprinkle's restaurant across the way. I've got a craving for some of her chili, and we can watch the store in case someone comes by and looks as though he wants in." She put her coat back on. "See you later." She left with a little wave of her hand. Mick settled in glumly to review the drawings.

After a few hours, however, his enthusiasm for the project was renewed. She was a genius! There was no doubting it. He was hard put to decide which designs *not* to use, and in the back of his mind, he lodged the fact that he could always bring her more stones in the future to fit the ones he discarded for now.

Several customers came in, and he turned on the charm. Selling was easy for him when he believed in the product, and he believed in Maggie's jewelry. By the time noon rolled around, he had not only completed his task of selecting designs, but had taken in almost five hundred dollars. His stomach started to warn him of the hour and he settled back, waiting.

Meanwhile, Maggie had spent an utterly delightful morning with Davey. The boy's problems with constructing some of her more complicated designs had been easily overcome, and in the next hour she gave him some lessons in metalwork. He learned even more quickly than she imagined he would, and before she left, she spoke privately to Nell, recommending that she start looking for schools that could offer the specialized training the boy would need to pursue a career as a master craftsman. "He's going to be one someday, Nell," she said. "Someday soon."

Nell's eyes filled. "That's what Patrick says. I don't know how to thank the two of you. Since you came into our lives, we've had so much hope and happiness. Davey's friends try to come by, but it's hard for them to relate to his physical condition. And for a widow in a small town, things can be difficult. People regard you as a kind of grim reminder or, at best, a fifth wheel. First Patrick and you and Mick. Now Tad." A tear spilled. "Well, I just pray I can repay your kindness someday."

Maggie could say nothing. She just gave the older woman a hug and left, tears dimming the sight in her own eyes.

On the way home, however, a disquieting thought occurred to her—not really disquieting, but unsettling. Patrick and Nell?

It had certainly been long enough since her mother's death. He was coming out of his depression, finally: his response to Tad and to her problems proved that clearly enough. However, she found it hard to think of her father as courting again. Nell, she decided, must only be responding to his kindness. That was it, of course.

Of course.

It was well past noon when she left Three Pines, heading for the Springs, so she assumed Mick would have gone ahead and eaten on his own. The late November air was crisp and cold and her appetite was sharp by the time she pulled into town. That appetite reminded her of something else.

Thanksgiving was in three days.

Maggie mentally slapped herself. How could she have let the holiday slip up on her? At first, after they were alone, she and Patrick had dutifully trekked to family gatherings in the San Francisco area, but now they both preferred a quiet, simple meal here at home. This had not gone without grumblings from such as Aunt Mildred, but it was their choice. Now, it was almost too late to thaw out a bird—much less make the other goodies! There was a possible solution to her dilemma, however.

She roared past the shop, not even stopping to explain her mission to Mick, pulled up at Beth Sprinkle's Springs Café and raced through to the kitchen. Beth, a large woman who moved around the small kitchen like a ballet dancer, looked up and smiled at her. "He's waiting out front, Maggie," she said, pointing with a wooden spoon that dripped thick chili sauce. "I must say, you picked a good one this time."

"Beth." Maggie scarcely heard her. She gasped for breath. "A fresh turkey. Can you get me one in time?"

"There's one been waiting for you," a familiar masculine voice said behind her. "That is, if I understand the Yank slang right."

She turned. Mick was lounging in the doorway, regarding her with a wry, but pleased smile. "Glad to see you could make it," he added.

"Oh, Mick." She automatically smoothed a stray hair back. "I'm late, I know. I thought you would have already eaten. I came here for—"

"Fresh turkey?" Beth interrupted. "Got some coming up Wednesday. You can have one. What size?" She sounded amused.

Maggie turned back around. "Uh." She hadn't given a thought to anyone but her father and herself. Clearly, she wasn't going to get away with that. She turned to Mick. "It's about Thanksgiving," she said. "It's a big holiday where—"

"I know about it." He wasn't smiling now, but she could see in his eyes that he knew he had her on the spot and he was tickled pink about it.

"Would you like to celebrate with us?" she blurted.

He looked over at a casserole set on a counter. "We've already agreed to. I thought you knew." Muscles at the corners of his mouth twitched. "We settled it on the phone about an hour ago. Thought Nell woulda told you."

Maggie turned back to Beth. "Your dad just ordered a twenty-five pounder," she said. "Be here early on Wednesday. I guess he figures on your feeding a real mob."

"Oh." Maggie felt more than a little stunned and very much swept away by other people's plans.

INDEED SHE WAS. Patrick had suddenly been bitten by the bug of hospitality and Maggie cooked all day Wednesday and much of Thursday for a list of guests that included not only Mick and Tad, Nell and Davey, but also Charlie and his current girlfriend—a young woman who looked as though she stepped out of a *Ski Magazine* ad—and Sam Glover and his wife, June. Everyone brought something, but it was Mick and his pumpkin soup that astonished and impressed Maggie the most.

He entered the forbidden area of the kitchen without so much as a by-your-leave and requested the final moments before the meal was served. "You got to add the egg yolk just before the tureen's brought to table," he explained, clearing a work area for himself. Tad had staggered in behind him, laden with a huge pot of a steaming mixture. With his father's help, he set it on the counter and ran out for more stuff. "You can keep this hot until we eat," Mick added.

Maggie wiped sweat from her forehead. "It's hot enough in here to fry eggs on the floor, or haven't you noticed?"

"Soup bowls?" He was regarding her with a strange expression.

"I've had enough." She pointed a cooking fork at him. "Now, *git*!"

"I can help."

"No, I—"

Tad came back in, carrying a large, lovely soup tureen, complete with ladle. Davey wheeled in behind him, his lap holding several cartons of eggs. The young O'Shay solemnly set the tureen on a clear section of the kitchen table, removed the lid and took out a can of beer. "It ain't Foster's, Da," he said. "Charlie brought it, though, and he claims it's good stuff. Go on, give it a try."

Mick opened the bottle with a turn of one big hand, lifted the beer to his lips and downed half of it. "Ah." He sighed. "No, it ain't like at home, son, but it ain't bad." He handed the bottle to Maggie, his eyes watching her again with that unreadable look. "Try some?" He continued staring at her while he rolled up his shirt sleeves.

She declined, preferring wine with turkey, but the little scene resigned her to a kitchen full of Australians until dinner.

And he was helpful. The boys left after a few minutes of getting in the way, and soon he fell into a smooth pattern

around her work. Sooner than she had expected, dinner was
on the table in front of what was obviously a grateful and
ravenous horde. Before Mick brought out his soup, Patrick called for both of them to come sit down and join in
the thanksgiving. Mick put down his beer, gave Maggie that
enigmatic look and offered his elbow.

She took it. It was the closest they had been since the day
of the workroom incident and blowup. The touch of his
skin, bare arm against bare arm, caused her insides to twist
with frightening pleasure.

Mick led her to the place of honor at the end of the table
nearest the kitchen. Patrick sat at the other end. Mick took
a place by Maggie's right, and Tad sat next to him, flanked
by his new mate, Davey. Mick felt an upwelling of emotion so strong he closed his eyes before Patrick called for
prayer. He barely heard the phrases uttered by the others,
but when his turn came, eloquence came to him like a gift
from above.

"Father in Heaven," prayed Mick O'Shay. "You've been
patient with me, and I thank you for that. You've brought
me to a good place with good people." His hand moved out
and covered Maggie's. "I thank you for that. And whatever happens to me in the future, I know somehow, I'll be
thanking you for that, too." His fingers tightened over hers,
and he felt her squeeze his hand in reply. It was the longest
prayer he'd ever said, aloud or silently.

Maggie managed to murmur a simple thanks. That was
all she could do.

Mick's pumpkin soup was the hit of the meal.

CHAPTER NINE

AFTER THAT memorable Thanksgiving dinner, there was no longer any question in the minds of Sullivan Springs society that Mick O'Shay and Maggie Wellington were a hot number. Gossip carried by well-meaning persons, spread rumors of romance where none actually existed. That is, not on the overt level. Though they worked together every day, and were frequently seen at Bath's café for lunch or walking in the direction of their respective homes at night, they both conducted their business relationship as just that: business. Nothing more. The chemistry between them grew stronger every day, but they each practiced their own versions of self-denial. And both of them were quietly going crazy. However, a great deal of work was getting done.

They selected stones to match Maggie's designs, and she started forming the wax models for her creations. Mick performed the unskilled tasks, including giving the workroom a daily cleaning, a luxury Maggie had never enjoyed before. She cast, he cleaned. She polished and taught him how to do the preliminary polishing. His big hands proved adept, and their work progressed nicely.

The level of erotic tension between them also progressed. While they were polite and distant in their interaction, each moment they spent together—and each moment they spent apart—served only to increase their desire for one another. Maggie tried denying it by calling on her sense of mission; Mick, on his sense of fairness and honor. Both succeeded in self-deception; neither succeeded in eradicating their truest emotions and instincts. Pressure built, but like the finest pieces of metal, neither broke.

Maggie decided one night as she lay sleepless, thinking of Mick in spite of her determination to put him out of her mind, that she had developed invisible antennae—a kind of twisted radar that homed in on him, regardless of whether he was nearby or not. When he was near, she heard music in the sound of his breathing and the scuffling of his boots on the floor. Her nostrils found perfume in the smell of his clean body in the morning, and his sweat in the evening. Her artist's eye found beauty in the smooth, muscular movements of his limbs and hands as he worked, and she yearned to see what he looked like without his shirt and jeans, though she denied herself speculation on this at all but the weakest moments.

Those frequently came when she was at her most creative, when a project was going without hitch—when she needed to concentrate the most. However, to her amazement, her erotic fantasies didn't interfere, but seemed to fuel her energies and abilities. When she was most aware of Mick, she worked the best. A strong, curving line in metal was the line of his back and shoulders as he bent over a task. A rough, masculine design on a thick piece of gold was an abstract of the hands she imagined touching her at night. The emerald light hidden in some of the finest stones were pale reflections of his eyes. She wanted him, needed him and tried desperately not to let herself dream of having him.

But she dreamed anyway.

Mick was suffering similar exquisite agonies. He didn't have her advantage of having admitted his love went beyond lust, so his conscience was burdened by a number of guilts—guilts he had no way of relieving or dealing with. His life experience hadn't prepared him for thinking of himself as a bad man, but the more he desired intimacy with Maggie, the more he became convinced that he had slipped over the edge from good to evil. His black-or-white cosmos was eating him alive.

He began punishing himself for his desire. Keeping his temper in check, he maintained a mild exterior, all the while seething, ready to bust loose and break things in his heated frustration. He made sure his relations with Tad didn't suffer, and spent quality time with his son in the mornings and evenings. He suspected, from the way the boy studied him from time to time, that Tad wasn't entirely fooled, but he hadn't mentioned the revenge quest since the first day, and Tad seemed content with his father's new obsession—which was becoming a hair shirt made of porcupine quills!

Each morning when he arrived at the shop, he'd pause by the front door and breathe in the lingering scent of her from the night before—or her fresh perfume, if she had arrived first. The shop bell would tinkle when he came in, and if she was there she would call out from the back or raise her head and smile if she was manning the counter. If he was alone for a little while, he would wander back and forth from the shop to the workroom and relive the day before, seeing her in his mind as she moved gracefully and skillfully through the workday, pleasantly serving her customers, and looking at him on rare occasions.

He began to wonder if she still loved him. Her concentration on her work seemed so sustained and solid, that he couldn't imagine her ever thinking about anything else. They worked from early morning until well after dusk, and it seemed that she didn't have the emotional energy left to deal with affections so recently conceived. She seemed now to pour all her love into her work.

Her work. Mick decided his judgment of her as a genius understated the case. The gold and silver seemed to move in her small hands like a living thing. The settings she made during the first week in December were beyond exquisite, and when she added his stones he wanted to weep at the beauty of what they had created together—he by finding, she by making. Precious metal flowed around and cradled his opals, showing off their color and fire as never before. He remembered the long, pleasurable hours he had spent shaping his stones, and those hours seemed more than worthwhile as the products of his labor melded with Maggie's in a symphony of creative delight. At times he trembled with the emotions he felt, but he was unable to let a single one out. They built, and were bottled and stifled inside of him.

On December fifth, a little after four in the afternoon, Maggie set the last opal in a necklace designed to resemble an ancient Egyptian piece. "Okay," she said, loud enough for Mick to hear her from the front of the store. "That's it for now. I've got three days left to concentrate on the weekend craft fair."

"What?" He came to the door of the workroom. "You can't stop! You're on a roll, Maggie. At this pace—"

"At this pace, I'm going to burn out." She stretched, making him ache with the sight of her body arching like a lithe, lean cat's. "No, I need a break, and I need to get things ready for the weekend. You won't believe what a wonderful, crazy zoo it'll be around here from Friday to Sunday night."

"Maggie..." He wasn't sure he could stand not watching her work on his stones. At times he felt as though her fingers were touching him when they were actually holding and caressing his treasures....

"This isn't open to debate, Mick." She stood and held the necklace in front of her neck. "Like it?"

He couldn't speak.

"See." She set the piece down carelessly. "I'm already losing my touch. I need time..."

"It's beautiful." He could only whisper. "Beautiful."

She cocked her head, regarding him. "Are you all right? You sound—"

"I'm fine." He cleared his throat and walked into the workroom, picking up the necklace from the table. "It's . . . exquisite. I've never seen the like."

"Fake Egyptian," she said, smiling at his uncharacteristic choice of praise words. "I kind of ran out of original ideas. I do need to charge my batteries." She glanced at her watch. "Let's knock off for the day and take a walk around the square to check out the competition."

Mick worked the necklace through his fingers, wishing it were her hair. "I don't understand how you can stop like this. When I have a rich vein, full of stones, I don't stop mining because the mood leaves me. I just keep on digging until I've run the strike. That way, no one else can get—"

"It is different, Mick." She took the piece of jewelry and set it in the safe on a velvet pad. Closing the safe, she turned to him. "No one else can ever mine what's in here." She touched her forehead. "It's all safe. But my mind's not made of rock and it needs rest." She frowned and reached out, as if intending to touch his face, but then she withdrew her hand. "And so do you," she said. "You look exhausted."

"I'm fine."

"You don't look fine," she said softly. "You look like I feel. Wiped." She moved until she stood so close to him he could hardly breathe. "Come on, Mick. We've been at this hammer and tong. Time for a break, okay? Dad and the boys won't be back from their outing in Denver until late. Let's catch dinner at Beth's and relax afterward instead of coming back to work."

He swallowed hard, abandoning his principles, just happy to be so near her. "All right. Whatever you say."

Maggie studied him. That was an unusually meek thing for him to say. His tanned face had new lines each day, she had noted, and his eyes were circled by bruised-looking skin. It was nothing the casual observer would note, but then, she was hardly a casual observer. He *was* tired. She took his hand. "Let's get our coats on."

They locked the shop and walked up the street toward the town's main square. Snow fell steadily. Christmas decorations festooned the streetlight poles and the lines across the road. Real evergreen boughs, Mick noted. And colored lights. Snow had accumulated on the ground and on tree branches, adding a festive touch. He slowed his pace, realizing for the first time that he was going to experience a storybook Christmas—during a snowy winter instead of a sweltering summer. For the very first time in his life, he ached for the things he had missed as a child and gave thanks that at least Tad was going to get them in the shank of his own childhood.

Maggie wondered at his strange mood. She could sense the emotions emanating from him, although she couldn't fathom them. He certainly wasn't thinking of revenge at the moment. Nor, probably, of his desire for her. His features had softened and he looked younger. She thought again how handsome he was in his own way. How unique a man. Her love for him welled unchecked, and she slipped her arm into the crook of his elbow.

Mick felt the contact like a shock. He knew immediately it had nothing to do with lust, and his eyes stung. She was getting some signal from him. She knew he needed that human touch right now—needed to know he meant something to her. More aches and regrets from his past loomed on his emotional horizon, but he pushed them aside, concentrating only on the sensation of walking with this woman at his elbow.

At the end of the block the sidewalk became a picturesque wooden structure. Mick's boots rang like those of an old-fashioned Western hero as they walked along. The storefronts here also reflected the look of a bygone era. "I tried to get store space up here," Maggie said, her hip brushing his. "But you almost have to wait until someone dies. It's prime real estate."

"They don't have the prime goods you do." He gestured with contempt at a small, cutesy shop selling English bath goodies and candles. "All that Pommy stuff. Why, we'd use it to clean the toilet back home."

"Pommy?"

"English. It ain't a term of endearment, believe me."

She laughed, and the sound—like soft touches all over his body—sent chills up and down his spine. "You have strange prejudices, Mick O'Shay. Oh, look." She pointed at a huge black stove being set up on the snow-covered green of the central square.

"For roasting chestnuts," he said, pleased to recognize the thing.

She looked up at him.

"Picture books. I remember seeing one as a kid. We didn't have many books, and I memorized every one I got hold of."

Maggie tightened her hold on his arm. "My dad says Tad told him you read all the time. That you fall asleep with a book on your chest many nights and encourage him to read as much as possible."

He shrugged. "Only way to get an education. I like to learn. Tad does, too."

She sighed, wondering how it was possible to love him more and more each day—how it was possible to feel this way, yet not *like* the man. How many tricks would her heart play on her before this was over?

They rounded one side of the square and Mick stopped to admire the three tall pine trees decorated with lights and snow. "Those are like the picture books, too," he said, smiling for the first time. "At home, we get a little branch of gum tree and stick stuff on it. Serves the purpose, but this is much more like it. Makes me *feel* like it's Christmas."

"Next week, we'll go out and cut trees. Have a decorating party. *Then* you'll really get the true spirit."

Mick thought to himself that if anyone could infuse him with the true spirit of anything, she was holding tightly onto his arm right at the moment.

They had an early and relatively silent dinner at Beth's, and enjoyed the turkey casserole the cook had made from leftovers. Both still had good appetites, in spite of the emotional turmoil that had disturbed their sleeping patterns. They downed rolls and salads as well as substantial servings of the main course. When they were on dessert, Beth wandered over.

"My, my," she said, grinning. "And I thought you two were good lunch customers. Working up appetites, are you? All day in the store?"

Maggie blushed, knowing what Beth was thinking. "We're working overtime, trying to get ready for the holiday blitz. It makes us hungry."

"I heard Davey Abrams was doing your Christmas stuff, honey. How come you're so busy?"

Maggie glanced at Mick. So far they had managed to keep the opal project a secret. He looked totally unconcerned. "She's doing some special order stuff," he said, wiping a roll in the gravy on his plate. "I run the store, she works in the back." He popped the roll in his mouth and chewed it with obvious relish. "Real good food, Mrs. Sprinkle. Real good." He swallowed some coffee and yawned.

"Well, I guess you been workin' hard at something."
Beth laughed. "Don't wear yourselves out, now. Too many
parties comin' up in the next few weeks."

Maggie groaned. She had actually managed to forget the
hectic social rounds that were demanded of the permanent
residents at holiday time. If she thought she was tired now,
just wait!

Beth left them then and they finished up in silence, if not
in peace. Mick drank his coffee and studied Maggie.

She was weary—he could read that in the shadows under her eyes. Her porcelain skin would always reveal the
state of her physical health, he realized. It was a clear in-
dicator for anyone who cared enough about her to be concerned. Her eyelids were drooping a bit, too, and the long,
dark lashes brushed her cheek from time to time. He began to wonder if they were as silky soft as they looked.
Then he began to wonder what she would look like early in
the morning while she still slept. Those silky crescents
would lie so softly on her pale cheeks. Her breathing would
be steady and even, her full lips slightly parted . . . moist.

Abruptly he pushed his chair back. This line of thinking
was going to get him into a state that would be embarrass-
ing, at the very least! "I should go home," he said. "They
ought to be back by now, don't you think?"

Maggie frowned. "I hope so. I never like it when the
weather gets messy and Dad's out. He's a careful driver,
but he's not all that good on snow. If we have to go somewhere in the winter, I usually drive."

"You can't be doing that for him the rest of your life."

"No. I know. I suppose I've grown a bit strange about
Dad. He was so lost for so long after Mother—"

"He's not lost now, Maggie." Mick's hand covered hers.
"He's being a pal to Tad, and I'm grateful for that. You
have no idea how grateful."

She looked down at his hand—square, tanned and scarred, with blunt-cut nails. It was a hand a woman could trust, believe in. Sadness overwhelmed her. Why couldn't she trust the man it belonged to? Why couldn't she somehow make him see how self-destructive his hate was? Could she ever be that strong? That much woman? She looked up and caught his gaze.

For a second, he was naked and open to her. His eyes reflected the confusion *she* felt in her heart. Maggie drew in her breath with a gasp. What she had thought she had seen the night she had taken her hike in the woods was plain to her now. He did have feelings for her. How deep they ran, she couldn't tell, and he closed up almost immediately. But she *had* seen yearning and vulnerability.

Mick O'Shay's armor was not impervious!

Mick felt a panic rising in him. He was right on the edge of making a complete fool of himself—of telling her he couldn't stand another minute without her in his arms; of allowing his own desires to override his conscience. All the pressure he'd exerted on himself over the last days seemed to be pushing at his willpower. Thankful that circumstances wouldn't allow him to be tempted to do what he wanted to do, he gruffly suggested they get going, and he paid for dinner. It was his turn.

They walked home. Mick had become acclimated to the cold and his enjoyment of outdoor exercise had led him to abandon the luxury of a car except on the rawest days. Tonight, the snow was falling heavily, but the air felt warmer than usual and he was quite comfortable. Comfortable with the weather, at least. His reactions to Maggie were making him as nervous as a cat on a hot rock, and he was anxious to get to the relative safety of his house, which he would after he left her at hers. He wasn't out of the woods yet, however. Good manners dictated he see her to her door first.

Maggie didn't argue with him over the little courtesies he seemed compelled to offer. In fact, they had become one of the more endearing things about him. She could sense that he was ready to bolt for his own place, but equally determined to do what he believed was right by a woman.

"The snow's going to be good for this weekend," she said quietly. A white blanket had covered the street and sidewalk and muffled all sound, making the area seem like an enclosed space. "If they get the roads cleared, people will come up to ski as well as hit the crafts fair."

"This means a lot to the town," he said. "To you."

"It's getting me a reputation. Maybe just on the local level, but—"

"San Francisco's going to put you international, mark me." His arm went around her shoulders. "You'll amaze—" He stopped. "Your Pa's not back."

Maggie looked. Their Jeep wasn't parked at either her place or Mick's, just down the street. "Oh, God," she said.

They hurried to her house. She fumbled the key, and he took it from her, opening the door quickly. "Nell," she said, catching her breath. "I'll call Nell first. She may have heard from them."

Nell's line was busy.

"Okay," she said, talking as much to herself as to Mick. "There's still no reason to panic. She may be trying to call us." Her hands twisted together for several moments before she realized what she was doing and jammed them in her pockets. She began biting her lower lip.

Mick slipped off his coat. "Listen, Mag. I think they're all right. In fact, I know it."

"You can't know any such thing. You have no idea what the driving conditions around here in a blizzard can be like." She hugged herself, determined not to give in to worried, frightened tears.

"I can know it." He came around to face her and put his hands on her shoulders. "You live out in the bush, live with the aborigines, and you learn things you can't explain. I knew when Ian died, Maggie. It was as if something had been wrenched right out of me. If Tad was in any danger, I'd feel it."

She looked into his eyes and believed. "Mick O'Shay, who *are* you?" she asked.

His hands tightened, then slid down her arms. "At times like this, I'm not sure myself."

"Mick—"

"No, Maggie. I—"

The phone rang. Both of them dived toward it. Maggie won. "Hello?" She listened for a moment. "It's Nell," she said, joy in her voice. "They're all right. The roads are really nasty up here, so they're staying over in Three Pines tonight." She spoke eagerly into the phone, but Mick didn't hear what she was saying. Relief filled him as it sank in that the boy was all right. He did believe in his premonitions, but it was so good to hear her speak the words.

It was also good to hear her speak and to watch her, her love for her father showing as plainly on her face as if it were written there with jewels and gold. His noble resolve dissolved as she hung the receiver up and turned the full force of her generous, loving personality on him. "They're all right," she repeated. "And it sounds as though they had a great time. You said you were grateful for what Dad was doing with Tad. Well, I'm even more grateful for what your son has done for him. He sounded so happy, so energized. So full of life and confidence. Actually, from the tone of his voice, I'm surprised he didn't try getting on home."

"I'm sure he has reasons other than the weather for wanting to stay over at Nell's." Mick felt a tightness in his throat and chest. He was having difficulty breathing, and his heart was pounding so loudly, he was sure she'd hear it and comment.

Maggie looked at him more closely and felt her body temperature rise by several degrees. His need, his desire for her was so evident it made her ache. She held out her arms. "Mick, we're alone for the night."

"No, Mag. It's not right." His voice was hoarse.

"An hour ago, it wouldn't have been—even five minutes ago. But don't tell me it isn't right now." She took off her coat. "Because it is. If you're half as perceptive as you say you are, you'll—" The look on his face made her stop talking. Such naked passion needed no words to fuel it. He held out, fighting his inner demons, a moment longer. Then he gave an inarticulate cry, and she was in his arms.

She couldn't believe such sensations existed. He held her in an iron embrace until she thought their bodies would meld together. His kiss was hot and deep and thorough, and left her breathless. Her body felt as if jolts of electricity were being poured through it, and perspiration broke out all over her. His lips and hands worshiped her face hungrily and then began to move to the rest of her body.

Mick retained only a fraction of control. Every moment of desire he had felt for her came surging up, filling him and sweeping him headlong into a maelstrom of passion. It had never happened to him before like this! His fingers twisted themselves in her hair and he inhaled deeply, breathing in the most wonderful perfume in the world.

"Is there a bed down here?" he managed to ask. "'Cause we'll be on the floor in a moment." He buried his face in the side of her neck and felt the rapid, strong pulse flowing under the skin.

"Not downstairs." Her voice was barely audible. "Only up—whoops!" He had her in his arms and up to the second floor almost before she knew what was happening. Unerringly, he found her room and, kicking the door open, carried her inside and laid her on the bed. He turned on the bedside light and started on her clothes.

"I have to see you," he murmured, his hands swiftly removing her sweater and the silk camisole she wore underneath. His palms, rough but tender against her bare skin, brought a cry of pleasure from her. "Have to see!" His lips followed his hands, increasing her delight.

"I want to see you, too." Her hands, trembling, worked at his shirt until his chest and shoulders were bare. His muscles, under tanned skin, looked as if they had been carved from oak. The light from the table gave his body a golden hue. "Oh," she whispered. "My!"

Mick paused in his mad rush to possess her completely. He sat up and pulled off his shirt, watching her intently. No woman had ever looked at him like that, and it was making his need for her almost unbearable. Boots, socks and jeans followed the shirt, and then his hands were on her again.

It was like live electrical wires touching. They both gasped and cried out. His control fled and he stripped her in less than half a minute, pausing only to worship the rest of her briefly with his lips and fingers before rising over her, his body aching to plunge into her.

Maggie lay beneath him, her heart and soul savoring the moment before they joined. It was as though her existence had been destined to be divided into two parts, and when Mick O'Shay entered her, the second part would begin. She had never felt such fire in her body. She was sure he felt the same way: veins stood out in his neck, and his passion for her was evident.

But he held back. "Are you sure?" he asked, harshly. "Do you really want me, Maggie?" The effort the question and delay cost him was tremendous.

"Yes!" she screamed, and with all her strength, she pulled him down and into her.

The cosmos exploded almost immediately for both of them. Maggie screamed again and locked her body to his. His shout echoed hers, and they convulsed together in throes of passion that sent the bed smashing against the wall and the lamp crashing to the floor. Their bodies danced and rocked, throwing erotic shadows on the far wall as the light from the lamp on the floor lit them. She cried out yet again, this time in disbelief at the intensity of the pleasure coursing through her, sending her from peak to peak of ecstasy.

Mick was buried in her, wrapped in her. From head to foot his body was shot through with pleasure so keen it was near to pain. And it wasn't over all at once. The need he had bottled up came bubbling out of his soul, giving him extraordinary powers. His strength seemed to increase with each incredible moment, and if she hadn't been meeting his with almost equal ferocity, he would have had to stop before he exhausted her. *Once more,* he told himself with the fraction of his brain that remained aware and rational. Once more, then he would have to quit to spare her. Joy flared through him, and he rode it, forcing himself to begin relaxing.

But when she felt this, she screamed in anger and passion, "No, no! Not yet!" and her body writhed beneath him.

They ended up on the floor, tangled in sheets, pillows, blankets and the quilt. One last bone-rattling climax, and then they finally had to give up, their bodies still joined, but limp and spent. For a long time, the only sound in the bedroom was that of gasping and sighing.

"Oh. My. God," Mick managed to say after a while.

"Yeah." Maggie opened her eyes carefully and licked lips already swelling from passionate kisses. "Exactly. Should I call the rescue squad?"

"Nope. I think I'll be able to walk without help in a day or so." He raised himself up on an elbow and looked down at her. "Well, Mag. You were right."

"About what?"

"You are in love with me. And I am in love with you."

CHAPTER TEN

MAGGIE LAY very still. "Are you sure you know what you're saying?" she asked, unwilling to spoil things, but not wanting him to create an illusion out of the incredible physical experience they had just enjoyed.

"I'm sure." He looked quite serious.

"Mick—"

"But it doesn't change anything." He stroked her hair. "I wish I could tell you I love you enough to do anything you say, but I can't."

"Or won't."

An expression of pain crossed his face. "Maggie, I didn't say that, and you shouldn't either."

She reached up and caressed him tenderly. "Oh, dear. What are we going to do about all this?"

His grin was wry. "For the long run, damned if I know. For the short..." He leaned down and gave her a long, slow, deep kiss. After a moment, she responded enthusiastically, and matters proceeded naturally from there.

THE EARLY MORNING sun was pale and watery, but bright enough to wake her when it slid across her eyes. Maggie groaned and stirred, feeling every single muscle in her body as she never had before. It was painful, but not entirely unpleasant. What in the world had done this? she wondered.

She sat up abruptly, remembering everything—every hour of loving, every moment of ecstasy. She was alone in the house—she could sense that clearly enough. Gathering the wrinkled, twisted sheet around herself, she got up, murmuring his name, sick with disappointment that he had chosen to leave her like this.

Downstairs, however, she found he had understandable reasons, ones she had been too caught up to think of. A note on the kitchen table explained it all in his neat hand:

Maggie, my love. Thinking of you every waking moment, but I figured it'd be better if I was home when Tad got there, and not in your bed when your Dad arrived. About us—can we just let it happen and not worry about it? When I woke up and watched you sleeping beside me, I felt happier than I can ever remember feeling. You are beautiful—more beautiful than any treasure.

It was signed, "Love, Mick." Maggie folded the paper and put it in the envelope. He was right, of course. They had other people to think of besides themselves.

That, however, didn't stop her from wishing she had been able to wake up and look up at his face, as he had watched her.

Patrick arrived about thirty minutes after she had showered and grabbed a quick breakfast. He sang Nell's praises as a hostess and cook and explained rather too glibly that he had spent the night in the guest room while Tad had bunked on the couch. Maggie wasn't sure whether to feel embarrassed or smug. She was hardly in a position to demand explanations about sleeping arrangements from anyone! Patrick added that he and the boys had had a great time and that they were laying plans for further expeditions, school vacation time allowing. Maggie said she thought that was a fine idea, and her mind began to play erotic scenarios that could be enacted when she and Mick were alone again.

As soon as she could, she hurried to the shop, but it was another hour before Mick showed up. When he did, her heart seemed ready to jump out of her chest, and her skin tingled until she wanted to rip at it with her fingernails.

He stood in the front doorway, just looking at her, his expression unreadable. Then, not taking his gaze off her, he shut the door and turned the sign around to CLOSED. Memory of the first time he had walked into her shop and her life hit Maggie like a ton of bricks, and the strength went out of her legs. It didn't matter, because his arms went around her immediately and his lips covered hers. Any doubts she had been harboring about the reality of the previous night's experience fled.

"Oh, Maggie," he murmured, kissing her throat softly. "Do you have any idea how hard it was for me to leave you this morning?"

"No harder than it was waking up without you."

He drew back, still holding her. "But it's gonna have to be that way, love."

"I know." She smoothed hair back from his forehead. He hadn't had it cut since she had met him, and it was getting rather long, the red showing an occasional streak of gray. "It's not as if we're in this by ourselves."

He frowned. "I'm not a man who talks easily about the way he feels, Mag. It's going to be hard on you. You're going to have to have a lot of faith."

She smiled. "I never thought things would get this far. You shut me out so effectively after...after you told me why you came here."

"Still angry about that?"

"Yes and no." She gently pushed herself out of his arms. "How can I be angry about any reason that brought you to me? And yet, I won't lie to you about this—I'll never accept your motives as right."

"I know. I guess if you were any different, I wouldn't have learned to love you." He reached for her again, but this time his kiss was only a gentle brush of his lips.

Maggie sensed that for now she'd have to be satisfied with that.

After Mick turned the sign back around, things seemed to settle back to the way they had been before he and she had made love. She felt a sense of loss over the lack of intensity between them, but also a little relieved. If they were going to keep their relationship quiet, it was far better if they could learn to behave as if nothing had happened. Far better.

And far more lonely.

Mick fought himself all through the day, knowing that this was going to be the most difficult time of his life—loving Maggie, yet not being free to live that love as openly as he yearned to. He had her reputation to think of, after all. Another matter of honor she might not understand. He loved her, yet he knew there were irreconcilable differences between them. He couldn't give her up now, but he couldn't give up his quest for revenge, either. It was a painful dilemma.

They managed to work with their usual efficiency, putting the finishing touches on Davey's work and setting the jewelry out in glass-covered cases in preparation for the weekend. He missed watching her work on his opals, but this was important to her, so he took up his assigned tasks with good humor.

"I want to put different colored velvet in the cases," she announced, coming in from the workroom with an armload of material. "Black or blue are fine for the rest of the year, but Christmas is special. The brighter colors seem to attract the impulse buyer, rather than the serious jewelry collector. And it's the casual buyer we're after right now."

"How do you know all this?"

"I studied business as well as art." She grinned at him. "There's no point having stuff to sell if you don't know how to sell it, is there?"

His hand stroked the velvet and then her cheek. "Nope, guess not."

By midafternoon they had most of the display set up. Yellow, gold and amber stones sat on a pale beige bed, amethysts on a lavender one, and rubies and garnets were on pink. Diamonds remained on black. There were no opals. Those, by mutual consent, would be kept aside for greater things.

"It's beautiful," Maggie said, stepping back to the door and viewing the scene. Silver tinsel ropes were draped around the display cases and colored lights winked on and off in the window. "Jewelry stores should be decorated for Christmas year-round. It's always Christmas in a place like this."

"It's always Christmas in your eyes." Mick came around from behind the counter and lifted her chin in his hand. His lips touched hers, and then the kiss deepened. "*You're* beautiful," he whispered, pulling her close. His mouth covered hers again.

Neither of them heard the bell over the door until a male voice said, "Excuse me. I was looking for Miss Wellington."

Maggie broke away just as Mick released her. Embarrassment clouded her vision and burned her cheeks. "Sorry," she said. "We were sort of celebrating the holidays a little early. What can I do for you?" Then she focused on the man and barely managed to suppress a gasp as she recognized him from a number of years ago.

Mick caught her change of mood immediately. One moment she was soft, warm and pliant in his arms; the next, stiff as a board and brittle as all hell.

And all because of this guy. Mick stepped back and studied him carefully. He was big—taller than Mick—but not as broad in the shoulders and chest. He had black hair that was liberally tinged with silver and receding slightly at the temples. His face was tanned, although not as darkly as Mick's own, and lines ran from the corners of his eyes back to his temples. He looked rugged and tough, a man who might do an honest day's work for an honest day's dollar. But somehow he was too smooth to be a laborer. Mick felt his temper sour. The guy was good-looking enough, he guessed. An old boyfriend? Real old. He had to be forty-five, if he was a day.

Or was he someone more sinister? He was expensively dressed in a heavy, well-tailored camel topcoat over a gray suit. His boots looked handmade. And Maggie? Well, Mag was practically fawning over him. Mick's temper grew worse.

"Mr. Drexel," she said, smiling. "Now I remember you. San Francisco. It's been years. I just didn't recognize you out of context. How are your wife and family?"

"Just fine," Drexel said, smiling. "And Cat's why I'm here. The last time we were in your place in 'Frisco, she drooled over a piece of silver and turquoise you'd done for a friend of mine. The same Mrs. Mason you made that marvelous opal brooch for. Then you moved, and I was too busy to track you down. Well, I found you." He reached into his pocket and took out a velvet bag. "Can you make this up into a necklace for her by Christmas? I know it's short notice, but—"

"Miss Wellington's already completely booked up with another special project." Mick had come out of his musings like a shot at the mention of the opal brooch and had moved over to stand near Maggie. His jaw jutted pugnaciously. "I don't think she—"

"Mick..." Her eyes warned him to shut up. "Let me look at the stone, Mr. Drexel." She upended the bag and slid a huge, perfect, egg-shaped turquoise gently onto a velvet pad. Whistling softly, she picked the treasure up. "I would certainly like to have a try at this," she said, staring at it. "I certainly would."

"If you can't make Christmas," Drexel said, "how about Valentine's Day? I promised Cat an extension on the ranch kitchen and a couple of horses for her dude string before spring. I could get started on the remodeling and put a bow around the ponies for this holiday—save the jewelry for a more romantic one." He smiled, as if to himself, and his dark eyes gleamed.

"Valentine's Day would pose no problem, at all," Maggie gushed, setting Mick's teeth on edge. "How about if I send you some preliminary sketches as soon after New Year's as I can?"

Drexel smiled again, showing white, even teeth and said that that would be fine. He gave Maggie his card, telling her to be sure to send the sketches to his office rather than to his home. Then he shopped, picking out nearly five thousand dollars worth of trinkets for his family and friends. Mick decided the guy had to be in something extremely illegal to throw around that kind of money on impulse buys.

He also resolved to find out what it was. Chances were, he decided in his jealousy and confusion, that he was somehow connected to the thief who had sold Maggie Ian's opal. San Francisco. Years ago. There might well be a connection. And Maggie had not introduced him....

But after Drexel left, and he confronted her, Maggie hotly denied any such thing. "That man is Garrick Drexel, a highly successful, respected financier," she said. "I don't know the whole story, but I do know he used to work on

Wall Street and now lives in Wyoming on his wife's guest ranch.''.

"He sure throws money around. *And* he knows the lady you made that brooch for. I'm going to check him out, as you Yanks say." Mick went for his coat.

"Mick O'Shay, don't you dare!" Maggie's cheeks were pink with rage. "I didn't introduce you because you were acting so rudely. There was absolutely no other reason."

He hesitated. "I just didn't like the way he barged in here and demanded that you work on his stuff."

"That is what I am here for! People expect me to make custom jewelry—it's my *specialty*, remember?"

More doubt assailed him, but he was determined not to let a single possibility get away. He picked up the card before she could snatch it off the counter and committed the man's address and phone number to memory. After that, Maggie wouldn't speak to him and avoided meeting his eyes directly. He saw the tears, but wouldn't relent. By the end of the day, her chilly, sad silence had filled him with a terrible grief of his own, but also a deeper certainty this Drexel character had to have something to do with the mystery around the opal's seller. Knowing how Maggie felt, Mick wouldn't have put it past her to lie, to try to thwart him in order to keep him from fulfilling his deadly mission—for his "own good," she would probably tell him. But he wasn't about to let that happen.

Maggie's sorrow filled her heart and soul. How could she have imagined his newfound love for her would make a bit of difference? Hadn't he himself told her repeatedly that it would not? She was dealing with a man who had his purpose carved far more deeply on his heart than she could ever be. Her love was only temporary and futile.

But it was too strong to deny. Far too strong.

She said nothing when he left early, claiming a need to be with his son. She just nodded and waited until the door

slammed shut before crying quietly. Nothing she could do
or say would make any difference anyway, she thought. So
why bother? She walked out from behind the counter, tears
flowing down her cheeks, and surveyed the beauty they had
created together. She also thought of the opal jewelry that
was a joint creation. Slowly, the tears ceased and her fists
balled up.

Damn it! She wasn't going to sit around boo-hooing like
a little girl! If Mick O'Shay was too stubborn and stiff-
necked to listen to reason, she was going to upset his apple
cart so that he'd *have* to. Going back to the counter, she
reached down behind it and grabbed a sketch pad. First she
would have dinner with her father, then she would go on
her mission! Her thoughts boiled with plans and possibili-
ties.

"LOOK, ALL I WANT to know is how legitimate this guy is,"
Mick told Patrick Wellington. Tad had been, as Mick had
hoped, over at the Wellington house. Patrick had invited
him in for a beer while Tad finished watching a program on
television, and Mick used the opportunity to good advantage.

"Garrick Drexel is as legitimate as they come," Patrick
informed him. "In fact, he's so clean, he squeaks. I never
knew details, but professional gossip had it he was inves-
tigated by the SEC a few years ago and survived with flying
colors. A law school classmate of mine, Sheldon Sheri-
dan, in New York, was his lawyer. That's how I know what
I do know."

"He's rich." Mick took a drink of beer.

"So're you, my boy. That doesn't make you a bad man,
now does it? Tell me, what made Drexel stick in your craw,
anyhow? Does it have anything to do with your friend, Ian
Richards?"

Mick choked on his drink.

"No," Patrick went on. "Maggie hasn't said a word to me. Tad spilled the beans. He's very worried about you, you know."

"He shouldn't be." Mick kicked himself mentally for not having explained the necessity of keeping his mouth shut to Tad. He ought to have known his son would open up once he learned to trust Patrick. "I'm only doing what I have to."

The older man rubbed his hand over his chin. "There have been times in my life I thought that, too. It usually turned out I was wrong. How much does Maggie know?"

"Enough!" Mick slammed his beer bottle down.

"What's the fuss, Da?" Tad appeared in the doorway. His young features were twisted in a worried frown.

"Nothing, son." Mick downed the rest of his beer and stood. "Patrick, please don't say anything to Maggie about my visit. We...we had a disagreement this afternoon. I'd rather try working it out myself."

"Undoubtedly an excellent idea." Patrick stood and extended his hand. He had a fair notion what had already happened romantically between his daughter and this man with his archaic notions of justice, and he was tempted not for the first time to administer some common sense with harsh words. But Mick O'Shay was, as Maggie had frequently described him, a diamond in the rough. Tad was such a fine young man: intelligent, in spite of his occasional lapses of grammar and ignorance of things American; and sensitive, judging by his ability to befriend Davey and make the handicapped boy feel comfortable. A man who had raised such a son had to be redeemable. Patrick had decided to be patient and bide his time.

Mick shook hands, feeling unaccountably guilty. He had achieved his purpose by getting Jeff Wright's office number, at least. In the morning, he would call the lawyer and get him to set an investigation in motion. He *would* find out

what he could, in his own way. Then he and Tad put on
coats and headed home to dinner prepared by the patient
Celia Hawthorne.

On the way, Tad kicked a lot of snow. He said nothing
until they turned into the walkway leading to the front
door. "Da, if you'd quit all this other stuff, you 'n' Maggie could get married. We could stay here for good." He
gave a pile of snow a particularly vicious kick.

Mick felt as though his veins had been shot through first
with ice water, then fire. *Marry Maggie?* He stared at Tad.

"Da?" In the light from the front porch, the boy's face
looked younger, eager.

"Oh, Tad." Mick felt himself severely waver from his
purpose for the first time. "What'm I supposed to do? Just
let the bastard go free? How many times have we talked
about this?"

His son said nothing, but Mick saw the glimmer of tears
as Tad turned his head away.

Dinner was a painfully silent affair.

Meanwhile, at her home, Maggie was picking at her food
and listening to her father. He was talking all around the
subject, but she knew he was trying to get her to think logically about Mick. Unfortunately, logic and Mick were like
oil and water.

"...a man whose value system is so different from
yours," Patrick was saying. That cut through.

"All right, all right!" she shouted. "So I'm making another mistake with a man. I'm grown and entitled. Just as
you are. I suppose you think everything is going to be
hunky-dory with you and Nell."

"I'm not sleeping with Nell!" Patrick lost his temper,
too, and slapped his hand down on the table sharply. He
realized his error too late. Maggie blushed furiously and
pushed back from the table so quickly her chair fell.

"I'll be back when I'm back," she said tightly. "Don't bother waiting up." She ran into the living room, and he heard the front door slam a moment later. The roar of the Bronco engine sounded in the night.

Patrick Wellington covered his eyes with his hand and uttered an unaccustomed curse word. He sat silently for a few minutes. Then he stood and went into the kitchen. Taking the telephone receiver in his hand, he dialed. After a few rings, she answered. "Hello, Nell," he said wearily. "I really need to talk."

At that very moment, Mick tried calling Maggie and he listened to the busy signal with growing frustration and anxiety. Was she actually so mad at him she'd taken the damn thing off the hook? Tad's words echoed in his head: *Marry Maggie, marry Maggie, marry Maggie.* He could not get the refrain out of his mind to save his life. Maybe if they talked . . .

But he wasn't getting any talking done this way. Mick slammed the receiver down and paced the floor, cursing quietly to himself. It had all been so clear for so long. Now everything was getting confused. *Marry Maggie, marry . . .*

"Bloody *hell*!"

"Why'nt you go see her?" Tad came into the room. He was dressed in his pajamas and had a book under his arm. "I'll be okay."

"Naw, I'll catch her in the morning." He didn't even try meeting Tad's gaze. "You go on to bed."

"No, bloody hell!" The book sailed across the room, barely missing Mick. "You go see her! I ain't gonna go to bed like some damned little kid. *You're* the only one actin' like you ain't got out of nappies yet."

Mick swore viciously. Tad stood his ground, glaring at his father. Mick collapsed as if he'd been punctured by a knife. "Oh, my God," he moaned, sinking onto the couch with his head in his hands. "I'm sorry, son. I'm so I don't know my own mind today." He sobbed—a long, deep and agonized cry.

Tad came over and sat by his father. Awkwardly, he put an arm around Mick's shoulders. The two Australians sat like that for a long time. Finally, Mick straightened. "I'll go see her," he said hoarsely. "We'll talk, I promise. You get on to bed. Please."

"Good on yer, Da," Tad said softly. He leaned over, kissed his father on the cheek, and then he got up, grabbed his book and ran from the room.

Mick sat for a while longer, tears running down his face unchecked. Then he went to the bathroom and washed his face, put on his coat and left his house, this time on a quest of an entirely different nature from the one that had haunted his life for so long.

MAGGIE SLUMPED in her chair and daubed with a finger at a tiny puddle of beer on the table. She'd had one beer, one lousy beer, and she was wasted. Wasted. It kind of fit the way she felt about life in general right now. Mick, her dad—it all seemed as if it was going directly down the toilet. The only stable thing in her life was her work. The jewelry, the stones.

The opals.

But stones couldn't hold you when you were cold or lonely, or talk to you in front of a fire on a snowy night or . . . Or love you. She took another sip of beer.

She wasn't drinking alone. In fact, she wasn't really drinking—just playing with the beer. Next to her at the table in the corner of the tavern was a friend, Joey Steele; an artist, a young man with a properly lean and hungry look. Next to Joey sat a worried-looking Charlie Jensen. Joey was sketching on a pad. Several drawings lay crumpled on the table, all rejected by Maggie.

"You really ought to get a police artist, Mag," Joey said, putting down his pencil. "I'm no pro at this kind of thing."

"I don't know any police artists." She regarded him balefully. "I just know you. Draw. I'm paying for it."

"You're wasting money," Charlie cautioned.

"'S my money. Come on, Joey. Make the ears a little bigger."

"Just what's this guy done to you?" Joey wanted to know. "He owe you money or something?"

"Lots more than money." Maggie drank beer. "Lots more."

"Is the Aussie really worth it?" Charlie asked quietly, showing uncharacteristic insight into her problems.

"Yep."

"Maggie—"

"Charlie, have you ever been in love? I mean really in love?"

The skier thought for a moment. "No, I guess not."

"Joey?"

"Once. I think." He picked up his pencil and made a few changes in the portrait. "I don't know. I'm living with a girl now, but love? I don't think so."

"If you don't know, you weren't. I've been 'I think I'm in love,' and it's different." She looked at the portrait. "That's better. Now make the nose a little wider and the mouth thinner.

Joey sketched. Maggie sat back and stared at the rest of the tavern without really seeing much. Smoke hung in a thin haze around the tables; conversation was lively but not rowdy. This establishment catered to the townspeople rather than the tourists and skiers. She had gone looking for Joey, ran into Charlie and they had located the artist here. Maggie had sat down and offered him a phenomenal sum to come up with a facsimile of the man who had sold her Ian's opal. Once she had that, she figured, she could get

Jeff to see what kind of police action she could get on the matter—police action that Mick couldn't interfere with. If they could catch the man, Mick wouldn't have a chance to carry out his terrible plans.

But coming up with a drawing that really fit her memory was far more difficult than she had imagined. Firstly, it had been several years, and she hadn't had reason to pay any particular attention to the guy's face. Secondly, Joey was clearly reluctant to take the task. He was a decent man and a good enough friend to balk at taking money from her he felt he couldn't earn. Thirdly, the argument with her father had upset her more than she had realized at the time. And, of course, finally, there was Mick.

There was Mick!

He stood a few tables away, looking like thunder. She raised her chin and stared at him defiantly. Charlie made a small noise and pushed his chair back. Joey said, "Whoops," and closed the sketch pad quickly.

Mick couldn't move for a moment. He wanted to do any number of things. He wanted to grab Maggie and shake her. After hearing Patrick's misery over the fight they had had at dinner, he was burning with remorse over the rift he had caused between parent and daughter, but part of that remorse had turned to anger at her. Why had she taken her fury with him out on the father she clearly loved so much? He also wanted to paste Charlie and the other man just for sitting with her. But mostly, he wanted to embrace her, kiss her and hold her next to him forever.

He settled on going over to the table and sitting down. "I've been looking for you," he said mildly. "I need to talk to you."

"About what?" She wasn't going to give him a damn inch, no matter how much she wanted to get up and go to him, and throw her arms around his neck and tell him that she loved him, no matter what he did.

Mick looked at the other men. Charlie stood. "We're outta here," he said. "See you, Maggie. Mick."

Joey stood, too. Then he opened the pad and tore out the picture. "Take this, Mag," he said. "I can't charge you for it, since it's no damn good. Sorry." The portrait landed on the table between Maggie and Mick. Joey and Charlie beat a hasty retreat.

"What's this?" Mick grabbed the paper. Glancing at the portrait, he looked up inquiringly at Maggie.

"It's an attempt to construct your man," she said, suddenly very tired. "I thought if I could show the police what he looked like—"

"They'd get him, and I couldn't. That the idea?"

She nodded.

"I've been pretty much of a fool, Maggie." He set the picture down. "It took some real hard kicks in the gut from some people I love a lot to show me that, but I think the light is finally dawning." He tapped the picture. "This could be a good idea. Why don't we try it?"

She stared at him. "Do you mean that?"

"What I mean, my darling love," he said, reaching across the table, "is that I have realized you, Tad—and Patrick—are more important to me than revenge. Ian's memory will be far better served if I don't murder in his name. I'll not stop until the man is caught, but I won't execute him. I want a new life now. A life with you. Are you willing, Margaret Wellington?"

CHAPTER ELEVEN

"TELL ME what happened." Maggie watched him carefully. "Why this sudden change of heart?"

"It's hard for me to explain, Mag." His grip on her hand became firmer. "Can you just accept that I've—"

"Try." She struggled to keep her emotions off her face. He was saying exactly the words she had longed to hear. But she didn't trust him as far as she could throw him.

"Maggie, don't you understand?" He was pleading now. "I'm asking you to think about marrying me."

She nearly fell off her chair. "*Marry* you? Mick, I don't *know* you."

"That's not so. You know me better than any woman alive. What do you want to know? Go ahead. Ask." He was now squeezing her hand between both of his own.

"Do you intend to squash my hand?"

He let her go as if she was burning him. "Sorry. I got carried away."

"Exactly. Carried away enough to barge in here and scare my friends."

"Why are you making this so hard?" It was dim in the place, but she could still see the light of genuine pain in his eyes. Her heart started tearing.

"Because." She put her hands over his. "I don't believe you can change your stripes just like that. I believe *you* think you have, but I don't."

"Aw, Maggie. I—"

"Tell me what happened between the time you left, hell-bent on pinning Mr. Drexel to the wall, and now? Why should I believe you've really come to your senses?"

"You," he said, "and Tad. Patrick, too." His expression started to take on the old, stubborn look. "It wasn't sudden, either. It's been cooking in me ever since I first met you. Look, I'm a simple man. I don't explain things too well. But I do understand when my mind's made up. It is, and I'm going to convince you of it."

"I honestly don't know how you're—"

"I'm going to do it the way I've done everything else in my life, Maggie. I'm going to *work* for it. I'm going to work and earn your trust. By the time I'm done, you won't be able to believe I ever felt any other way than I do now. That I ever thought I could live without you." His determination was a palpable thing.

She took a deep breath. "All I can give you is time, Mick. We're committed until April and San Francisco. By then, we should both know our hearts. Fair enough?"

"Probably." His gaze was so intense it seemed to probe her mind. "Let's go home."

"What?"

"Let's go home." He ran his hand up her forearm, causing an erotic thrill to go through her. "I want to make love with you."

"Where's home, Mick? My dad's in one, Tad's in the other. We can't—"

"Oh, yes we can." He got out of his chair and came around to sit next to her. Sliding his arm around her waist, he pushed her hair away from her ear and put his lips so near, she could feel his breath. Her insides went hot and liquid. "Tad's asleep by now," he whispered. "His room is way down the hall, and we don't have to make as much of a fuss as we did last time, now, do we?" There was so much silky seduction in his tone, she had to look twice to make sure this was still Mick O'Shay. "Come on, Maggie. I need you."

It took her all of one second to make up her mind.

The house was so quiet, she felt like tiptoeing, but Mick boldly barged in, clearly unconcerned about alerting Tad to their presence. "Shh," she cautioned as he removed her coat and kissed her neck, murmuring his desire. Goose bumps rose in spite of her nervousness.

"It's all right," he said. "He sleeps like he's been coshed. Take a bomb to wake him up. Besides, he ain't likely to mind, since my marrying you was his idea in the first place."

"Beg pardon!"

"Easy, Mag. I just meant, he said I should, and I got to thinking about it like I've never thought about anything else before." He traced the line of her cheek. "You're going to make a beautiful bride, love." His arms tightened around her, and his lips covered hers, giving her no more opportunity to discuss the matter. Unable—and really unwilling—to help herself, she melted against him, sighing with desire and surrender.

Once they were in his bedroom, behind a closed and locked door, he loved her with such tender skill, she thought she couldn't live through the intensity of the pleasure he gave. Whereas the first night he had been raging with need and passion, tonight he was a different lover: slow, tantalizing and exciting beyond measure.

Under his hands, their clothes fell away as they had before, but now he took the time to turn back the bedcovers and lay her gently on the cool sheet. Maggie's nipples peaked as she shivered again, and Mick said, "Ah," with a smile. He kissed her lips softly, then went after her body. Not much later, the goose bumps were a memory and her skin was slick with perspiration. He licked and tasted her all over until she was ready to scream with the delicious sensations he caused.

"I want to do this every night for the rest of my life," he whispered, gazing down at her, the heat in his eyes matching the heat in her body. "Every night, and at least once or twice during the day."

"An ambition I approve of," she managed to gasp. "Whoever said make love, not war must have known you well."

"Nobody's known me like you do. Nobody! Nobody ever will." He entered her then, and soon they were soaring together silently. It seemed to last forever, and when it was finally over, Maggie couldn't even focus her eyes. Mick murmured, "Marry me, Maggie," into her ear and promptly fell sound asleep.

She lay there for a while, trying to think. His desire and passion were undeniable, his earnestness unmistakable. But she just couldn't accept that he had managed to throw off his purpose in a few hours. No one could change so quickly.

Her body throbbed with fading pleasure, and she moved to ease the tension in some of her muscles. Mick's arm, already around her, hugged her to him more tightly. In his sleep he shifted so that his head rested partly on her breast. She looked at him.

Well, he certainly wasn't tense anywhere. She smiled. Sweat beads from his erotic exertions were still evident, giving his skin a golden sheen. The lines usually marking his face had eased in sleep, and he looked remarkably like his son. His firmly carved mouth was relaxed and partly open, and he was puffing soft, even breaths on Maggie's skin. She felt a renewed surge of love for him.

But she couldn't commit to him for life. He was a cipher, in spite of his claim to simplicity. He was like a loose cannon on a sailing ship; there was no telling when the waves would send him careering into the side of the vessel, tearing a gash that would send her to the bottom.

Maggie gently lifted his arm and eased out of bed. He made an unhappy sound and his hand moved around for a moment, then settled and relaxed. She would have loved to stay and wake up with him, but she had to get home. There was the breach with Patrick to repair, a serious apology to be made. Perhaps she would even offer an explanation. If he knew about Mick's obsession—his supposed *former* obsession—maybe her father would understand why she had flown off the handle so easily. She owed him that much. Dressing quietly and quickly, she bent down and kissed her sleeping lover, then left his house.

PATRICK WAS still up. When she opened the door and saw him sitting in the living room in his special chair, she suddenly felt about sixteen years old. "Have I missed curfew?" she asked, smiling in a conciliatory fashion.

"Come on in, honey." Patrick sounded tired. "No, you haven't missed anything."

"Oh, I am so sorry." She dropped her coat on the floor and went over to hug him. "I don't know how I could have behaved the way I did. Can you forgive me?"

"I'd forgive you, if there was anything to forgive." He patted her shoulder. "Go sit down. I suppose we need to talk."

She sat, folding her hands in her lap. "Mick asked me to marry him."

"Why am I not surprised? Are you going to?"

"Dad, he's . . . Well, he's an unusual man. He has some real hang-ups involving his past. He . . ."

Patrick waved a hand. "I know all about that, Maggie. And have you asked yourself if you want to marry a man who might end up in prison or worse?"

"How do you know about it?"

Her father smiled sadly. "Tad can be quite talkative when he chooses. One day he started talking about his friend Ian, and one thing led to another. A tragedy, a real tragedy."

"Yes."

"But one that'll be far worse if his father ends up playing judge, jury and executioner. I don't know, Mag. As a man, I appreciate Mick's desire for vengeance. As a former servant of the court, I wonder if I ought not try to knock some sense into him."

"He says he's giving it up. He told me tonight he won't try going after the man himself. He'll let the authorities handle it."

"Do you believe him?" Patrick's eyes bored into her.

"No."

"Then you must not join your life to his."

"I know." Tears came, and she let them flow. "Oh, Dad. I don't know what to do. I love him so much!"

Patrick shut his eyes for a moment, fighting the emotional pain. Then he rose and sat beside his daughter, putting his arms around her and comforting her as best he could.

The next day, her romantic problems notwithstanding, Maggie rose before dawn and hurried through her morning routine, bolting breakfast and saying good morning to her father as she put on her coat. "I'm feeling better," she reassured him. "I know I don't have to decide anything yet, and time may provide the answer." Patrick mumbled sleepy approval and went back to snoring softly. Maggie left and walked briskly through the lavender dawn to the store. It was only a few hours until the time when hundreds, hopefully thousands of tourists and shoppers would hit the streets of Sullivan Springs.

There was nothing, she thought as she unlocked the shop, like the promise of such a day to help one forget one's problems for a time.

But the sight that met her eyes made her scream with anguish.

MICK WOKE when sunlight hit his eyes. He rolled over, feeling for Maggie, and muttered with disappointment when he found the other side of the bed empty. Well, he reasoned, she'd had to go home and talk to her dad. He lay on his back and wondered if she had told him about the proposal. He smiled. Married, they could hammer out their problems. It *would* work. His thoughts strayed briefly to the drawing of the man Maggie thought might be the thief, and he had a brief twinge of guilt over folding it up and slipping it secretly into his coat pocket. Then he remembered what day it was, and strangely enough, a sudden sense of anxiety overcame him.

Twenty minutes later, he was on his way—*sans* breakfast—to the shop.

MAGGIE DID HER BEST to behave calmly while Sam and another officer went over the shop, looking for clues. It was her fault, she berated herself. All her fault! If she hadn't rushed out yesterday, intent on getting the sketch done of Mick's villain, she would have remembered to follow her routine of putting the jewelry away in the safe and setting the nighttime alarm. The loss was far more than financial. If she had been the only one to suffer for this, it would have been tolerable, but there was Davey Abrams to consider. Almost all of his careful work was gone. And Mr. Drexel's fabulous turquoise. Mick's opals, of course, were all still safely stowed in the big iron box. But she herself was ruined.

"It don't exactly look like a professional job to me," Sam said, standing and dusting off his pants. His sergeant was still on the floor, searching for minuscule clues. "I'd be willing to bet my pension it was just some yahoo who's been casing the town and who lucked out on you with your guard down."

"Is that good or bad?" Her voice trembled in spite of her attempt at self-control.

"Good and bad." Sam frowned. "If he gets careless and tries fencing or selling the stuff right away, we might nab him. 'Course, he's not going to do that here in town. I'll have to alert Denver. Fort Collins, too."

"And the bad?"

"He might be smart. Hang on to the stuff for a while. Take it to another state. Back east. To the coast. We can't cover every pawn shop and fence in the country. Nope, Maggie. I think you'd better start getting together a report for your insurance—"

"Maggie!" Mick's shout sounded tormented. "Maggie! Is she . . . ? Maggie! Are you all right?" She was swept into a bear hug that drove the breath right out of her. All her resolve to be brave broke and she sobbed, unable to say a word.

Mick held her tightly, comforting her with his arms as best he could. "What bastard did this?" he growled, turning to the police chief. "Have you caught him yet?"

"Not yet, Mick, but—"

Mick swore, long and colorfully, ending with the words: "...just like with Ian. You don't stand a snowball's chance of finding him. It's gonna be up to me, and I—"

"Whoa." Sam Glover held up a big hand. "This is the U.S. of A., O'Shay. Second half of the twentieth century. It isn't up to the citizens but to the cops to catch the bad guys. Now, you just relax and take care of your lady. Leave the detecting and catching to us. That's what they pay us for."

Mick started to deliver a hot reply, but Maggie had recovered and gave him a warning kick in the shins. He let her go, but kept an arm around her shoulders. "All right," he said. "Earn your keep, Chief. But remember, this is Maggie's life you're looking at." He stared at the wreckage. The glass-topped cases had been smashed, the colored velvet strewed and torn. A few pieces of jewelry were left, but he could tell at a glance they were not high quality, just the inexpensive costume line. His heart ached for her.

"They didn't get any of the opals," she said in a weak voice. "Nothing that was in the safe. Just the stuff I carelessly left out. Oh, Mick. Davey's work. It was all for nothing." His arm around her tightened.

"Ho, now!" The sergeant, a young man with a scraggly blond mustache, stood up, holding a scrap of crumpled paper. "What's this?"

Sam Glover took it and smoothed it out on the wooden counter. Maggie looked at the piece of paper and gave a cry of recognition. "Joey," she said. "It's a scrap of one of his drawings. Oh, but he couldn't have—"

"That the skinny kid with you and Charlie last night?" Mick's expression was frightening "*He* did this?"

Sam studied the drawing. It was a partially rendered depiction of a man's face. "There's no signature," he said. "No way to be sure—"

"The hell there isn't." Mick reached into his coat and took out the finished portrait. Unfolding it, he laid it down next to the evidence. "See," he said in dark triumph. "No mistake. Drawn by the same hand. And Maggie can swear he did it. She gave him the instructions?"

"That so?" Sam looked at her.

She nodded. "But, Sam, Joey is a friend. He's a gentle person who wouldn't harm anyone. You know how he is, always taking in stray cats and people in trouble. He would never—"

"Let's go ask him." Mick felt inside his coat and found the butt of his gun. "Give me a few minutes with him, and we'll find out—"

"O'Shay," Sam said mildly. "Let me have your piece."

"It ain't necessary. I won't—"

Sam held out his hand and wriggled his fingers. Reluctantly, Mick withdrew the weapon and gave it over. "I don't need it, anyway," he said. "Just five minutes."

"And if he ain't guilty?" Sam regarded Mick steadily.

"What's the damn drawing doing here?" Mick's jaw jutted.

"Mick." Maggie put her hand on his arm. "Let them take care of it. Please!"

He turned and looked at her, and his ferocious expression softened. "I can't stand the idea of someone deliberately hurting you," he said. "Just can't stand it!"

"But I can't believe it was Joey."

"You were with him last night?" Sam asked. "And he did do this second drawing?"

"Yes." She pushed her hands together to hide their trembling. "I . . . I was upset. I thought this drawing might solve some problems. . . ."

"What problems?" Sam's voice was stern.

A few minutes later, he knew about Mick's partner and the odyssey the Australian had made to find his killer. He rubbed a hand over his forehead. "Whew, if I'd known what a time bomb I had in you, O'Shay—"

"I'm not any more." Mick raised his hands. "I found something far more important to me." His hands went out to Maggie. She stepped back into his embrace a shade reluctantly. That he had taken and hidden the portrait bothered her at a gut level. He believed in his change of heart, she knew. But had there really been one?

"Uh-huh." Sam looked just as skeptical as Maggie felt. "In any event, you try getting near Steele before we've had a crack at him, and I'm liable to throw your butt in jail for obstruction at the very least. Do I make myself clear?"

Mick nodded, feeling rage seething, but trying his best to put it aside. "Yeah. I hear you, Chief. He's all yours. Besides, I've got a lot of work to do around here, if we're going to be ready for the fair."

"Mick," Maggie said quietly, "we're cleaned out. There's nothing to sell."

"Oh yes, there is." He hugged her to him.

Sam and his sergeant hung around a while longer, sifting for any more clues and learning from Maggie that she hadn't tried to hide her emotional state from Charlie and Joey. She had to admit that they were both aware she wasn't functioning on all cylinders, and that either one might have deduced she had been less than careful with her security. By the time they left, she was almost convinced Joey was guilty in spite of her friendship with the artist. The door closed, making the bell tinkle, and she felt fresh tears come.

"All right." Mick rubbed his hands together. "We've got a couple of hours before opening time. Let's get to it."

"There's no point." She bent down and picked up a tattered piece of velvet. "The place is a mess, and I've got nothing left to sell."

"The safe is full." He took off his coat and tossed it on an overturned chair. Slipping off the empty holster, he put it next to the coat.

"But . . . but only with your opals and some unset stones of mine."

"Exactly." He was rummaging in the narrow closet on the back wall, where she kept cleaning equipment. "Go in the back and start organizing them. I'll take care of the mess in a jiff."

"Mick, the opals are for . . ."

"The opals are mine. For whatever I want." He emerged with a broom and dustpan. "Now, get at it!" Maggie scurried into the workroom.

Two hours later, thirty minutes before the shop was officially open, they had restored its appearance. But...

"I cannot feel good about selling the jewelry I made for you," she said, miserable. "It's like I'm cheating you."

He kissed her hair. "You could never cheat a gnat. And we can't show all this stuff anyhow. You'll just have to outdo yourself before April."

"But it's not just the jewelry. These are your special stones."

"The only thing that's special about them is where they came from." He shut the closet door and dusted off his hands. "Not to worry..." His hands fell slowly to his sides. "What in the hell?"

Maggie turned. Joey Steele and Sam were walking down the sidewalk toward the store, carrying boxes. Her heart leaped and sank at the same time. No sooner were they in the door than Mick was on Joey. "You little son-of-a-bitch!" he yelled. "I oughta—"

"Hold your damn water, O'Shay!" Sam balanced his burden on his hip and blocked Mick with his right arm. "He ain't the burglar. It was his roommate, Darlene Turner."

Mick stepped back, breathing hard. "Roommate? You mean a *girl*?" Sam nodded.

Maggie took the box from Joey and opened it, crying out with joy. "It doesn't matter! Here's all Davey's work." She rummaged. "And Mr. Drexel's stone! Oh, Sam, Joey. I don't know how to thank you!"

Joey looked extremely unhappy. "Don't thank me, Maggie. If I hadn't shot off my mouth, you wouldn't have had this trouble."

"Are you serious about your girlfriend doing this?" she asked. Joey literally hung his head.

"Serious as a heart attack."

Sam handed his box to Mick, who took it over to the counter and started unpacking. Maggie glanced at his back and could tell immediately he was listening with every fiber. Said Sam: "Joey told this young woman what a state you were in while they were... Well, I expect you get the picture. Anyhow, after he fell asleep, she took off, broke in here and hid the loot in the alcove where he stores his old canvases."

"It would have been months before I looked in there for anything," Joey explained. "It was probably the safest place in town. God, Maggie. I feel just awful about this. I had no idea Darlene was the light-fingered type."

Sam said, "Her one mistake was picking up your discarded sketches and keeping them for lists and such. The one that fell out of her pocket led up to your place."

"There's no doubt it was this Darlene and not him?" Mick had turned and was scowling at them. "No doubt, at all?"

"Mick!" Maggie felt a surge of resentment and anger.

"Of course, there's doubt," Sam said. "She's innocent until proven guilty. It's a system of justice our countries have in common."

"If she's so damn innocent, how come you arrested her?"

Maggie sighed loudly and took the box from Sam. "Because, Dirty Harry, they had what's called 'probable cause.' That means she can be arrested and held for trial. I didn't spend my life as a lawyer's daughter without learning something about the legal system," she added, winking at Sam.

"Oh." Mick scratched his head. "Who's Dirty Harry?"

Sam laughed loudly. "Ask your kid. I bet he knows. Maggie, I'm gonna need a statement from you. Come on down to the office as soon as you're done here."

"Oh, dear." She looked around. "This is going to take some time, and I won't be able to open until around noon. We have to get all the opals back—"

"I'll help," Joey said. "It's the least I can do."

"Mag." Mick came over and put his arm around her waist. "You go on with Sam. Joey and I'll put things right. Don't worry about it."

"But—"

He kissed her forehead. "Go on. When you come back, you can take over." He hesitated for a moment, then said, "It's cool." After a brief pause, he announced, "I got that from my son."

Maggie left, wondering what she would find when she came back.

After giving Sam her statement, she asked if she could speak with Darlene Turner. Curiosity had filled her, and she just had to know why the woman had taken the risk of breaking into the shop. Sam had answered the question of how.

"She's an electrician," he said. "Probably a semi-professional thief. She crossed up that alarm slicker'n a snake on ice. If I was you, I'd get myself a better system right away." Maggie agreed.

Darlene was a pretty woman, but her attractiveness was marred by a hard sullenness. Maggie could see why she had appealed to Joey, however. Her face was all planes and hollows; she was a perfect artist's model, capable of many expressions, and the dark shadows in her eyes made her fascinating to watch.

"I ripped you off because you were easy," she said, her voice a snarl. "My profession is stealing, and I've been casing this town ever since I moved in with that idiot, Joey.

He talks all the damn time, you know. I just waited until the right fish fell into my lap.''

"I see.'' Maggie looked directly at the woman until her eyes slid away. "So you went when you knew I was vulnerable, was that it?''

"That. And I saw the Wall Street type go in that afternoon. I know enough about you to figure he didn't drive all the way up here just to shop—he had to have something special he wanted made up.''

"He did. And I would have hated to tell him it was lost.''

"People like that can afford it.''

Maggie's temper flared. "Maybe they can. But sometimes things are worth more than money. That turquoise is going to be made into a special necklace for his wife. It holds some emotional value for him. If you just want money, rob banks. Jewelry has spirit and personality and meaning for the people who own it.''

Darlene just smirked. Maggie left with invisible steam coming out her ears.

"She's not at all remorseful," she complained to Sam before she left the office. "How can a person be that callous about other people's feelings? Joey must be terribly hurt.''

"I expect he was." Sam frowned. "She said some pretty tough things to him when we took her out.''

Maggie thought about that all the way back to her shop. When she got there, she received several pleasant surprises. Mick and Joey had two other helpers. Tad and Patrick were putting finishing touches on the Christmas trimmings. Her father dropped his work to come over and hug her. "Mick gave us a call," he explained. "Oh, honey. Are you all right?''

"Sure. Now. But if Sam hadn't found the stolen merchandise, I don't know—''

"Davey would have been devastated." Patrick frowned. "I called Nell. They're going to drive over this afternoon. I thought we ought to have a kind of celebration tonight. An impromptu party, perhaps."

"That's nice, Dad. But I'll probably be too tired. This has already taken a chunk out of me. And the day hasn't even begun yet."

"Don't worry," Joey piped up. "I feel so lucky to be rid of that woman, I want to party. I'm going to help your father and Nell get things ready. All you have to do is show."

"Okay." Maggie smiled. It was good to know that Joey wasn't going to brood.

Mick watched her, enjoying the play of emotions across her lovely face. She grew more beautiful to him with each day, he realized—and with each experience, good and bad. And each new aspect of her character showed in her face like a facet on a fine gemstone. "Before you go off to plan this blowout, Patrick," he said, startling everyone with his sudden speech, "I'd like to ask for some help."

"What can I do?" The lawyer's face indicated he was far from settled about Mick and his daughter. Mick shrugged that off. Time would take care of that problem. But since Sam had left, he'd been brooding on something else. Something related to his other problem.

"Sam said the woman who broke in here was innocent until proven guilty. Now, I knew that was part of the law, but I don't understand it. Do you have anything I can read, Patrick? I figured since you were a lawyer..." He rubbed the back of his neck, feeling the weight of his ignorance in front of all these people.

Patrick smiled broadly. "I sure do, son," he said. "I have about a ton of stuff. If you want, I can make you an expert on constitutional law. How would that be?"

"I think it's what I need," Mick replied.

Maggie listened to the conversation with astonishment. Was she ever going to be able to predict what this man would do next?

CHAPTER TWELVE

IN SPITE OF the inauspicious beginning, the day went extraordinarily well. The highway was clear of snow and ice and the skiers and shoppers descended on Sullivan Springs like a wave of beneficial locusts. Sidewalks and slopes teemed with the visitors, and local cash registers worked overtime. Maggie couldn't have been happier with the response of the public to the jewelry she had designed and Davey had made. As she sold and wrapped each piece, she inserted a small card stating the name of the craftsman in bold letters beside her own name as designer and dealer. A number of people indicated interest in seeing more of Davey's own work, and she decided to ask the youth if he would be willing to allow her to display some of his sculptures as well as the jewelry. When he and Nell arrived later that day, she put the question to him, and it was like seeing a Christmas tree light up.

"Geez," he said, almost rising out of his wheelchair in his excitement. "You mean they really want to see *my* stuff? Not just stuff I copied?"

"That's the ticket, Davey." Maggie did some quick calculations on her adding machine. "And I've got more good news for you. Our jewelry is selling so well, I've decided to give you a cut of the profits. So far, it amounts to this much." She tore off the sheet and handed it to the boy. Davey whistled softly and showed it to his mother. Nell took one look and clapped her hand to her mouth, tears in her eyes.

"We've been worried," she said, when she had gained control of herself. "So worried about the money it would take to send him to the right school. With this—"

"This is just a drop in the bucket," Maggie said. "But it is a start." She was interrupted by the entrance of another large group of customers, but she was warmed clear through by the happiness on the faces of both Abramses.

Mick observed all this quietly. So much good was coming out of his teaming up with Maggie; so much good for people who had been perfect strangers to him just weeks before. Even that artist fellow had come out on top, getting rid of a girlfriend who had been poisoning his life without his knowing it.

So much good. He tucked himself back in a corner, behind the crowd swarming around the counters, and watched her.

Why hadn't he seen it from the very first moment they'd met? She was an earthbound angel, spreading goodness to those around her as if she just couldn't help herself. She was an angel, and he was going to worship her for the rest of his life!

By the middle of the afternoon, satisfied the shop was well under control with Nell helping Maggie at the counters and Davey acting as general gofer, Mick left to take a short stroll through town. Maggie had suggested that he check out the action, and at this point, there was little she could ask of him that he wouldn't bust himself to do. Putting on his jacket and abandoning his empty holster without a tinge of regret, he went outside.

The town looked different with all the people. He didn't think he liked it as much, but crowds meant customers and customers meant sales and sales meant Maggie's success, at least at the local level. He itched for the day when she would be recognized far and wide. Trying not to bump shoulders with strangers, he made his way to the square.

Here, the throng was thicker, but friendly and full of the holiday spirit. Around the north side of the square various community groups and organizations had set up food booths, serving a wide assortment of goodies. Mick elbowed his way over to the one selling Polish sausages and sauerkraut on thick buns. The smell of the spicy food made his mouth water even before he took a healthy bite. Although a hint of snow was in the air, the sky was blue, and he looked up at it in appreciation before chomping down on the sausage.

"God, what a great shot!" An unfamiliar male voice rang out, startling Mick. He looked around and saw two men coming through the crowd toward him. One had a large camera balanced on his shoulder. The one in the lead carried a microphone and recorder. Mick jammed the rest of the sausage into his mouth and chewed it up quickly.

"Hey, guy," the lead man said when he reached him. "You're one hell of a picturesque dude. Local?"

"I live here. That what you mean?"

"But you're not..." The man was blond and slender, and reminded Mick vaguely of a dingo on the prowl. "Say, mind if I interview you, pal?" the dingo asked. "It's for the Denver news."

Mick thought for a moment. This could be turned to an advantage, if he handled it right. "I'm working down at Wellington's Worthies, a jewelry shop," he said. "Mind doing it there?"

The man's expression brightened. "You mean the place that was burglarized. Oh, hell, yes! You know the chickie who did it's wanted all over the country?"

"Say again?"

"I got it from a source in the police department. Seems she's connected with a ring of thieves who—"

Mick reached out and grabbed the lapel of the man's coat. "Talk to me, mate," he said, his face inches from that

of the surprised reporter's. "And keep the bloody recorder and camera turned bloody off. Understand me?"
The other man just nodded quickly, fear filling his eyes.

SAM GLOVER LOOKED up, startled, as Mick O'Shay burst
into the office. The Aussie's face was a clear indication of
his dark feelings, and Sam prepared for trouble.

"I want to see the prisoner," Mick snarled. "Now!"

"Hang on, O'Shay." Sam rose slightly from his chair
and shot a glance at his dispatcher, willing her to make
contact with his officers. The woman ducked her head behind the radio, and he heard soft words spoken. "What's
this all about?" he asked.

"You know damn well what it's about." Mick's fist
slammed down on the chief's desk, causing papers to scat-
ter. "That woman. She might be a link to my man!"

"She's no link to anything that concerns you." Sam kept
his voice low, but put steel into his tone. "So butt out."

"Sam." Mick's tone was now low, too, but far more
menacing. "I like you. But I will talk to her. With or without your approval."

Sam held his ground, but felt a trickle of sweat run down
his back. "You're gonna be lucky to get my approval to
stay in town, if you keep on threatening me, mister."

Mick took a deep breath and turned away, trying to control his anger. "I found out you've connected her to a
thieven ring, Sam," he said. "She might know the man I'm
looking for. I know it's a wild chance, but I have to try." He
turned back, willing the chief to see his deep need. "Isn't
there some way?"

Sam relaxed a bit. The Australian was in the grip of
fierce emotions, but he wasn't out of control or dangerous. He sat down. "Mick, she's got a lawyer who's on his
way here right now from California. She's wanted in that
state as well as half a dozen others. It may take years for her

to be tried for breaking into Maggie's place—the other charges are far more serious. But if you go roughing her up, you could blow everything."

"I won't touch her, Sam." Mick ran his fingers through his hair in frustration. "I only want to ask her some questions. How could that foul things up?"

Sam sighed. "You got a lawyer? If you had legal representation, I might be able to let you do a short interview."

"I got a lawyer. Give me the phone."

MAGGIE LISTENED to Tad's scared young voice on the telephone. "I don't know what's goin' on," he told her. "Only that me Da called your Da and he needed a lawyer. He's down to the jail."

"Okay, Tad." She tried to put reassurance in her own voice. "You just sit tight. Joey's at the house with you, right? I'll go see what's happening, and I'll let you know as soon as I do." She heard the boy swallow, then agree.

"Nell, Davey," she said, hanging up the receiver. "Can you manage here for a while? I think Mick's in trouble." Eyes wide, both of them nodded assent. Heart pounding, Maggie left the shop and hurried up the street. She was almost to the door of the police station when a hand grabbed her shoulder and a masculine voice called her name imperatively.

"SO YOU CLAIM you've never seen this man or anyone looking like him?" Patrick asked, his tone gently persuasive as he spread the drawing of Maggie's memory out in front of the woman once more.

Darlene sneered slightly and shook her head. "I wouldn't remember, anyhow," she said, her eyes not really studying the drawing. "He looks like a jerk. The men I hang around have more class." She rattled on, yakking about the important people she knew in California and about the sharp lawyer who was going to get her off, scot-free.

Mick, his temper now coldly under control, sat behind Patrick, saying nothing and doing nothing but listening. She was lying. It didn't take much instinct about people to realize that.

It gave him something akin to joy. A joy that settled into his bones like the kind of chill he had felt when he had first come to this mountain land.

With the proper stimulus, he reasoned, she might be counted on to lead him right to his quarry—to help locate, expose and betray the man he sought. In his mind, he began working a trap as complex and clever as any he had used to trap the wary animals of the Outback when he had needed food to survive.

"Miss Turner," Patrick was saying. "You know that if you cooperate, things will go much better for you. That if you—"

"Stop wasting your time," Mick said softly. "It's plain she'd rather rot than make any sort of deal to her own advantage. Come on, Patrick. Let's get out of here. The atmosphere is smelly, and I'd like to report to my superiors as soon as I can." He had thickened his accent, but given it definite upper-class tones. Darlene Turner, who hadn't heard him speak before this, looked up at him in surprise and not a little shock. The Australian accent *did* have an effect on her. Interesting.

Patrick looked surprised, too, but covered it quickly when Mick dropped one eyelid in the ghost of a wink. "Whatever you say, Colonel, uh, *Mr.* O'Shay." He stood. "Miss Turner, if you decide to talk, please have Chief Glover contact the Col . . . contact me or Mr. O'Shay here. I certainly can't make you any kind of guarantee, but I know if you chose to give the authorities information, *any* information about other crimes, particularly concerning gemstones, it couldn't hurt your case."

Darlene hadn't taken her gaze off Mick since he'd spoken. She lit a cigarette, her fingers shaking slightly. "You an Aussie?" she asked.

Mick nodded.

"Cop?"

He shook his head negatively. She didn't look as if she believed him. "I know something about opals," she said, drawing deeply on the cigarette. "Something you might—"

Mick never learned what it was. At that moment, Maggie burst into the interrogation room, closely followed by a bellowing Sam Glover. "Mick, Mick," she cried, throwing her arms around his neck. "Whatever you've done, we'll stand by you. I don't care if you've killed someone! Dad will—" She stopped cold, having just seen Darlene.

"So that's the way it is," the pretty thief said tightly, stubbing her smoke out directly on the tabletop. "Nice try, *mate*," she added. "But you ain't getting one more word out of me. I want my lawyer with me before I make another move. That's my right."

Mick reeled with anger and frustration. He had been so close! Barely restraining himself, he grabbed Maggie's wrists and pushed her away. At that moment, he felt he had no love for her at all. "Ask Patrick what was happening," he said between clenched teeth. "Ask him!" Then, his expression cold and bitter, he left her.

Maggie turned to her father. "Dad, what...?" She was too shocked by Mick's behavior to cry, but she could feel the tears in her eyes and throat. Her father raised an admonishing hand, his expression not much friendlier than Mick's had been. They waited while Sam led the angry prisoner back to her cell. Then Patrick told her what she had done.

Maggie was too crushed and too angry at herself to cry after that. The tears became acid that burned her heart and soul. She had ruined Mick's chance for a lead to Ian's killer. She had done it with the best of intentions, but she had done it anyway. No wonder he had regarded her with such venom. She hated herself. Undoubtedly, he felt the same. "I didn't know what to think," she told her father. "This man, a reporter, stopped me on the street and asked me some terrible questions about Mick. Who he was and who he was looking to... to kill or something. Dad, the man seemed to think Mick was some kind of thug! What was I to think?"

"Oh, honey." Patrick's expression softened and he took her in his arms. "It wasn't anyone's fault. Just a series of misunderstandings. Go to Mick. Find him and explain. If he really loves you, he'll understand and forgive you."

Maggie shuddered, remembering the icy light in his eyes. "I don't know. It's beginning to seem that he pretends to himself he loves me, but when the chips are down, his need for revenge is still strongest. Can love ever really compete with hate?"

Patrick felt her hurt as if it was his own. "Yes, it can, Maggie. But you're going to have to fight if you really want to win. And I can't tell you how to do it this time. You are on your own, daughter. I can only pray."

She murmured her thanks, but wondered secretly if it would be enough—if all the prayers in the world would be enough to break through Mick O'Shay's iron wall of hate.

IT WAS NOW Mick's turn to take a hike. He stormed out of the station and shouldered his way through the thinning crowd, too angry and upset to think. His emotions tore at him more keenly than a sandstorm in the desert and it wasn't until he had blundered through the streets and reached the foot of the ski slope that he slowed down and tried collecting himself. He paused, leaning against one of the huge steel uprights of the chair lift, and breathed like a spent horse while he thought.

She had blundered in with both feet flying and had ruined the situation. It had almost seemed deliberate—as if she actually couldn't stand the possibility that he might succeed. If she really did love him, he could understand her not wanting him to go to prison, but to stop him from a line of inquiry that might let the police take over again? Was that love? Laughter from skiers hurtling down the last section of the slope mocked him. Mick hit the upright with his fist.

How was he to know if she loved him? Did he really know what love was? How far did it go beyond sex, beyond the kind of pull she had on his heart and body? He had asked her to marry him, had leaped on the idea like a wombat at a waterhole. But was that what he wanted? To be yoked once more to someone who didn't understand him? Didn't agree with his aims, his beliefs? Ah, bloody hell! He hit the upright again, bruising his hand this time. He swore, quietly and viciously, aiming his cursing more at himself than anyone or anything else. He was too damn thick to know his own mind, much less anyone else's. He had to love her. There was no other explanation for her getting under his skin the way she had. No other explanation for him chucking a willy like this.

Was there? He considered taking another swipe at the upright.

"Hit that pole again, O'Shay," a cheerful voice called out, "and you're liable to bring the whole lift down." Charlie skied to a sliding stop inches from Mick's boots. "Give it a break, man," he said. "Maggie got you crazy again?"

Mick almost smiled. "Yeah. And not just her. I'm doing a fair share on my own. Times like this I think I ought to just go back and crawl underground. I knew what I was doing there."

Charlie pulled off a mitten and scratched his head under his ski hat. "I'm not one to give advice, but that sounds a lot like a man who wants to bury his head in the sand. Only thing ever comes of that is you get real damn vulnerable in some important places, know what I mean?"

Mick did smile this time. Then he frowned. "I got to get my thinking straight, Charlie. I just can't see clear to what's right and what's wrong these days."

Charlie grinned. "Come with me. I think I've got the cure for you." He stepped back and skied down to the lodge in a graceful, flowing motion. Intrigued, Mick followed, his footsteps clumsy in the smooth wake of the skier's tracks.

MAGGIE LAY in her bedroom, listening to the sounds of people partying. Swearing her father to secrecy over her terrible blunder, she had covered her own wretchedness with smiles and congratulations to Davey and had stayed downstairs only as long as absolutely necessary. When she finally pleaded a headache, the others seemed to accept her excuse without a thought. Nell offered to bring up some herbal tea, but Maggie said all she needed to do was close her eyes for a few minutes.

A few years was more like it.

The more she thought about it, the harder it was for her to believe she had actually gone raging into the police station in her anxiety about Mick. What had she thought she was going to do for him if he had been arrested? Had she even been thinking at all?

It was doubtful. Thinking was hardly something she'd proved adept at lately. Her mental processes had been in turmoil since the moment Mick O'Shay had set foot in her shop.

Maggie rolled over and pounded her pillow, tears squeezing out of her eyes. She did love him, damn it. There was no other explanation for this pain. The affair with Jerry had upset and humiliated her, but it had never hurt; had never made her feel her heart would break if she never saw him again.

If she never saw Mick again, she had no doubts that it would. She was too old and too smart to have gotten into a situation like this, but here she was and she had no idea how to deal with it. No idea at all.

DOWNSTAIRS, Patrick forced himself to enjoy the gathering. A few months ago, even a few weeks ago, it might have been impossible to come out of himself and delight in the company of friends. He was not about to lose that because Maggie had made a mistake. She would recover, as he had, and they would go on with life just as they had before.

Well. He smiled across the room at Nell. Maybe not just as they had. His feelings for Nell Abrams had ventured beyond mere friendship, and he hoped that, in time, what they were cultivating would turn into love. Maggie would get over O'Shay. She'd gotten over that bastard in San Francisco easily enough. His girl was tough, and once she made up her mind to be rid of the Australian that would be it. Patrick smiled again and Nell came over, a look of quiet concern on her face. Although he wasn't sure he wanted to hear what she would say, he took a moment to admire the lovely line of her aristocratic features and ponder the wonders of the heart that gave her such a caring nature.

As she sat beside him, he took her hand. "What is it, my dear?" he asked, using the term of affection that had first come so hard and now fell easily off his lips. "You don't look happy. This is a happy occasion."

Nell glanced around the place. Nearly a dozen people their own age chatted comfortably in the living room.

Davey, Tad and a bunch of boys were in the den, sharing lies over the din of MTV. Joey Steele and a group of young people Maggie's age were dancing and flirting in the kitchen and dining area. Everything looked just dandy. But . . .

"Where is Mick, Patrick? And why did your daughter take herself off to bed so early? Surely she can't sleep away a headache with all this commotion. Have they had a falling out?"

He didn't meet her direct gaze. "You might say. Nell, there's a lot more to Mick's story than just that of a charming character who managed to dig a fortune out of the ground—a lot more to divide him and Maggie than just their backgrounds."

"Of course, there is." She patted his hand. "That's what makes their relationship so interesting and romantic. Mick has more than a little air of danger about him. I expect Davey knows the reason. He gets a wary look in his eyes when I get a bit too nosy about what Tad's told him. And they have spent a lot of time together talking, as you well know."

"Yes." Patrick let more guilt settle on his back. He had told Nell only about his concerns that Maggie would be hurt again, not the specifics. Her intuition had served her admirably, as had her tact in not letting her curiosity force the issue. He was so used to keeping confidences, especially about matters of the law, that he had been unable to share Mick's dark purpose. Now, he knew he had to take the chance. "Come with me," he said, standing, still holding her hand. "We need to talk about this, and I know of only one place in this house where we can count on being alone tonight." She surprised him by giving him a flirtatious look and raising one blond eyebrow. "No, it's not my bedroom," he added, somewhat embarrassed. Nell only laughed softly and squeezed his hand.

He took her to a place he rarely went, but was one reason that he had bought the house. The doorway was almost hidden by the kitchen pantry, and the stairway was lit only by a dim electric light. But the basement office room was warm and when he went over to his dusty desk and turned on the light, it was bright enough. Nell looked around, understanding in her blue eyes. "Everything's here waiting for you, isn't it?" she asked.

Patrick nodded. "I thought someday I'd try my hand at writing. Fiction, probably. Or at the very most, faction. I'd get my socks sued off if I tried relating reality as I experienced it in three decades of practice." He made a gesture with his hand. "All this has just been sitting here, though."

"Until now?"

"Nell, Mick is after a man he believes caused the death of his partner, Ian Richards."

Her expression grew sad. "I was afraid of something like that. Tad always got funny when he talked about him, and Davey definitely looked strange. I suppose he knew."

"Tad talked to me, but I expect he was too shy to tell a woman. His experience with older people seems to have been limited to his father and Ian."

"When you say Mick is after that man, do you mean what I think, Patrick?" Her hand touched his arm.

"I'm afraid so. He's not a man used to relying on others to carry out his purposes. For a while, it seemed he had gained some sense. After the burglary, he asked to see material on constitutional rights. But then a reporter told him the woman who did it was involved with a ring of thieves. That set him right off. He called me to do the actual interview, but he had almost tricked her into revealing some names. When Maggie burst in, thinking he'd been arrested, it tipped his hand and the woman shut up like a trapdoor. And Mick—"

"Was furious. Oh, my. Poor Maggie. She only meant to help him, didn't she?"

"I don't think O'Shay saw it that way."

"Patrick, isn't there something that can be done to salvage this situation? If that person does know something, can't she be persuaded to talk? Don't you call that making a deal?"

He smiled sadly and kissed her fingers. "Dearest Nell, it's out of my hands. I'm not even licensed to practice any more. Sam let me act as Mick's lawyer for a few minutes, but if we tried to push it we could both end up in jail. No, I'm afraid it's a mess I can't help with."

"But you did practice in California. And you do have a nephew and relatives there who still do. Can't they do something?" A fighting light was now in her eyes.

"Well." He thought. "Jeff is a criminal trial lawyer. I do have a few old favors I could pull in. There is that sketch of the man who sold Maggie the opal that Joey did." He rubbed his chin. "You know, we might just be able to put something together. It's all a long shot, but you never know about a thing like this until you try."

"That's the spirit!" Nell raised a clenched fist. She was smiling broadly. "That's my guy!"

Patrick looked at her. They both stopped smiling at the same time—with their lips, that is. Their eyes smiled still, and when they kissed he knew his heart had finally come full circle.

AROUND TEN, Maggie decided she had spent enough time in self-pity and mourning. Fixing her face, taking extra care with makeup and jewelry, and changing to a festive sweater and slacks, she forced herself to smile and go downstairs. She was greeted enthusiastically by the guests, but her smile started to hurt when she realized Mick had never shown up.

Only Joey, of the adults, seemed to sense something was very wrong. He started to ask questions, but she shushed him up quickly. Her pride wasn't ready for a public beating. "Where's my dad?" she asked the artist. "And Nell?"

Joey shrugged. "I thought I saw them go off into the kitchen a little bit ago. For that matter, where's Charlie? I know he was invited."

"I saw him." One of the female ski instructors offered the information from the arms of her dancing partner. "He and that fellow of yours were out at the lodge." She watched Maggie carefully. "They were with a bunch of tourists, and it looked like everyone was having a good time." Her tone indicated the tourists were not male.

Maggie clenched her teeth and smiled. So much for love and faithfulness. So much for Mr. O'Shay's proposal of marriage. *So much for him and his damn opals.* She was working on a suitably casual reply when the front door flew open.

Mick and Charlie entered with a blast of arctic air. Maggie's heart jumped into her throat and the blood seemed to fill every vein in her body to bursting. He wasn't handsome—he was gorgeous. His normally tanned complexion was ruddy from the cold and his eyes shone with excitement. He saw her immediately, and all fears that he had lost his feeling for her fled when she saw the expression on his face.

Mick hadn't known how he would approach her. Now, seeing her looking more beautiful than he remembered, he was paralyzed. Her hair was pulled back from her face and caught behind in a cluster of ringlets that framed her features. Her eyes were big and luminous, her lips moist and tempting. The sweater and pants she wore left little to the imagination regarding her delectable figure. His muscles regained the power of movement and he hurried to her, putting his arms around her and looking directly into her startled eyes.

"We have to talk, love," he said. "Now, and in private. It's a matter of life and death."

CHAPTER THIRTEEN

"WHAT DO YOU MEAN, life or death?" Maggie's mouth was so dry she could barely manage to get the words out. His urgent "now and in private" had caused her to take his hand, lead him immediately upstairs to her bedroom and shut the door, all thoughts of the problems between them aside. The words "life and death" had filled her with fear and caused her muscles to tremble violently. He didn't answer, but put his arms around her again, this time pulling her into a tight embrace.

"Mick, are you in trouble?" she asked, breathlessly. Her trembling eased slightly, her body warmed by his. "What's wrong?"

He chuckled softly. "Always it's what trouble I'm in or what might be wrong, love. Can't you anticipate anything right?"

She tried pulling away. "Not when you burst in, looking as though you've trekked across Antarctica and claiming a frantic need to talk to me alone. Mick, where have you been?"

"Skiing."

"Skiing." She lowered her arms to his chest and pushed. He didn't let her go. "Damn you, I've been in a living hell, while you—"

"I know and I'm sorry, Maggie." He looked serious and sincere, and none of the angry, manic light was in his eyes. He looked in control of himself.

He wasn't. Mick's muscles were jumping like kangaroos under his skin. He didn't want to talk—he wanted to tear off her clothes and wrap himself around her and bury himself in her. He wanted to kiss that look of hurt and reproach from her face. He wanted—

What he wanted would have to wait. "Listen to me, Mag. I was wrong to get so mad at you. You were impulsive, but you were only worried about me. I just ain't...am not used to a woman caring so much about me. I don't always react right."

She squirmed, but not desperately. "You can say that again, buster!"

"I don't always react correctly."

His grin warmed her heart, although she was determined to stay angry. His lopsided smile, that chipped tooth, the fight-damaged nose: oh, God, the man was dear to her! She abandoned any further resistance and molded herself to him, her lips parting for a kiss.

Mick reacted correctly. His mouth covered hers and carried her into that world where there were no thieves and murderers, no avenging warriors, no doubts, no fears. Where all things were right and good and fair.

Her response, coming on top of all the emotions and confusions of the day, triggered the elemental male in him. Mick fought a wave of desire so blinding, he lost control. She made a low, eager sound in her throat and started pulling his coat from his shoulders, and the need for sex with her almost overwhelmed his other need.

Almost, but not quite. With a tremendous shudder, he gently took her wrists in his hands and held her away from him. The pressure of passion kept him shaking, but he made himself speak calmly.

"Maggie, I need your help. This time I'm not going off half-cocked, and you're in on it. Mag, I think I've found a way to try flushing the bad guy."

"By skiing?" Her eyes were wide and dilated, and her breathing ragged.

He continued to hold her wrists trapped with one hand, and with the other he smoothed back the hair that had fallen loosely around her face. "I went up skiing with Charlie for a while, until it was just too dark to see where I was about to fall, love. I ain't ... I'm not much good yet, but the exercise and concentration helped clear my mind. When I was done, I could see things. Things that finally made sense to me."

Maggie waited. Something in his eyes told her this was indeed vitally important, if not exactly a matter of life and death. She relaxed, he let go of her and she went over to sit on the bed. He remained standing, his coat still on.

"No matter how much I love you," he said, "or you love me, my obsession with Ian's death is going to hang between us like a kind of ghost. Right?"

She nodded.

"We keep hurting each other over it." Now he did take off the coat and toss it down on the bed beside her. He was wearing his gun again, she noted with rising alarm. "Look at you," he said. "I've got the piece on again, and your blood pressure goes up. Think, Maggie. Would Sam have given it back to me if he was worried about me?"

"No." She swallowed. "Of course not."

"All right." He nodded and began to pace the room slowly. "After Charlie finished helping me learn to bash myself out on the snow, we went into the lodge to take back the equipment I'd borrowed and have some coffee before coming here, and we met—"

"I heard about who you met."

"Give me a fair go, will you?" He raked his hand through his hair. "The sheilas're telly people. Not like the mug who tried taking my picture this afternoon, but real newspeople. They want to do a spot on us for one of those hour shows. Not a big spot, but it might get the attention of the right people.''

''Do you really think the man you want will watch a news program? He might not even be in the country, Mick.''

''He is.'' That cold light was in his eyes again. He didn' need to add that he just knew it. ''But that isn't the only reason for doing the spot. You—''

''Mick, don't do that.'' She rose. ''Don't make me an excuse for your—''

''Damn it, woman, I'm not!'' He grabbed her upper arms, his face less than an inch from hers. ''What do I have to do to make you believe how much I love you, how much I care about your art? Die?'' He stared at her for a moment before slamming his mouth over hers again. This time, there was no gentleness; only passion. No skill, only desire.

Maggie could only hang on for the wild ride. She knew he was going to stop with the kiss and go no further, but that didn't stop her senses from reeling as if she and Mick *had* been making love. When he finally let her go, abruptly so that she fell against the bed, she gasped out, ''No, you don't have to die. I don't know what you have to do, Mick O'Shay. But it's not that!''

He held out his hands. His chest was heaving as he tried to overcome his obvious passion. ''Will you take me on faith, then? It's all I have to offer.''

''I . . . I suppose it's all I have to offer, too.'' She tried a smile, wincing when her bruised lips reminded her of what had just happened. ''We're quite a pair, aren't we?''

''Too right.'' He reached for her and pulled her to her feet, but made no attempt to drag her close again. ''Too right by far. Now, let's try thinking, and let me tell you what I have in mind. Then let's go down and clear things with your dad and my kid.''

They were downstairs in five minutes, and learning Patrick was still unavailable, they explained to Tad where they would be for a while. He looked relieved to see his father, but didn't take much time away from his friends to satisfy any questions he had about the events of the last few hours. Maggie and Mick left the house and went to the shop, where the television crew were already setting up under Sam's watchful eye.

What Mick had in mind was a perfectly sensible and promising idea. The television women had wanted to do a short spot for a Sunday news program on local craftspeople, but Mick had persuaded them that the story of his and Maggie's artistic symbiosis would make a far more interesting and unique documentary. Everybody and his brother, he had said, was doing the local crafts bit.

The ladies were enthusiastically convinced, Maggie deduced with amusement, not only by the logic, but also by Mick's outrageous charm. He played the humble miner to the hilt, acting, as he said, like the typical Aussie ocker, a man of little culture and less breeding. Then he would switch natures and become an informative and charismatic personality. All Maggie had to do, which suited her just fine, was stand by, show a few stones and explain how the jewelry was made. He let her show only the less spectacular pieces, however.

"The best of Ms Wellington's work will be submitted to the San Francisco Exposition," he explained. "We just can't show any of that, finished or in progress. But if there are any true lovers of the finest opals and jewelry, they should plan on being in San Francisco in April to see the public display after the judging."

Thus, thought Maggie, the bait is laid. She then sat quietly while Mick talked about his life in Coober Pedy.

"The name's aboriginal for 'white man in a hole,'" he said. "We mine underground and many of us live underground. But each man can only claim 165 feet square. You can have up to three partners and join four claims, no more than that. It's a democracy. An opal miner's a bit like a bee," he explained for the fascinated reporters and camera crew. "A honey bee, that is," he added, his brawny arm draped over Maggie's shoulders. "He don't exactly know where the best vein is, he just senses it. Truth is, dumb luck plays a major part in success."

"What about trained geologists?" one of the reporters, a pleasant-looking woman with short brown hair asked. "Haven't such people done better than those who just...look?"

"Naw." Mick picked up a large crystal opal and displayed it. "Take this, f'r instance. The vein this beauty came from I found by just dropping me hat over my shoulder. Luck, miss. Luck is the secret. Now, I had a partner who... But that's another story." He dropped his smile and pulled Maggie closer. She stiffened, then relaxed, resigned. This was Mick's show, and after the fiasco she had made of the afternoon, she owed it to him to carry on as he wished.

Of course, that was all that was needed. By the time the interview was through, a thoroughly enticing version of Mick's association with Ian Richards had gone on tape. The reporters didn't make any promises about what parts would be aired, but they encouraged viewing of the program the Sunday after Christmas, which was when it was scheduled. Mick promised solemnly that he would watch it. Maggie was sure wild horses couldn't keep him away from the set.

When everyone had packed up and gone, however, Mick turned to her, and it was clear what was on his mind. "Let's go home," he said thickly, "see where the mob has crashed, then find out where we can be alone. Even if we have to check in a motel. I've got to be with you tonight." The hunger in his face caught at her heart and heated her body until she felt moisture break out on her skin.

But . . .

"Mick, we can't. We can't keep thinking only of ourselves. We both have family—"

"Of course we do, love." He touched her cheek. "And they have us. Do you know, before you came roaring into the jail and stirred up such a fuss over me, I had been thinking you were an angel on earth?"

"Oh?" She frowned, having no idea where he was going with this and concerned about the negative implications. His hand, however, stayed warmly on her cheek and his smile was so loving!

"That's right. But you aren't an angel. Just a human being trying to look after yourself and everyone close to you. You can't be an angel, love. Why don't you quit trying?"

"I have no idea what you're talking about. If you're after sex, this is hardly the way to get it!"

Mick measured the anger and hurt in her eyes and decided he had to pursue it. "Somewhere in your life, you got the idea you were put here to help people, weren't you? Well and good, Maggie. But it's got to balance, doesn't it? Now me, I'm a taker. I've taken from almost everyone I've ever known or cared about. My profession is taking from the earth itself. I need to learn from you, but I think you need to learn from me. At times, you act like a little kid who always has to please in order to be loved." He had gone too far. The anger flared into rage, and he barely caught her hard little hand in time as she swung it at him.

"You conniving, tricky *bastard*," she cried. "How dare you sit in judgment on me! You, who are ready to murder to fulfill some macho notion of justice. You...you can just go to hell!" She tore loose from his grip, grabbed her jacket and stormed out of the shop, slamming the door firmly behind her.

He stared at the door for a moment, then nodded. In a few minutes, he had straightened up the shop and placed the valuables in the safe. Turning on the alarm, he left and loped up the sidewalk until he saw her figure silhouetted against the snow by the streetlights. He caught up with her about a block from his house. "Does the truth always make you run away?" he asked, his breath white in the cold night air.

"I'm not running. I'm going home. You'd better not try to stop me!"

"I won't. I'm going home, too. But if you should decide you want to see me about anything, talk about anything, feel free to come on over."

His tone held no mocking edge, but she felt the level of her fury at him rise. "I wouldn't hold my breath if I were you. You're liable to suffocate before I ever talk to you about anything again."

"Aw. Does this mean our opal deal is off? Let's see, this must be about the fifth time you've—"

Maggie stopped dead. She turned and faced him and started swearing at him with every terrible word she had in her vocabulary. He listened, attentively, then began responding in kind, but with phrases and words she'd never heard before. Soon the air around them was blue with curses, frosted from their breath and electric with undischarged sexual tension and energy.

"And furthermore," she snarled, "I wouldn't dream of calling off our deal, you snake. You think I'm always Miss Goodie Two-Shoes? Well, put this in your pipe, or anywhere else you see fit: I'm using you just like you've been using me! Why do you think I've put up with your arrogance and ignorance and macho sexuality? Only so I could

use your opals to make my mark! What do you think about
that?''

"That you're real damn quick to think up lies. You
wouldn't know how to use a toothbrush if your Ma hadn't
taught you. And I'm not ignorant, only uneducated. As for
my sexuality, you haven't had any objections so far. In fact,
you seem to enjoy it rough. Quite a contrast to that lady-
like air you put on when you want to impress people."

"I don't put on airs! What about that good-old-boy act
you put on for the television? Oh, they were all so impressed. If only they really knew what you *used* them for!"

"I didn't use them to help me murder anyone," he responded quietly. "On the contrary, since I figured out how
much I love you, I haven't done anything but plan ways to
fulfill my obligation to Ian's memory without endangering
myself or those I love. You know that's true, Maggie. You
know it." He paused. "You know I love you."

Her near hatred and rage blew away like a feather on the
wind. "I know." Her voice cracked with emotion. "I love
you too. Why is it that at times I just can't stand you?"

"By God, Maggie." His hand cupped the back of her
head, and not gently. He pulled and her face was lifted to
him. "I'm beginning to think the two of us were brought
together solely to torment one another. That is, when we
aren't doin' things far more pleasant." The following kiss
seared her to her soul.

A few minutes later, they were in his bed, naked and
screaming like wildcats in their passion. On the way to that
state, Mick had retained barely enough sense to check and
see that Tad's bed was empty and to assume that he was still
over at Patrick's or with Davey. Unselfish fatherhood went
only so far, and he was determined that tonight he would
make Maggie realize once and for all that she was more
than his mate, friend and lover. She was his soul, as he was
a part of hers. He didn't know what it meant, but he knew

it was true. And tonight—now—he meant to show her. Whatever it took. With a cry torn from the deepest part of him, Mick surrendered himself to the woman he loved.

Maggie felt the change in him. One moment he was a stallion, on top and plunging into her for all he was worth. The next, he was worshiping her with his hands and lips, his maleness filling her more completely than ever, but his body still except for the trembling of his muscles as he forced that stillness on himself. Her mind swam and refused to accept the reality of what was happening, but her heart and body knew immediately.

She opened her eyes and gazed into his. "I love you," she whispered. "I never have and I never will love anyone as I love you." The light that entered his eyes at those words was warmer and brighter than summer sun seen through the finest, clearest of emeralds. Then his eyes closed, and beneath the fringe of thick lashes, she saw traces of moisture. She touched his shoulder and gently pushed him over until he lay on his back and she was astride. Then Maggie began to make love to her lover.

He groaned, the role of receiving pleasure rather than taking it bringing such wonderful sensations, he thought his body had taken on a whole new set of nerve endings designed only to drive him up one wave of delight after another. She rose above him, a goddess, giving him the gifts of love and life. He shuddered and shook, struggling to control his need for release and yearning to explode into her and to escape the terrifyingly delicious torment. His fingers dug into the sheets and then her hips. And then his hand covered her lower stomach, his thumb questing into the glistening black hair that was entangled with his reddish patch. The bed became an acre of paradise.

Maggie threw her head back and pressed down with all her might, pulling him as deep into her as possible. There was no need for movement now. She slid her legs wide and locked her calves around his thighs. Her arms went behind his shoulders, her fingers digging into the muscles. Her head dropped forward, her eyes stared into his, and her hair made a silky, thick veil grazing both their cheeks. His breath was hot on her face, and their sweat blended as hers beaded and fell on his skin. Then the wild sensations began, starting in the muscles at the small of her back and spiraling down until all of her pelvis region was afire. The fire blazed there and spread until it was consuming all of her in its immediate and timeless joy.

Mick felt it when she started to go. Felt it with every cell of his body. Like a swimmer releasing his body to rapids he thinks may kill him, he, too, let himself go and allowed the power of his passion to flood unchecked. He hooked one arm around her neck, and with the other, imprisoned her hips. He made himself one with her until he was screaming hoarsely with the devastating energies surging through him.

They rose higher and higher, reaching a peak of physical ecstasy that took them far beyond sex. Their bodies racked and shuddering with spasms of unbelievable pleasure, they thrashed and cried out, calling each other's name in voices reduced finally to whispers—whispers that gradually trailed off into the gentle, even breathing of sleep. Even then, they remained joined for a time, their slumbering flesh determined not to give up that oneness. Hours passed, and they warmed and comforted one another while in deep sleep.

At one point, Mick awoke just enough to reach over to turn off the light and pull the tangled blankets over them. Maggie, her head on his shoulder and her face pressed into his neck, didn't stir. She was still holding him, and it occurred to him that if he died tonight, he would go to his reward the happiest, most exhausted man who ever lived. He remembered nothing more until morning.

PATRICK REACHED OUT and squeezed Nell's hand briefly after she had set breakfast on the table in front of him. He still found it hard to believe that the previous night had actually happened. "Would you have come with me if we hadn't found the boys asleep on the den hide-a-bed last night?" he asked, watching her expression closely, needing the truth.

"I don't know." She sat down, picked up a fork and poked at her own food. She wore one of Maggie's high-necked quilted bathrobes and, Patrick knew, little else. Straightening his back, he pulled in his stomach and forbade himself jam on his toast. "What happened," Nell went on, "was so right, so magical, I can't even imagine everything not being perfect for us." Her smile dispelled his anxieties.

"What did Maggie have to say when you went in, wrapped in my blanket to ask for a robe?" he asked, wondering what his only child was going to think when he told her she was going to be getting a new mother, and a brother in the bargain.

"Um..." Nell took a bite of scrambled eggs. "She didn't have much to say, Patrick."

"Still asleep, eh. Well, that business with O'Shay did knock her for a loop. I'm not—"

"Maggie wasn't in her room, darling. And her bed was mussed, but not slept in."

"Not...not in? Where the hell...?" His knife clanked against the side of the plate and then fell onto the table.

"Calm down." Her voice was kind, but firm. "Didn't it occur to you to wonder why Mick hadn't come by to pick up Tad? Or why the boy wasn't up at dawn to pester you about his father?"

"You think...?"

She ate and swallowed some more food. "Of course. You and I don't have a premium on stolen nights in each other's arms. Maggie is with Mick. In his bed, I imagine."

"But, damn! She's—"

"She's a grown woman, and knows exactly what she wants. Now, finish your eggs before they get cold, but keep room for the pancakes. I need to shower and dress so I can wake the boys before I make them."

Patrick's anger and anxiety subsided slightly under her loving bullying. But he reserved judgment on whether Maggie actually did know what she wanted.

MAGGIE WOKE SLOWLY and deliciously, thinking that she was an idiot for being so happy. Her head lay on Mick's chest, and she could hear the steady beat of his heart. The air in the bedroom was cold, but she was warm, warm, warm. A contented sigh escaped her lips. Mick's chest rumbled as he chuckled.

"Mornin'," he said, stroking her hair with his hand. "Sleep tight?"

"You know it." She moved and moaned. "Ow! I didn't know I had muscles there."

"You've got muscles in the sweetest places, love. I'm personally grateful to every one of them."

"Mick," She sat up, brushing hair out of her eyes. "What are we going to do about us? We fight like cats and dogs, then jump right into the sack and have a spectacular time. Are we really in love?"

"Yeah," he said, gazing steadily at her. "We're definitely in love. Our problem, y'know, is that we don't like each other. We gotta work on that."

"I don't understand how I can love you and not like you. I just don't understand! I've never even heard of a situation like ours before."

His smile was gentle. "That, dearest, is because you're too civilized by a fair shot. It ain't really a question of understanding, but of living and letting things work out."

"How can things work out if we don't—"

His grin widened. "Shut up, Maggie," he said, grasping the back of her head, tangling his fingers in her hair. "This is how things'll work out."

After a few minutes, she had to agree he was probably right.

They loved until sunlight beat strongly on the bedsheets. Then she insisted they get up and make themselves presentable to their various family members and friends. He muttered some more—good-naturedly, though—about her "civilized" behavior, but cooperated. Soon they were dressed and were heading down the street to her house. The day was lovely: relatively warm and clear. A steady wind sounded in the tops of the trees, but was only a gentle breeze at ground level. Maggie felt her spirits rising high. She did love him. Walking by his side, with his arm across her shoulders, she felt so treasured and so safe.

Mick's muscles tensed as they walked up to her front door. It was easy enough to chide her about her need for parental approval. It was another thing to face the father after you'd spent the night with the daughter. He wasn't sure what to expect, but when he tried putting himself in Patrick's place, he realized it was probably best to be ready for anything.

To their mutual surprise, however, the house was empty. Breakfast smells filled the air, though the kitchen was spotless. "Dad never cleaned up like this," Maggie said, looking around. "I do believe I sense Nell's fine hand."

Mick came out of the den. "The boys slept on the sofa. Thing pulls right out into a fair-sized bed. But where did they all get to?"

"Look who's worried about family now," she teased. "Come on. I'll fix you breakfast. I *know* you're hungry. I sure am!"

"What a way to work up an appetite, eh?" He came over and embraced her, and breathed in the clean womanly scent of her hair. It stirred him, but his stomach made it clear he had to satisfy that particular appetite first and foremost. Maggie giggled at the rumbling and pushed him away.

"That's real romantic, Mick." She teased him over her shoulder with her eyes. "Now, what would you like to appease your tummy? Eggs, pancakes, waffles?"

"Let's start with some coffee." He didn't respond to her joking, but looked suddenly serious. "I feel as if my brain's full of cotton."

"Coffee, it is," she agreed and made a pot strong enough to satisfy the fuzziest of minds. Mick had sat down at the kitchen table and accepted the steaming mug from her without a word. His expression was blank, unreadable. Frowning, Maggie tossed some bacon in a pan and beat a few eggs. What was eating him, anyway?

Mick sat completely still. The coffee cooled in the mug, but he took no heed of it. Something was wrong. He strained his ears, listening for any sound that was slightly out of the ordinary. Outside, the wind had picked up a bit, though it had a gentle call to it compared to the howling he'd heard in sandstorms. Snow and cold could kill you, he mused. There wouldn't be the torture of suffocation by grit and heat, but you'd be just as dead....

"Maggie." He stood up so quickly his coffee spilled. He paid no attention. "You have a weather station? One that warns of dangerous conditions?"

"Sure." She gestured at the radio on the counter. "But what are you worried about today? The weather's perfect."

"Turn it on!"

"Mick, what is it?" She moved to obey even as she asked the question. Something in his eyes impelled her.

"They're in some kind of danger—Tad, Patrick. I don't know what it is yet." The radio came on and an announcer spoke in measured tones about what Maggie had already told him was a perfect day. Then...

"Chance of an avalanche in higher elevations. Skiers and snowmobilers are urged to take precautions—"

"Bloody hell!" Mick swore, running to the radio and taking the thing in his hands as if he could get a direct answer from it. "Where are they?" He looked at Maggie with anguish in his eyes. "Where's my boy?"

CHAPTER FOURTEEN

SHE COULDN'T CALM him down. The more she tried, the worse he got. Before he could become totally unreasonable, she agreed to call the highway patrol office and see if any avalanches had been reported, particularly between Sullivan Springs and Three Pines. None had been.

"Mick, you're overreacting," she said, hanging up the phone. He wasn't watching her, but was staring off into space and biting his thumbnail. "We don't even know they've gone out of town, much less where they might be if they did. Don't you think—"

He stood up and wiped his hands over his face. "You're right. I'm not thinking. But something's churning deep inside me. It goes beyond knowing." His expression turned wilder and more upset. "If he was lost in the bush, I'd know what to do; where to go. Here, I'm blind and deaf. I'm as lost as . . ." He swore. "He's *lost*. That's what it is! Tad can't see anything."

"Mick, you can't know that. You aren't psychic, are you?"

"Call it whatever you want." He grabbed her shoulders. "I have to get out there. Get a hold of Charlie."

She was getting scared now. "Not unless we know for sure there's a problem."

"Maggie, I know!"

She reached for the phone. "I'm calling Nell's house. If she, Dad and the boys are there, will you quit this craziness?"

"They aren't," he said darkly.

They weren't. She let the phone ring twenty times before giving up. Mick had his coat on and was out the door as soon as she put the receiver down. Maggie threw her coat over her shoulders and hurried after him, imploring him to use his head. It did no good.

They got Charlie out of bed. He had partied long and late at her house and hadn't gone to bed alone, although he was by himself now. Mick's alarm amused him at first, until he began to see how deadly serious the Australian was.

"You got second sight or premonitions, Mick?" he asked, trying to swallow a scalding cup of coffee handed to him by Maggie. "That what you're saying?"

"It ain't something I can bloody explain." Mick's hair was standing up on end where he had raked his hands through it repeatedly. "I only know I feel Tad's in danger. And the man on the radio was talking about avalanches."

"I can't get Search and Rescue out on something as flimsy as your hunches," Charlie said gently. "I'm sorry, Mick, but you'll just have to wait. Now, if you get something more concrete, you can count on me for anything."

"I can, eh?" His shoulders hunched.

Maggie shuddered. That dark, elemental part of him was ruling now. There was no telling what Mick would do if he truly thought his boy was threatened. And he did seem to feel that! She waited, fearing he'd draw his gun on Charlie; knowing that if he did, she was going to have to do something drastic to stop him. She wanted to speak, but could think of nothing to say in light of his current madness.

Then he threw one of his special Mick O'Shay curves.

Charlie had replied that sure, he could count on him. Mick relaxed. His body had been tight, strung out as hard as steel rope. Now every muscle and joint seemed to loosen. "You don't look too busy this morning," he said to Charlie. "How about we go for a little drive? You were wanting to show me how to cross-country ski, weren't you?"

Charlie nodded, clearly surprised at the turn the conversation had taken. "Sure, no problem. Maggie, you want to come, too? I can get us all in my Suburban with our equipment."

"I wouldn't miss it," she said, giving Mick a hard look. "Not for the world." He poured himself a cup of coffee and ignored her. Only the slight tremor of his hands showed he was keeping a tight check on his emotions.

He tolerated the time she took to throw a quick breakfast together—they never had gotten to the one she'd started to prepare at home—while he and Charlie loaded the Suburban. But he ate like a man with no appetite, his eyes had a far-off look and the expression on his face made him seem as if he were in another world.

Before they left, Maggie made one more attempt to reach the Abrams house. This time, Nell answered almost immediately. Maggie nearly fainted with relief. The relief lasted all of the five seconds it took for Nell to tell her Patrick and Tad had left a while ago. When Charlie finally pulled out of his driveway, Mick didn't say a word, but pointed his finger—in the direction of Three Pines.

When Charlie started to protest that better skiing lay in the other direction, Maggie almost snarled at him to follow Mick's lead. The spooky stuff was getting to her, she realized, and she couldn't help but react. Mick's anxieties seemed to be pouring out of him and into her. He closed his hand over hers and squeezed, although he didn't take his attention from the road. His touch only made her feel more scared, and she did not like that one little bit.

But she did know she was closer to him in that moment than she had been all the time she had spent with him in bed.

The wind picked up as they drove. No one said a word. She noted that the snow that blew against the windshield turned immediately to droplets of water, another sign the weather was warming.

And another sign that the high snows could be loosened.

As they neared Three Pines, Charlie cleared his throat nervously. "You know, we could have stopped almost anywhere along here and found a nice meadow to ski. But I guess you got me going along on this crazy hunt with you, don't you?" He glanced at Mick and Maggie where they sat beside him.

"Yeah," Mick said.

"And I ain't supposed to stop in Three Pines?"

"No," Mick said.

How he knew what he knew, Maggie fervently hoped she would never find out. But not a mile beyond the town, traffic was stopped. Mick was out of the Suburban before Charlie had braked into place behind the last vehicle in line. Mick still had a death grip on Maggie's hand and dragged her with him as he raced up to the head of the line where a highway car stood, its bar lights flashing like bizarre Christmas decorations. A patrolman, dressed in uniform and a lined leather coat, was speaking into a microphone.

Mick grabbed him by the shoulder. "What's going on?" he said, barking the question.

The patrolman turned, annoyed. "Get back in your car, buddy. We got some snow on the road is all."

"That ain't all!" Mick started past the patrol car. Maggie braced herself for a scene. The man was young and big, taller than Mick and ham-handed. She couldn't think of a thing to do except smile as winningly as possible.

It seemed to throw the patrolman off. He frowned at Mick. "You folks can't go out there," he said. "The snow's too loose."

Maggie's heart lurched painfully. "Is anyone...was anyone on the road when it hit?" She shaded her eyes and looked beyond at the ten-foot-high drift of snow that covered the narrow highway. There was no sign of the Bronco. No sign any vehicle had been swept down the side of the mountain, though it would be hard to tell, the snow was so deep.

"No, not that I can tell. But the lead car there said they thought they'd seen a blue four-wheeler drive out of Three Pines just before—"

Mick spun Maggie around. "Tell Charlie to bring the bloody skis!"

She glanced back. Charlie was already on his way, laden with skis, poles and boots. "Shut up, Mick!" she said. "This is an avalanche area. Don't make any more noise than you must."

The patrolman now took offense at the situation which had slipped beyond his control. "You people are gonna have to get back in your car," he said. "I've got a snowplow on the way up."

"And three people on the way down." Mick released Maggie and moved until he was eyeballing the younger man. "My kid's down there somewhere. And this lady's—" he pointed at Maggie "—Pa. No snowplow's gonna get them out."

"It's okay, Gene." Charlie arrived and dropped the skis. "This guy's a little crazy, but trust me when I tell you it'll be easier to let him do what he wants than to try stopping him."

"Well, I'm stopping him!" Maggie spoke firmly, cutting off any reply the patrolman was about to make. "Mick, if you're sure they're down there, you can't go. I can, and Charlie, if he's careful. But you have to stay here."

"The hell—"

"She's right, Mick." Charlie stepped forward, around the cop who was turning red trying to decide how to regain his authority when everyone was ignoring him. "She's light enough and I'm good enough to be relatively safe on the snow. You get out there with your weight and make a misstep, or worse, fall, you could bring more of the mountain down on us."

"Too bloody right," Mick said softly and moved back. Maggie never loved him more than she did at that moment.

It took a few more moments to convince Gene that letting them go was all right. Charlie's position as a leader in Search and Rescue tipped the balance. Gene was wisely nervous about Mick, but Maggie extracted a promise of good behavior plain enough to ease the cop's misgivings. Then, with the familiar ski equipment in place on her feet, she slipped off down the slope, searching for signs of a buried vehicle, fearing she'd find Patrick and Tad, and more afraid she would not. Charlie, a far better skier, telemarked behind her, probing the snow with a telescoping pole.

She had gone several hundred feet when she sensed Mick say, as clearly as if he were standing by her, "There, love. There." Maggie stopped.

Goose bumps that had nothing to do with the snow or the chilly air broke out on her skin. Looking up, she could see that this was exactly the spot where a car driven off the road by an avalanche might have ground to a halt. Charlie was a few yards above her. She held up her hand. He slowed and stopped.

Mick squatted down on his haunches, ignoring the questions the cop was asking him. Below, he could tell she had gotten his signal, amazing as that was. She and Charlie moved carefully over the snow until they were almost exactly where he wanted them. Charlie began to probe.

"Whatever you people use to dig cars out," Mick said quietly, "you'd better get it up here. My boy's down there, and he's still alive."

"You're plain crazy, mister," the patrolman said. "There's no way you could know any of that. And if there is a vehicle down there, I can't see how anyone could still be alive in it."

Mick stood. He looked at Gene. "You'd better hope there's someone alive in it," he said. "You'd better get some help out here. Now. And I'm going down there to dig my kid out by hand if I have to!" He started down the slope, sinking up to his hips in the soft, deep drifts and moving as carefully as if the whole side of the mountain was treacherous quicksand. Maggie looked up and saw him, and from her gaze he felt such strength and love flowing that he thought he might float down to her side.

Help did arrive, the car was exactly where Mick knew it would be and everyone except Maggie was awed by Mick's prodigious feat of strength—he pulled his son *and* her father from the wreck. She had long since decided that nothing Mick O'Shay could do would surprise her. She loved him; his ways and values were completely alien to her; but she loved him.

Patrick was badly bruised, but otherwise unhurt. Maggie felt tears flowing down her face when Mick handed him out to the paramedics. His complexion was almost as white as the snow, but his eyes flashed with the kind of fighting spirit she hadn't seen since her mother's illness had been diagnosed. He was, she realized, healed. Injured on the outside, but healed in the heart and soul.

Tad was another case entirely. The boy was just as conscious as Patrick, but he was suffering from a broken leg. Her heart seemed to climb into her throat as she watched him struggle to keep from crying out with pain as his father gently and tenderly prized him from the tangled metal.

She could see Mick speaking in a low, soothing tone the whole while and Tad nodding from time to time. The rapport between them in this crisis seemed to be total, and she found she yearned to know what it was like to be joined so to another human being—to be joined so to Mick. Finally, Tad was free and in the hands of the capable professionals. Mick turned from the wreck and came toward her, moving through the snow like an irresistible force. She didn't hesitate, but threw herself into his arms.

Both of them cried.

FOR THE NEXT few days, Maggie had little time to reflect on the events. She had no further contact with her lover except one terse phone call during which he only communicated that his son was all right. Tad was taken down to Denver, where his injury was treated, and Mick went along, demonstrating his loyalty as a father and his complete antipathy to any form of communication with Maggie other than the face-to-face kind. Patrick, confined to bed by doctor's orders for twenty-four hours and on enforced rest after that, was good-humored only when Nell arrived to visit. The rest of the time, his temper would have put a cornered rhino to shame. Maggie found her patience with the two adult males in her life sorely tried.

"I should have known better," Patrick said, for perhaps the thousandth time, as Maggie served him breakfast in bed the third day. "I wanted Tad to see some of the wild back country beyond the main roads. What a fool I was!"

"You weren't a fool, Dad." She straightened the napkin around his neck. "Just in the wrong place at the wrong time."

"He won't trust me anymore." The words were new, not the usual complaints she'd been hearing. And they were muttered, not shouted.

"Oh, Daddy." The extent of his guilt hit her. She sat down on his bed. "No one but yourself blames you. You have taken on a load you don't deserve."

"I deserve..." His expression was thunderous, but his words were interrupted by the ringing of the doorbell downstairs. Maggie murmured soothing words and got up to see who it was. Nell had taken to coming right on in, so she was certain it wasn't anyone who could help her relieve Patrick's mood.

She was wrong.

"G'day, Maggie." Tad, on crutches, followed by his dad, lumbered in. "Can I see Patrick?"

"Tad! Are you...?" She looked at Mick, who was smiling and managing to give her a sexy message with his eyes at the same time. "Is he...?"

"He's fine," Mick told her. "Too ornery for the doc to keep in bed one more minute. Wouldn't let me take him home. Had to see Patrick first. How's he doing?"

"Mean as a snake. He's blaming himself for the accident. As if he could have prevented—"

"That's garbage!" Tad hopped over to the stairs. "He couldn'ta known half the mountain was coming down on us." The boy's eyes flashed with an angry fire so familiar to Maggie it brought a lump to her throat. He maneuvered himself up two steps. "I'll tell him what for, that's what I'll do!"

"Just watch the language, son." Mick, still grinning, lounged back against the banister. He didn't watch Tad struggle up the stairs. He watched Maggie. When Tad finally made it to the top and his hearty greeting to Patrick rang out, Mick stopping smiling.

"I missed you," he said.

"A phone call might have helped." She folded her arms so he wouldn't see how she was suddenly trembling.

"Naw." His eyelids dropped to half-mast and he eased away from the banister. "Phones are for bad news or business. Once you knew Tad was all right, there was no need to keep you posted on every detail." With his fingers he reached out to touch her cheek and then caress her hair. "If I'd just been able to hear your voice, it'd-a driven me half crazy. No, I was waiting for this, love." His kiss reaffirmed everything that had happened between them, and more.

Maggie felt herself ignite with desire. She had missed him, too, and only now realized just how much. It was as if he was returning part of herself to her with his touch and caress. She made a low noise and pressed her body against him, longing for more. He responded by whispering her name in a rasping voice and embracing her tightly enough to take her breath away.

"It was thinking of you kept me sane when I didn't know how the lad was going to be," he confessed. "I'd imagine him crippled, losing the leg, and you'd be right there, telling me not to worry. That everything would be fine. You're in my mind as well as my heart, Maggie Wellington."

She was about to reply in kind, when a knock sounded at the front door. Turning, still in Mick's arms, she saw Sam Glover standing outside. He grinned, clearly enjoying her embarrassment, then his expression turned grim. "Gotta talk to you two," he called through the barrier of the glass outer door, which was closed. "It's important." Maggie extricated herself and let him in.

"It's about that Darlene Turner," Sam said when he had settled on the couch with a cup of coffee. "The one tried burglarizing you. Remember?"

"Not bloody likely either of us'd forget," Mick muttered.

"Well." Sam took a sip of coffee. "She's jumped bail."

"What?" Maggie almost dropped her own cup.

"Jumped bail?" Mick looked puzzled. Puzzled and worried.

"Escaped." Sam set his cup down on the coffee table. "She and her fancy lawyer managed to get some judge to set her bond low enough she musta figured it was worth the loss to split and—"

Mick swore. "So the law can't catch her and punish her for doing what she did to Maggie or anybody else?"

"Take it easy, Mick," she said. "This is upsetting, Sam, but why make such a point of telling us? I did get all my jewelry back. Why are you so worried?"

He hesitated. Then, "Seems she took a special dislike to you two. According to the police back in L.A., she was all the time talking about how she was going to get even—how she blamed all her troubles on you."

"That's insane!" Maggie forced her hand not to tremble. "She brought it all on herself."

"Sure, but—"

"She coming after us?" Mick's tone was quiet. Maggie glanced at him. His expression was feral.

"I don't think so." Sam was totally alert. "I don't think she's got what it takes. But she did brag to me about knowing people. Important, powerful people. I just thought you ought to know so you could kind of watch your backs."

"Consider it done," Mick growled. Maggie shivered at the sound, but deep inside, she felt so safe it canceled out the negative news. She slipped her hand into his and almost melted when his fingers closed over hers protectively.

IN SPITE OF the warning, however, the days through Christmas and New Year's went without incident, except for those caused by the interaction of six people whose lives were increasingly intertwined.

Patrick, absolved by Tad of any further guilt feelings, rose from his bed and returned to his pursuit of Nell and the organization of his professional memoirs with renewed vigor. Maggie was pleased, but only prayed he hadn't jumped to conclusions about Nell's feelings. If she did not return his affections, it could spell emotional disaster.

Nell was being careful, Maggie sensed. She visited regularly, particularly when the boys wanted to hang out together, but she never intruded on Maggie's role as woman of the house; never said or did anything that would make anyone think she was more than just a very good friend to Patrick. Maggie wasn't sure whether this was because her feelings didn't run deep, or whether it was plain good manners. Her father seemed happy, however, so she warned herself not to be concerned. After all, she had enough to do keeping her own love life straight.

The boys found a deeper camaraderie during the period of Tad's recovery. Though his injury was temporary, it formed a bond Maggie realized could have been forged no other way. When Tad was back on both feet, she knew, he would have a lifelong appreciation for the difficulties Davey would always face, and probably a thankfulness for his own good fortune. As well, his adventure in the avalanche made him an instant celebrity among the youths of both towns, aiding his integration into teenage society, which was vital if he was to be happy in America for the long term. She told herself that this development wasn't really so important, as the day would come—sooner or later—when the Aussie father and son would return to their homeland. But it pleased her, nonetheless.

Then, there was Mick.

Daily, they worked together on the opals. He seemed less driven to get all the work done as soon as possible now, and she was able to work on other projects from time to time, with him looking on. In contrast to his critical attitude at the beginning, he was now only full of praise. Now and then he made a suggestion, but it was usually on target and helpful. This was never more the case than with Drexel's Turquoise, as the large stone had become known to them.

"The cobber's crazy about his wife," Mick commented one evening as he examined the stone while Maggie worked on sketches of possible settings. "You just don't see stones like this every day."

"No kidding." She erased a line. "I expect it cost him a few commissions."

"You're planning on using silver, aren't you?" He set the stone down and leaned over to check her sketch.

"*Heavy* silver. But not in a southwestern design." She moved the pencil over the page. "I've got in mind something more...Norse. A necklace a Viking queen might have worn."

"How do you know it'll fit the owner?" His tone wasn't critical, but it was skeptical.

"Easy." She reached into a drawer, fiddled around until she found the right envelope and handed it to him. "Drexel sent me a photograph."

Mick opened the envelope and took out a brief, typed letter and a snapshot. The woman in it was good-looking, with strong features. Not a beauty, but nice on the eyes. She held a huge black horse by its reins in one hand and a struggling toddler in the other. She appeared to be very much in control of both. Mick grinned. "Yeah, you're right. She's tough. The Viking style will befit her."

"I'm delighted you agree." Maggie continued to work, a small smile playing over her face.

"Too right, I agree." He leaned farther and kissed her. "I always agree when you're hitting the nail on the head, love."

She returned the kiss. "And you don't agree when I don't."

"You need that." His smile was wicked, and the light in his green eyes made her insides warm and twist with anticipation.

Their passions had been curtailed by circumstances, however when they did have an opportunity to steal a few hours of lovemaking, the experience was overwhelming and explosive. Maggie began to wonder if life with Mick would continue to be one of constant erotic highs or if someday it would all fall apart from the pressure. But she didn't wonder very hard. Things were going too well for that. She was loved and cherished, and for the time being, that was enough.

There were still clouds on the horizon, of course. Mick was far from ready to abandon his search, and proved that by persuading Jeff, who paid a brief preholiday visit, to take the sketch of the man who'd sold Maggie the opal back to San Francisco and have a private detective see if any leads turned up. Jeff complied, but he warned Mick not to get his hopes up and advised him that even if they did find the man, proof that he had committed the murder was totally lacking and, in addition, he would have to be tried in Australia, which would involve a lengthy extradition process. Mick just said he'd cross those bridges when he came to them. The first order of business was finding the bastard. He'd worry about the rest after that. Maggie tried to convince herself she shouldn't worry about it. And for the most part, she was successful.

Christmas was the best she could remember since she had been a small girl. The anticipation built during the days before the holiday itself. By unspoken agreement, the three families centered their celebrations at the Wellington house, bringing presents, decorations and food to be shared. On Christmas Eve they attended services together at the Sullivan Springs Community Church. Then it didn't seem right for the Abramses to drive all the way to Three Pines, just to turn around in the morning and drive back for the celebration and opening of presents. So with some judicious juggling and polite hypocrisy, Nell slept in Maggie's room while she bunked down in the den on the foldout. Davey slept over at Mick's.

Bright and early the next day, Maggie was awakened by eager pounding on the front door. Filled with excitement herself, she hurried to let them in. Davey wheeled in first, his eyes alight with anticipation and happiness. Tad, now agile on his crutches, actually gave her a quick kiss on the cheek before racing to the tree. Then Mick sauntered in.

"Morning, love," he said softly, gazing at her, his love so evident in his eyes that she nearly cried for joy. Their embrace was cut short, however, by the impatience of the boys and by Nell and Patrick emerging from upstairs. The time had come for exchanging gifts.

The boys went first, gleefully unwrapping and exclaiming over their various gifts just like much younger children. Maggie was particularly pleased to see Tad acting this way. The boy tended to be unchildlike to a degree she wasn't sure was healthy. He needed a chance to be a kid, she thought.

Once they were done, they went into the den to further explore their new treasures, and the adults were left to themselves.

"You two first," Patrick said, beaming. "We ought to do this in order of age, don't you think?"

"Suits me." Maggie reached under the tree and handed Mick a small box. It contained the ring she had made with that special opal of his. She had managed to keep the project a secret from him by working on it when he wasn't around, and hiding it in with some junk when he was. He opened the package and rewarded her with an astonished, delighted expression.

"How'd you . . . ?" He took the ring from its velvet bed and put it on his right hand. It was a perfect fit.

"Actually, the elves made it while I slept," she teased.

"Maggie, it's even more wonderful than I imagined from your sketch. I'll treasure this the rest of my life!" He showed his gratitude by giving her a sound kiss.

His gift to her was even more of a surprise. He took a velvet bag out of his shirt pocket and told her to close her eyes. She felt the cool smoothness of a beaded necklace around her throat and thought he had given her pearls.

But he hadn't. The exclamations from Nell and Patrick didn't prepare her for seeing a string of opal beads around her neck when she looked in the mirror. "Oh, Mick! I've never seen anything like this," she cried. "The *work* it must have taken!"

"They're all from one big stone," he said, clearly pleased with her reaction. "I've been carving it for a few years, just waiting to get it put together for the right person. You're that person, love." He looked proud and in love and happy.

"Well, I will treasure this always, too." She touched the opals, now warm from her skin. Her kiss got a little drawn out, and Patrick had to clear his throat several times before he got their attention.

"Nell's already given me her present," he said, taking a small box from the pocket of his dressing gown. "But this will seal it." He opened the box, revealing a large diamond engagement ring. Nell was smiling and blushing. "Maggie, Mick," Patrick said, "Mrs. Abrams has done me the honor of agreeing to be my wife!"

Maggie was stunned for a moment, then with a whoop of joy, she flung her arms around them both.

CHAPTER FIFTEEN

MAGGIE PAUSED on her way to work to listen to the music made by water running off roofs and down the gutters. Every day the sun shone as brightly as today, the snow melted a bit more. It was nearly the end of March—nearly spring. And, thank goodness, nearly time when she and Mick would be finished with Project Opal!

Thinking of the past three months both confused and hurt her. While her feelings for Mick had only deepened, her conviction that their love didn't have what it would take to last had also deepened. Maggie started walking again, slowly. She was in no hurry to get to the shop and have to face the man she loved.

It had started the Sunday after Christmas when the television show featuring them had aired. Maggie had been pleased that Mick's story about Ian had been edited out. Mick had not been. Grumbling darkly about fluff telejournalism, he had retreated into a mood that nothing she did could pull him from.

The mood had lasted for three months. A car drove by her and Maggie stepped back to avoid being splashed by the dirty, slushy water kicked up by the tires. Being with Mick now, she reflected, was like walking down the street these days: you never knew when you were liable to get a cold, dirty soaking—emotionally, not physically, but that was worse. She wasn't sure how much longer she could take it!

She had tried being patient; had tried to understand his disappointment over the show and his growing frustration that Jeff's detective efforts had produced nothing. She hadn't even objected when he'd spent the day with her and not said one word. There had been times when she had been tempted to take the nearest object and fling it at him, but she had restrained herself. She loved him; surely that was enough. Wasn't it?

Damn! It frightened her to admit it, but maybe it wasn't enough. Maybe she was doomed to love men who for one reason or another weren't appropriate life partners. She stopped again and closed her eyes, thinking of the happiness her father and Nell were sharing. They had been married on Valentine's Day, and Patrick had moved into Nell's place, since it was already set up to accommodate his new son's needs. The three seemed a happy family unit; they obviously enjoyed one another and were content with their lives. Tears stung her eyes, and she knew with a rush of humiliation that she was jealous.

How petty, she fumed. She should be overjoyed that her father had come out of his grief and found a new life and new love. She was overjoyed!

But she was still jealous, still unhappy about her own situation—still in love and still miserable.

If Mick and Tad had moved in with her, as she had assumed they would after she was alone, she might have had more of a chance to work on Mick's temperament. Her pride had kept her from suggesting it outright, and he had ignored all of her hints. In fact, he rarely took advantage of her solitude to make love, doing so, it seemed, only when passion swept him out of control and he couldn't help it. Then his love was as hot and wild as her most erotic dreams, and his protestations of unending love for her so believable she wondered how she could ever doubt him.

But that didn't happen every night.

Maggie forced herself to blink the tears out of her eyes. Her plodding pace had managed finally to take her within half a block of the shop. She saw Mick's Jeep parked in front, and her stomach started to churn. It wasn't the way she wanted to feel when she was about to spend the day in her lover's company, but the way she did feel, nevertheless. She sighed and continued to walk.

The door of the shop opened and Tad came out. His leg was fully healed now, and he walked with confidence. He saw her and waved. Carrying his schoolbooks under one arm, he ambled toward her, looking for all the world like a replica of his dad. Her throat tightened for a moment.

"Take it a bit easy this morning, Maggie," he said in that young-old way of his. "He's like a hornet in a bottle. Mind you don't get stung."

Her own temper flared. "Maybe he should mind *he* doesn't get stung," she snapped. "I've about had it with his moods."

Tad didn't reply, but he rolled his eyes and headed on up the hill toward school. Maggie turned and watched him. The farther he got from his father, the more relaxed the set of his shoulders became and the younger he looked. She was not the only one Mick's attitude was taking a toll on.

She entered the shop with her emotions on a razor's edge. Mick was seated behind the counter. "You're late," he said. "It's almost nine."

"I'm self-employed," she shot back. "I can come to work when I want."

"We have less than two weeks to San Francisco. I'd think you'd want to be putting in every possible minute—"

"Mick, we have selected the five pieces I'm going to enter. The photographs were sent weeks ago, and the jewelry has been approved. Nothing I can do now is going to make one whit of a difference. I can make jewelry until I'm blue in the face, but the people who like my work are probably going to want to custom-order, anyhow. I'm essentially wasting my time until I see what kind of market the show opens up for us. It's almost spring, and the morning's a nice one. I wanted to spend a little time smelling the flowers.''

"There ain't any flowers yet. Damn snow doesn't look like it's ever gonna leave. I wonder if flowers bloom here, at all.''

"I meant it figuratively." She jerked off her light jacket and jammed it on one of the hooks by the door. "And, yes, the flowers do bloom here like nowhere else. Come June, the high meadows will be carpeted with color. It's wonderful.''

"Too bloody fine," he muttered.

"That does it!" She grabbed her coat and put it back on. "Mick O'Shay, I'm sick to death of your damn gloominess and bad temper. I can't stand another minute of listening to you complain and find fault with every little thing I do. You can sit there all day and gripe to yourself if you want. I'm leaving!" Hardly noticing his astonished expression, she turned and left, slamming the door decisively behind her.

Mick stared at the door, watching her retreating figure through the glass. Every inch of her seemed to vibrate with anger and indignation. Even her hair stood up, lifted as it was by the slight breeze. Suddenly, he knew just how close he was to losing her. "You've been a proper ass, mate," he said softly to himself. "A true and proper ass!"

MAGGIE SLID down the slope, the softened, slightly mushy snow making her progress a fraction slower than it would have been in winter. She aimed her skis almost straight down the fall line, wanting as much speed as possible—wanting to blow Mick O'Shay right out of her mind.

She had done the right thing. With her own frame of mind as explosive as it was, if she'd stayed near Mick, blood might have flowed! It was much better to get away and be out here on the mountain, enjoying the crisp air, the bright sunlight and the sense of freedom only rushing headlong downhill could bring. She felt cleansed, if not healed.

The mountain was not too crowded this weekday morning, and she had most of the runs to herself. Ordinarily, she exercised like this on a regular basis, but her involvement with Mick and his project had done more to her previously well-ordered life than merely trap her heart and drive her half crazy. Her muscles reminded her that they were not as well-toned as they might be, and she had better take it easy if she didn't want to be in agony tomorrow. Maggie raced on, ignoring the warnings.

She did slow down, however, when she came upon a small grove of pine trees. Then she stopped. Her heart was beating hard and fast and her breathing was rapid. It had been a good work-out—just what she needed. She rested until her heartbeat slowed.

Sunlight, filtered by the trees, dappled the snow at her feet. Here, where shade had protected it, the white covering was still fine and powdery. Maggie bent and picked up a mitten-full, admiring the tiny star-like shapes of the crystals. They weren't enduring like diamonds, but they were just as beautiful in their way. She let the snow trickle from her hand to the ground. The gentle breeze fanned the soft flakes out into a plume.

It was like love, she mused—the kind she shared with Mick: as beautiful in its way as the kind of permanent relationship she hoped her father was finding with Nell; as he had found with her mother. In the ultimate scheme of things, who was to say which was the more valuable: a diamond or a snowflake—a love that flared like a comet, then fizzled into nothingness, or one that lasted a lifetime. She felt a sense of peace growing within. Who was to say, indeed!

She glanced upward and squinted at the sunlight that was already pouring life into the land. When summer came, she was sure he'd be gone. After San Francisco, they had no professional reason to be together anymore. A wave of sorrow whipped through her, and she tried to control it. But it was hard, knowing that summer could—and probably would—take him off on his hunt again, perhaps back to his home. She thought about Tad being uprooted once more and got angry. Maybe, if Mick left, he'd allow the boy to live with her or Patrick and Nell. Tad deserved a stable kind of home life as he entered the difficult teenage years. And her father's marriage hadn't lessened his interest in the young Australian, at all. In fact, it seemed to her that Tad spent as much time over in Three Pines as he did in the Springs. They could work something out for his benefit.

She felt better, having made that decision.

Her stomach then decided to remind her of the time, and she pushed back her sleeve to look at her watch. It was after noon. Time for a break. Time to eat. She ski-walked out of the trees and started to turn downslope.

"Look out, Maggie!"

The shout barely reached her in time. Maggie shot a glance upslope, saw the figure hurtling toward her and scuttled backward into the protection of the trees. The skier zipped past her, his arms milling about as he struggled to get control of his perilous course.

It was Mick.

Her heart pounding faster than it had when she'd been racing on her own, Maggie dug in and pushed off, hoping she could catch him before he broke his neck or someone else's. She gained on him in a moment.

"Mick," she yelled. "Can't you stop?"

"I don't think so!" His lips were pulled back from his teeth—whether in a grin or a rictus of terror, she couldn't tell. "No brakes on these things."

"Sit down!" They were flying along, and she couldn't figure out how he had managed to stay upright for as long as he had. "Fall back on your hip and don't use your hands to brace."

"What?"

"Fall on your fanny!"

"Only if you'll fall with me!" He executed a surprisingly agile move and they both sprawled in the snow. Somehow, he had managed to get his arms around her in the process.

Maggie tried to sit up, spitting snow. "Let me go, you idiot! I've got to check to see if any bones are broken."

"No bones, love. Just hearts. I came up here to grovel at your feet and apologize." His breath was warm on her cheek, and his embrace remained tight.

"Grovel at ground level," she said, struggling as best she could when much of her was buried under heavy, wet snow and the rest was being held by an intransigent Aussie. "Mick, let me up!"

"Not until you either refuse or accept my apology." He sounded as comfortable as if he was sitting by her on the couch in front of a warm fire. "I've been a right bastard to you. To Tad. To everyone. And I deserve a hearing, if not forgiveness."

Maggie turned her head so she could look directly at him. His eyes were inches from hers, and while his tone was light, there was nothing of the joker in the green depths. "All right," she said. "Speak your piece."

"I lost track of what was real and valuable," he said. "I took your love and Tad's love, for granted while I wallowed around in self-pity. Mag, I can't promise I won't do it again, about this or something else, but it doesn't mean I don't love you and my boy—love you so much, it would near kill me if I lost you."

She started crying, and all the peace she had felt in the grove vanished. "I believe you, Mick. But words and apologies don't make up for weeks, for months of—"

"Don't cry, love." His own voice sounded broken. "My God, what have I done? Maggie, we talked about marrying once."

"No, Mick. Don't! Don't torture either of us with that. I just don't trust you, much as I might love you."

That brought him up short. He was quiet for a long moment. Then he said quietly, "You don't trust me? Maggie, darlin', what does that mean?" His hold on her relaxed.

Maggie sat up and brushed snow off herself. "It means I don't really know who you are, Mick. I can't go on living indefinitely with a lover who's hot one day and cold as death the next. I can't live with a man who—"

"Who loves you?"

"Don't do that! You aren't living with me, anyway."

"That's for your sake." He sat up beside her. "What would it do to your reputation if me and Tad just picked up and popped over to your place the instant your dad was gone? People would—"

The tears were coming hard now. "Most people here expect it. This isn't the Dark Ages where lovers have to skulk around in the middle of the night to get some action. There must be dozens of couples who aren't married living together in the Springs. Hundreds and thousands in the city."

"That doesn't make it right."

She just shook her head. There was no reasoning with him.

"Well, it doesn't." His hand touched her cheek. "Not when a man wants to make the woman he loves his wife. Not when he wants to live with her and love her forever. Not when he wants to protect her in every way. Including what people say about her."

Maggie closed her eyes, heedless of the tears now flowing steadily. Since the beginning of time, hadn't woman yearned to hear those words from man? A century ago, twenty years ago, wouldn't she herself have jumped at them? So why did they not do more than make the pain worse? "I don't need protection, Mick. I need someone to stand beside me, not in front of me."

"Everyone needs protection from time to time. Even me. Right now, especially me. I need the kind of protection only you can give me, Maggie."

She turned to look at him again. He wasn't crying, but his eyes were as sad as she had ever seen them. "What kind of protection could you possibly need?" she asked, her voice now hardly more than a whisper. "You're strong and sure of yourself. You have a gun and the ability to use it."

"I need protection from myself, Maggie."

He said nothing more, but no apology on earth could have moved her as much. She couldn't stop her hand as it moved to caress him, touching his hair, his face, his lips. "Why?" she whispered.

"Because I forget," he said. "I forget what's important and start brooding on . . . other things. You know the one thing wrong with you, love? You take too long to lose your temper with me. You should have knocked me silly right away when I began acting nasty about that telly show. You're too good a person. Show me some teeth when I get out of line." He bared his own healthy ones at her.

Maggie stopped crying and started laughing. Why did she try to fight it? For good or ill, she was lost in her love for him. They fell into each other's arms and were kissing in the snow when the ski patrol finally came down to check out what had been reported to be two casualties, writhing in apparent agony on the slope.

SAN FRANCISCO! Maggie lifted the window shade and looked out at the city. It had never seemed so romantic and magical before, not even at the best of times before Mick.

Before Mick. Her whole life was divided by the man—before she met him and after. How strange, how wonderful that someone could make that much difference to her—could actually restructure her existence!

She turned from the window and looked back at the bed they had shared the previous night. He looked as though he was still sleeping, his features relaxed and handsome and a reddish stubble shading his cheeks and jaw. His hair, which had been trimmed in Denver before they had left, was neat in spite of the many times she had tousled it with her fingers as they'd made love during the night. He was, she mused, as different now from the man she had thought she'd known as he had been when he had demonstrated his strange insight over his son's accident. He had produced and worn suits with shirts and ties. His grammar was perfect and his conversation as urbane as that of anyone they had met at the gathering of jewelers, judges, buyers and sellers. It took a keen eye to discern the rough-and-ready Mick O'Shay today.

But she was becoming used to this: Mick surprising her at the most unexpected turns. She was beginning to think he was not ever going to fit a pattern, a style, a role, particularly if she or anyone else tried assigning it to him. He was unique, original, as rare and valuable as the finest jewel shown at the Exposition, and she loved him beyond her own understanding.

"Gonna spend all morning standing there staring at me, or are you gonna come back to bed and do something about what you're thinking?" Mick had been watching her since she had slipped quietly from the bed, his love for her wrapped around him like a silken blanket. Something about her had changed since that confrontation on the ski slope, and while he hadn't figured it out yet, he was hardly about to complain. She had responded to his love with a fervor he hadn't known she possessed, in spite of the passion she had always shown in lovemaking. Unskilled as he believed he was in reading her heart and mind, he knew her feelings had grown deeper, more committed, less subject to change at the whim of her own bad moods or his. She still wouldn't talk seriously of marriage, sidestepping every time he tried bringing it up, but he had more hope now than ever before. Holding his arms open to her, he invited her to experience another demonstration of why they should plan on spending the rest of their lives together. She smiled and came eagerly.

"I DON'T KNOW why you wouldn't stay with us, dear. We have so much room in the house now that the children are gone. I did so hope Jeff would move back after his divorce, but you know young men. Can't stand to be under Mama's thumb for one second." Mildred Wright set down her teacup and regarded Maggie out of eyes that resembled Drexel's Turquoise but were not as warm. Maggie thought with pride of how delighted the man had been with his wife's Valentine gift, and how much pleasure she derived from making jewelry that was to be a present born out of love.

"Aunt Mildred," she said, settling back onto the older woman's mauve velvet couch, "Mick and I have to be in the same hotel as the Exposition. We appreciate your offer of hospitality, but—"

"It's the same attitude your father has," Mildred interrupted, her lips tightening in annoyance. Maggie marveled once more at how much the woman resembled her late mother, and yet how different she was from her sister. Evelyn Wright Wellington had loved life and people and had never judged either. Mildred sat in judgment over one and all. "He married that . . . that woman," Mildred went on, "without consulting anyone in the family. I've no doubt she was after his—"

"No, Mildred," Maggie stated. "Nell Abrams had no motivation other than love and friendship when she agreed to marry Dad. Now, if you'd like to keep this tea peaceful, I suggest you not make any more remarks of that nature!" Mildred looked startled, but when she began talking again, it was on an entirely neutral subject.

Mick, who had ensconced himself in a comfortable chair some respectable distance from the two women, smiled. This was the Maggie he enjoyed being with—the one who took no guff from anyone. Including himself!

He thought back to the row they'd had before coming to California. He had planned on leaving Tad with Celia Hawthorne. The housekeeper-cook and the boy had a fairly good relationship. But Maggie wouldn't have it. Acting as fiercely maternal as if the lad was her own flesh and blood, she had insisted he stay with Patrick, Nell and Davey. The spring holiday was going to occur while they were gone, and Patrick had travel plans for his new family—which included Tad, as well. Celia didn't seem to mind the break either, saying she was going to take some of the money she'd earned as the O'Shay's domestic and do a little traveling herself. So everyone was happy—including Tad. Mick mused that he had been at least partly right months ago when he had thought of her as an angel. She certainly had many of the necessary qualities.

Fortunately, she was also quite human and occasionally delightfully devilish.

After concluding the obligatory visit with her aunt, they drove back into the city for another obligation: a cocktail party in conjunction with the Exposition.

"This is going to be nothing more than a meat market," Maggie complained as she eased herself into a simple black dress. Her only decoration was Mick's Christmas necklace.

"Meat market?" Mick raised his eyebrows, but didn't look at her. He was too busy trying to tie his bow tie.

"You know. People looking to do a deal, to do business. They like your stones, they'll try buying some. They like my work, they'll try selling me ones. I really don't think—"

"You look beautiful." He looked at her now, the tie perfectly in place. "Stay by me, and you won't have to worry about anyone bothering you. Some treasures aren't open for business."

She stepped into his arms, feeling more strongly than ever before that he was truly trying to bring his promises to life. If only she could believe them!

THE PARTY WAS exactly as she had anticipated: dealers dealing, wheelers wheeling. She and Mick were much sought after by both, but with his adroit maneuvering and sensitivity to her reactions, she was able to talk to only those people with whom she wanted to visit. After a while, she relaxed, enjoying herself as old friends—artists she had known when she lived in the city—came over to her and congratulated her on the fine technique and style she had developed. A substantial number of dealers, representing the finest jewelry stores also showed definite interest in buying and displaying her work. Mick had been right—this was a turning point in her professional career. A turning point that could lead to great opportunities. She could almost feel her head swelling over the praise, and tried hard to keep taking the words with a grain of salt. Mick's opals, she kept telling people, were so inspirational she couldn't have done poor work if she'd tried.

But what was really making her feel higher than a kite was being with Mick. She knew that right down to the farthest recesses of her heart and soul.

From time to time during the evening Mick had the sensation that he had to reach up and gently pull her off the ceiling. It was a happy, delightful sensation, one that brought him much joy. The praise her colleagues were heaping on her for her work warmed him. He paid no mind to her words about his stones. They were the best, he knew. So was she. They were meant to be brought together, whatever the original reason he'd had for contacting her had been.

A slight shadow passed through his mind at that thought. Two days earlier, when she had been busy with formalities for the show, he had taken off for Jeff Wright's office to receive the final report from the lawyer's detective. It had been inconclusive. A number of witnesses had said they thought they'd seen someone who looked like the drawing, but no one could name names or give addresses. Mick knew his prey was out there—he could sense it. To know their paths might never cross, however, was painfully frustrating. He would have to be luckier than sin, he realized, if he wasn't going to spend the rest of his life wishing he could bring this unhealthy chapter of that life to a close. He would have to call on all of his skills to aid him if—

"Mick!" Her voice was low, but urgent. He opened all his senses.

Darlene Turner, masterfully disguised, stood across the room, watching them. But Maggie wasn't looking at the woman. Her eyes were fixed on a thin, dark man standing beside the thief. Mick's muscles all tensed at once.

"No!" Maggie was whispering now, so that only he could hear. "There's nothing you can do! I can't be absolutely sure it's the same man. He just looks familiar."

"It's the same man," Mick hissed. "Look who he's with."

"I don't— Oh, my God!"

"No, the Devil. Come on. Let's get out of here, but slowly, so they don't get suspicious and figure we've recognized them." He took her hand and led her toward the door, nodding polite dismissal to those who looked as if they might stop them to chat.

"Mick, what are you up to?" She followed him willingly enough, but he heard the fear in her voice. "What are you doing?"

"Calling Jeff. He can tell us how to get those two to the police."

Maggie almost fainted with relief at his answer. But Jeff was no help.

"I'm going to report the Turner woman as soon as you hang up," he told Mick. "But as for the guy, unless he's wanted for crimes in this country, or in this state you're out of luck. If he's in collusion with her, you might get a conspiracy charge—that is, if one of them confesses to plotting harm to you or Maggie. But no cop is going to arrest him without some kind of probable cause. That's—"

"I know what it is," Mick snapped. "I've been reading Patrick's law books. You're telling me unless this bastard pulls a knife or takes a shot at one of us, the law can't touch him?"

"You got it. Sorry."

"All right. Don't dob in the sheila. I have a better idea what to do about both of them." He listened to Jeff for a moment. "No, don't worry. I won't." He hung up the phone, and Maggie saw he was trembling with suppressed rage.

"I won't let you do it!" she said, standing in front of the door. They had gone back to their room to make the call. "If you want out of here, you're going to have to go through me, and I'll fight you with every breath in my body. I love you that much!''

Mick smiled, the expression genuine, not forced. "Darling Maggie, I believe you'd cut me off at the knees to save me. But don't you worry, love. I have no intention of going out there and ruining our future. Oh, no. You're famous now, and I love you.''

"But you said... What about...?''

"We go through the rest of the week, acting as if everything is normal.'' He put his hands on her shoulders, steadying her. "They don't know we know who they are. It's like hunting. Make the hunted think it's hunting you.''

"What?''

"It's so simple, love. Our success is the bait. Once this Exposition is over, I take you home, then I go back to Australia. They'll follow me, thinking you'll come after.'' He paused, and his eyes turned dark. "Once I'm home, I'm the hook that's going to finally do them in, for good and all!''

CHAPTER SIXTEEN

MAGGIE SETTLED BACK in her seat on the 747 and closed her eyes. The sleeping pill Mick had suggested she take was making her drowsy, and she knew she was about to drift into slumber in spite of her nervousness.

It had taken the hardest fighting of her life to get where she was, next to her lover on the way to danger. When Mick had declared his intention of luring the killer to Australia and setting himself up as bait, she had stated he wasn't going anywhere without her—that if he really wanted people to believe he was going back to dig more opals, he'd better let her go along. She would add credulity, since they were clearly regarded by the jewelry community as a duo. She had been prepared to throw herself on the runway if he tried flying out without her! Mick hadn't given in easily, but eventually he had agreed to her company.

"Comfortable, love?" His voice, low and warm, soothed her even more. "Need anything?"

"Uh-uh. I'm jus' fine, thanks." She turned her head so that she was resting on his shoulder. "Just fine."

In fact, if it wasn't for Mick's purpose for going home, everything *would* be just fine, she reflected. The Exposition had been an unqualified success for her professionally. She had placed second in the show, an exceptional honor for one so young and untried in the business. Requests for special orders had flocked in after that, and she had fended off—with difficulty—all but the most juicy ones. If she had wanted, she could have returned to Sullivan Springs with enough contracted work to keep her busy for years. Busy and wealthy. The money she'd been offered still astounded her. The senior artist who had placed first had advised her in a fatherly way, saying that she now had the prestige of a winning name and her work could consequently be worth far more than before. Her admiration for the man and delight in his unsolicited praise and interest had added enormously to her pleasure in receiving such an honor.

But more important to her than any honors or money was her love for Mick. She was going to be as close to him as a heartbeat! Hadn't he *asked* to be protected from himself?

Mick leaned his head slightly to his left so his cheek touched her silky hair. Her breathing settled into a steady pattern. She was finally sleeping. He reached over and took her hand where it lay relaxed in her lap. It was tiny as a bird in his big paw, and like Maggie herself, seemed quite delicate. Yet it was a strong, capable hand. Maggie herself needed to be protected, but she was determined to make her own way. And strong enough to give love and comfort in a lavish style that never failed to amaze and bring him joy. She was going to Coober Pedy with him, but she was *not* going to be in any danger. He was going to see to that!

THE LAND WAS the most desolate Maggie had ever seen. For as far as she could see from the window of the small plane, wasteland stretched. "My God," she whispered. "It's the back side of the moon!"

"The back side of paradise, you mean." Mick, who had been dozing in the aisle seat since they had left Adelaide, tipped his hat back from his eyes and leaned forward to look out the window beside her. "That's some of the richest dirt in the world, Maggie."

"You could have fooled me." She smiled, taking the sting out of her sarcasm. This was his home. She ought to give it a chance.

"You'll see." He returned to his sleeping position, hat over eyes. "You won't be disappointed. I promise." He breathed deeply once and his whole body relaxed again.

Maggie watched him. They had spent several days in Sydney, recuperating from the long flight and enjoying the city. Each day, he'd shed more of the civilized veneer he'd worn so well in San Francisco, until by the time they had flown to Adelaide, the capital of South Australia, he had been stripped down to the natural man he'd been when he'd arrived in Sullivan Springs. From a friend's home on the outskirts of Sydney, he had retrieved a small trunk from which he had gathered some old clothes. His suits, shirts, ties and city shoes had gone into storage at the hotel, pending his return. Maggie, following his counsel, had done the same with her good clothes and had purchased a meager wardrobe of rough-wearing clothes, a hat for protection against the sun, boots and a gallon of sunscreen. "Your skin will look like a dead leaf in days without this stuff," Mick said. "And while I'd love you just as much if it did, I'd hate to let it happen without a fight. Bathe in it!" She promised she would.

He had used the lotion, too, just before they had left Adelaide. "I'm white as a grub," he complained, studying his forearm. It looked tanned to Maggie. "My old mates won't recognize me, or they'll think I'm a ghost come back to haunt the digs. Well, a week or so, and I ought to be back to normal." He rubbed his callused palms together and shook his head disapprovingly. "Soft," he muttered. "Soft." Maggie, who had been caressed rather vigorously by those palms not so many hours before, reflected that soft was definitely in the mind of the beholder. About the only thing soft on his body was his eyelashes!

The small plane's engines changed pitch, and she looked out the window again. If they were nearing the town, she couldn't tell. On and on the unchanging landscape went. She shivered. To be lost, to be injured out there, would spell certain death for most humans. Her foot jerked and hit the side of the bag she had stowed under the seat in front of her. In it was a set of jewelers' tools—she intended to do some work while Mick carried out his plan. The very idea of just sitting and waiting for something to happen had almost driven her crazy! She could only imagine what she would be like if she actually had to do it.

"Comin' in," Mick said, not moving from his slouch. "Hang on to your breakfast, love."

"What?" The answer came not from Mick, but from a sudden, sickening lurch of the airplane. Maggie stifled a scream and grabbed at the arms of her chair.

Mick's hand covered hers tightly. "Just hot air currents," he said. "Be through 'em and down in no time."

Maggie managed a quick look out the window. "There's nothing down there but rabbit holes," she cried. "I don't see any town, at all. Oh!" Another air current rocked the plane.

"Those are mines." Mick squeezed her hand. "They look like bunny holes from this high up. They're big enough for a man—sometimes two—to dig in. You'll see."

Maggie closed her eyes, not certain she was ever going to see again.

They did land eventually. The pilot brought the plane through the worst of the turbulence and set her down with hardly a bump. When Maggie felt stillness, she opened her eyes. Mick was sitting up, smiling at her. "Welcome to my home," he said.

They got off the plane, along with the two other passengers, taciturn men who had nothing to say to each other, much less to strangers. The copilot unloaded the luggage, tossing each piece to its owner from the minuscule baggage compartment. Maggie had a suitcase. All of Mick's belongings were stuffed in his ancient canvas carryon. He spoke to the copilot while she struggled to drag her belongings to one side of the runway. The sun was blazing, and a steady, hot wind carried a diet of dust and grit with it. She adjusted her hat to keep the rays out of her eyes.

"Now, then." Mick came over and picked up the suitcase easily. His bag was slung over his shoulder, and on his hip he wore his gun. No longer hidden in a shoulder holster, it looked menacing. Maggie widened her eyes. He didn't notice. "We're looking for a hitch into town," he said, scanning the horizon.

"There's no limousine?" She looked over at the tin-roofed building that served as a terminal. "No cab service."

"Very funny. This is the Outback, Maggie. Stick close or it'll eat you alive, and I wouldn't want that to happen." His expression was serious, as was his tone, but his eyes gleamed with humor.

"Mick? Mick O'Shay!"

Mick turned, saw the tall, dusty figure loping toward him and whooped with pleasure. Maggie watched, feeling extremely out of place as he traded shoulder-grabbing and light punches with the newcomer, a man so lean and leathery he looked as if he had dust, not water in his veins. She grew more uncomfortable when two other men, not so lean, but equally leathery, emerged from the terminal and joined in the male-bonding.

It got worse.

They got a ride with the trio, whose names Maggie barely managed to decipher during Mick's introductions. Her lover's accent—which seemed to grow more pronounced by the second—rendered his English mush to her ears. Trev, Jack and Georgie, she thought, were polite as could be to her and then seemed to dismiss her presence. As she rode, squished between Mick and the side of the open Land Rover, ducking her head against the heat and grit and listening to the guffaws and incomprehensible language, she thought she must have been out of her mind to insist on accompanying him.

But the painful pressure of the gun at Mick's side grinding into her hip reminded her she had good reason to accompany him. His old friends all wore guns and she noted a sinister looking shotgun strategically placed by the driver. It was like stepping back into time, she thought—back to the Wild West where the law had been governed by might more than right. As that passed through her mind, Mick's arm went around her shoulder.

She knew immediately when they were in town. The "rabbit holes" gave way to dusty streets and buildings, some of which looked fairly new and modern. Others were made of corrugated tin and weathered siding—no wood. There were many trailers. She scanned the unpromising scene, expecting to be taken immediately to Mick's old home and dumped.

She wasn't. The Land Rover pulled to a stop in front of a ramshackle building declaring itself a pub and the men poured out. Maggie sat, wondering what to do, but Mick reached in and lifted her to the ground, holding her for a moment and studying her face. "I have to shout a few for the lads," he said. "Mind?"

"What?" She brushed hair and sand from her perspiring face.

"Buy a few beers for the boys," he explained, grinning. "I'll even stand you one, if you want."

"A beer just might save my life," she declared, swiping at the grit on her jeans with an open palm. Mick's smile broadened, and he looked as if he would have liked to have a go at the dust himself. But he refrained. She followed the group inside, thinking that drinking herself into a stupor was probably one of the best ideas she'd had in quite a while.

But it got better. Much better. Two beers into the celebration—which was joined by a growing number of women as well as men as the word got out Mick O'Shay was back, he introduced Maggie to the crowd. "This is me darlin' Maggie," he said, reaching over and lifting her out of her slumped position on her chair to sit on his lap. "She's an artist." He fumbled inside his jacket and brought out a packet of photographs. When he tossed them on the table, she recognized snapshots of her jewelry. "She made these beauties," he added.

"When did you take those?" She half listened to the appreciative noises made by the crowd as the pictures made the rounds. Mick just grinned.

"She ain't no artist, Mick, she's a bloody genius!"

"We oughta get Lew over here to take some photos for the newspaper."

The friendly praise rolled on until Maggie was embarrassed but pleased. Now she wasn't just a sheila tagging along with old Mick, but a person of worth in her own right. Mick kissed her on the cheek and let her get back to her own chair and beer. The time passed quickly then, and she didn't even finish her beer, she was so busy talking to new acquaintances.

Finally, Mick called a halt to the party, and Maggie was glad. While she had satisfied her hunger with a hot meat pie, she was exhausted. The heat, the beer and the attention had sapped her strength to the point where she wasn't sure she could stand steadily. When Mick announced they were heading home, however, she did.

"Somebody tell Nigel I need to talk to him," Mick added. "When you see him."

"He'll be in later tonight," a man said. "Out checking on a dispute." Mick nodded, somber for the first time since arriving. Maggie felt a quiver of anxiety. Nigel had to be the law man around there, she decided.

They went outside with Trev, who had volunteered to drive them to Mick's home. Maggie gasped when she looked up at the sky. Not even in the mountains had the stars seemed so brilliant and so close. "It's so..." she said, unable to find the right words to describe the scene.

"Beautiful," Mick finished. "And so're you. Come on, love. I've got a need to make our homecoming official," he said in a low tone. Maggie scrambled into the Rover, energized by the promise in his voice.

The night air was still quite warm, though she could feel it cooling quickly. The wind had died and the annoying grit no longer besieged her teeth and eyes. The buildings she could see seemed transformed by the darkness into welcoming havens; light poured out of the windows and people moved about behind them in domestic fashion. She wondered what she would think of Mick's dwelling and steeled herself to accepting primitive conditions with good grace.

No good grace was needed. Mick's "cave" was an underground paradise. He had wired ahead to have a friend clean and air it, stock the kitchen with food and make up the bed with clean linens. She stepped through the door, down a flight of stairs into air-conditioned comfort. "Ah." She sighed. "That feels wonderful! Can you turn it down—it's almost too cold."

"It ain't air-conditioning, love." Mick waved goodbye to Trev and shut the door. He carried her suitcase into the bedroom and continued talking. "It's natural cool from the underground. Stays about the same all year long. Don't worry about being too cold. I can give you a jumper and, besides, we're going to bed, anyway."

"I believe I'm going to like it here." Maggie turned around, admiring the simple decor, the walls lined with books, the primitive carvings that were clearly part of a collection. "I can't imagine why you wanted to leave here in the first place."

"I'm glad I did." His gaze held a myriad of meanings. "Very glad."

Overwhelmed by emotions she wasn't able to name, Maggie moved into his embrace.

Much later that night, Mick lay awake, his body weary, but his soul content. Maggie nested in his arms, her warmth and softness a balm to his spirit. Battles lay ahead, he knew, but for the moment, the war was far from his mind. He had brought his woman home, and she seemed pleased.

This wasn't a place he could ask her to stay forever, nor did he want to return totally to his old ways as a miner. But Coober Pedy was where he needed to be from time to time. He could feel the strength of the earth, feel the resonance with nature he enjoyed best here. Hidden treasures called softly to him, beguiling him and beckoning him to discover them and prize them from the rock and soil. Yeah, he was home. How long Maggie could take the life remained to be seen.

A lot remained to be seen. He shifted slightly on the bed, putting his arm over her. The ends of her hair tickled his skin pleasantly. She still hadn't responded to his talk of marriage, and he was strangely shy of bringing the topic up again. She knew what he wanted, and he would have to wait until she declared herself. Waiting wasn't the easiest thing, but he'd manage. He'd manage anything to spend the rest of his life with her. Once the other business was over, settled for good, he'd be able to concentrate all of his energies on her and eventually she'd have to succumb to the pressure of his love.

His eyes finally shut, weighed down by exhaustion. That she loved him enough to marry him, he had no doubt. Since the time he had challenged her in the snow to confront him, she had demonstrated the extent of her commitment time and again. To come with him into what she believed would be a dangerous situation was the final proof—she thought she was actually risking her own life to protect his.

She wasn't risking a thing, of course. During the Exposition, when she hadn't been around, he had spent enough time bragging about a certain rich vein of opals to lure a saint, much less someone interested in a repeat performance of what had happened to Ian. And that vein, he had made certain everyone knew, was nowhere near town— nowhere near Maggie's turf. It was so far from any place she could possibly be in South Australia that the chance she'd be in danger was about as great as the chance he'd fly to the moon! Mick had covered his bases.

He turned onto his side, still cradling her against his body. She was his special treasure and no harm would come to her. He fell asleep, dreaming of the life they would share in the future.

Nigel arrived before dawn. Mick awoke to a pounding on the door and to Maggie's sleepy voice telling the pounder to give it a rest, she was coming. Mick waited, grinning to himself.

Maggie threw the door open, fully prepared to tell the caller to go away and come back at a more civilized hour. But one look at the man in the doorway, and she stepped back, allowing him to enter without further delay. This was not, she decided instantly, someone you argued with. He was huge and fairly bristled with all manner of lethal weaponry.

The behemoth ignored her. He stomped through the living room and into the bedroom, one hand slamming the wall where the light switch cowered. Mick's sleeping form was illuminated. "Wot's the deal, O'Shay," the newcomer roared. "The lads said you needed to see me. Been up all night, and I ain't in the mood for this." He jerked the covers off Mick. "Who's the sheila?"

"Good t' see you, too, Nigel." Mick sat up, wrapping the sheet around his middle. "This is Maggie Wellington. She's to be my wife."

"Wife?" Nigel, who had to be seven feet tall and at least three hundred pounds—all muscle—turned and stared at Maggie. She wrapped her robe more tightly around herself and smiled, waving her fingers at the man in what she hoped was a friendly fashion. She'd deal with Mick's labeling of her later. Right now, anything that kept Nigel tamed was fine with her.

"When she comes to her senses and says yes, anyway." Mick got up, dropped the sheet and pulled on his jeans. "I need to talk with you, cobber. Come in the front room and sit."

Nigel complied, and Maggie took herself into the kitchen to make tea, rather surprised that Mick hadn't ordered her to provide refreshment. The whole atmosphere reeked of male dominance, and it was to Mick's credit that he didn't seem to be falling back into old patterns—unless his assumption about her future matrimonial state could be called macho.

And she wasn't sure they could be. When they had gone to San Francisco, he hadn't given her any flak about checking into the same room. It was different, he'd explained when she had asked why. The people in the hotel room next to her weren't her neighbors. While she didn't agree with him, his logic did make sense. Regarding Coober Pedy, he had explained that he was going to tell his old mates the truth—that he planned to marry her. If she chose to argue about it publicly, she was free to do so, but she didn't have to be told it would be very bad manners. Maggie sighed, not contentedly and not unhappily, as she poured the boiling water into the warmed teapot. Tea leaves swirled, and she wondered what they said about her future.

"So you flapped it about so the bastard could hear that you was comin' after the mother of all opals?" Nigel accepted the mug of steaming tea from Maggie with a nod of his massive head and a thank-you in his eyes, if not on his lips.

"That I did." Mick sipped his tea appreciatively. "If he don't take the bait, Bob's your uncle. Maggie's sure it was him, and that little Light-fingered Lilly was right by his side. Thick as thieves, you might say."

"And they don't know we made them," Maggie said, pulling up a chair and sitting at the table. Nigel looked at her, startled. "They don't know we recognized them," she explained, smiling sweetly. "We covered our original surprise and raced from the room, telling everyone I'd had a sudden inspiration for a design that I just had to get down on paper. We hammed it up a bit, and soon we were the objects of considerable attention. That left the field open for Mick to talk about his plans to return here. If Darlene does wish us harm, and the man does want to repeat his crime, they could hardly resist following us."

"Following *me*." Mick poured himself some more tea, adding cream and sugar as Nigel had. "You're not the bait, love. I am. Nigel here has agreed to keep watch on you to make sure there's no mistake."

Nigel smiled. At least, he pulled back his lips from his teeth. Maggie smiled back, knowing now was not the time to argue the issue.

But when Nigel had finally lumbered out of the cave, she turned on Mick. "I will not be baby-sat by King Kong," she stated. "I realize this might get dangerous, but I—"

"You don't know the half, Maggie." Mick put down his tea and regarded her with a serious expression. "Out here, you're no more capable of defending yourself than you are of... of walking to Perth and surviving. You can't call for help when there's no help to be had. No neighbors would hear you down here in the ground. You'll be stuck here most of the time, too. The heat's beyond what you can stand during the day, and nights, well, nights I don't want you wandering around without an escort for more reasons than fear of injury or death. You're a beautiful woman, love, in a place where beauty is not the more common commodity. I did have a reputation in the past that might have sheltered you, but I've been gone, and new men who don't know me have settled here. Not a one of 'em doesn't know Nigel, though."

"Who is he? The sheriff or something?"

"Or something. Nigel is Nigel. You stick close to him when I'm not around and you'll be fine."

"And where will you be?"

"Off diggin'. Where else?" He got up and went to the kitchen. He took out a rasher of bacon and used a large butcher knife to slice off some pieces. Then he retrieved a frying pan and placed it on the stove.

"Off diggin'." She came over to stand close behind him. "And I'm to cower here in the ground like a proper little sheila? Think again, mate!"

"Don't argue with me on this, Maggie. Mining's no place for you."

"And who's going to be guarding you? While you're down in some hole, that man could sneak up on you and brain you. Why can't I watch your back?"

"Because..." He faced her, exasperation written all over his face. "Because—"

"Because you don't think I'm capable. That's it, isn't it? I'm tougher than I look, Mick O'Shay. You ought to know that by now!"

His features hardened and his eyes became green stones. "It ain't...isn't open to debate, Mag. That's my final word, and nothing you can say will change my mind." He turned back to the stove and threw the bacon on the heated frying pan. The meat sizzled and hissed, hurling droplets of grease into the air and filling the house with a savory smell. Maggie retreated, sensing she would only waste her time. But she was already forming a plan to thwart him.

"THAT'S RIGHT, MISS. Squeeeeeze the trigger. Slooowly, slow..."

Maggie squeezed. The rifle bucked and her ears rang, but the beer bottle that had jumped off the rock burst into a thousand pieces. Nigel broke into an unintelligible stream of praise.

She had bided her time, waiting until Mick was secure in his mining routine and in his belief that she had given up her notion of helping him. Then she had given Nigel an ultimatum: teach her to shoot or spend the rest of his stint as a bodyguard wondering where she was going to sneak off to next. The big man had thought for a moment, then he'd agreed to the lessons. Clearly he had expected them only to be something to keep her from being too bored. When she had shown determination, then proficiency, no one had been more surprised.

Unless it was Maggie. She had always been a pacifist, and taking a weapon in hand with the idea of using it on another human being was alien to her. But a lot had happened that was alien to her, and she had embraced much of it. If learning to defend herself was what it would take for Mick to let her work at his side, so be it.

She was, however, far from bored. Mick had set up a small work area for her in the living room, and she had started several projects, utilizing stones belonging to his friends as well as his own opals. This increased her fame and popularity, and when he was gone overnight she never lacked for invitations to dinner from wives of the men whose discoveries she was transforming into treasures. Her alleged engagement to Mick seemed to make her immune to feminine jealousy, as well.

Not that she was about to fool around with her own personal Goliath. She and Nigel let each other alone most of the time, but gradually, as the days passed into weeks, they became friends, and she knew that protecting her was no longer just a job for him. He acted rather as she imagined an old-fashioned retainer would, respectful and devoted, asking nothing in return for his services but trust. She was careful not to actually manipulate him, but by demonstrating her own willingness to learn and to put up with discomfort, she eventually persuaded him to take her out into the mine fields and show her where Mick was working.

MICK GRUNTED with satisfaction as he prized out the chunk of rock that bedded the stone he'd been after all morning. Taking the most extreme care, he gently and painstakingly worked the section of rock free from the main vein. He'd find out the extent of his reward tonight when he freed the opal, but for now, he was pleased with his work.

"Good on you, mate," a familiar voice sounded behind him. "Why don't you stop for today and let me shout you a beer?"

Mick whirled, white rock dust flying from his hair and clothes. "Maggie! What in bloody hell are you doing down here? Where's Nigel?"

"Upstairs." She pointed to the surface. "Don't be angry with him. I bullied him into bringing me out."

Mick tried to build a head of steam, but the sight of her, dressed in tan slacks and a shirt with the sleeves rolled above her elbows, her dark hair hidden under a yellow hard hat, let the pressure right out of his boiler. He grinned and reached for her. Then he noticed the rifle in her hand. "What's this!" he shouted. "What the hell are you doing with a—"

"Being sensible," she replied. "Nigel isn't omnipotent and neither are you. It didn't sit well with me to just loll around, letting you men take care of me." She adjusted the rifle strap where it rested on her shoulder. "Now it just might be possible that I can take care of myself and you, as well. I'm a pretty fair shot, I'll have you know."

Mick groaned. So much for keeping her safely hidden underground. He ought to have known better. This woman would never submit to a passive role without a fight. "All right, love," he said, resigned. "I'll knock off for the day and you can buy me a beer. But don't let that rifle give you a false sense of security. It's been quiet up to now. I don't expect it to stay that way!" She nodded soberly enough to make him feel relieved that she was still taking the situation seriously. In truth, he was glad she had interrupted him. All morning he'd had an itchy sensation at the back of his neck. Things were going to break soon, he was sure of it.

That evening, Darlene Turner came into town.

CHAPTER SEVENTEEN

THEY WERE HAVING a beer with friends in the pub connected to the hotel when Maggie spotted her in the lobby, checking into a room. At first, she wasn't sure it was the same woman. Turner had dyed her hair a blond so pale it was almost white and wore clothing that made her look heavier and older. Only her eyes, darting this way and that, settling on her and Mick, gave her away. Maggie stifled a reaction of recognition and kicked Mick under the table.

"Ouch, love," he said. "What'd I . . . Oh!"

"Oh, indeed." Maggie leaned over and whispered in his ear. "What do we do now?"

"Not a thing." His hand covered hers. "We wait. We wait, and let nature take its course."

"Nature? What's nature got to do with any of this?"

He squeezed her hand. "Watch," he said.

What followed had obviously been rehearsed, but Maggie was impressed. Mick raised his voice and proposed a toast to his mates, both present and past. Trev and Nigel rose to their feet, lifting bottles to the ceiling, adding to the toast: "And to the luckiest mug what ever turned over color in South Australia: Mick O'Shay. To him what's on the trail of the richest vein in history!" Shouts of approval, guffaws and clinking glass punctuated the announcement.

Out of the corner of her eye, Maggie saw Darlene hesitate and listen before following the manager up the stairs to her room. *Bait and hook,* she thought. It might work, but it was like a knife in her heart to think that Mick was deliberately setting himself up as a target.

Later, back home, she tried not to let her feelings show. He wasn't going to stop, no matter what she did or said, so it was only right that she give him the best of climates to work in. That meant not making him worry about her.

"All right, love," he said when she emerged from the bathroom, clad only in a scrap of black nylon designed to drive any man out of his mind in a second. "Out with it. What's in your head right now?"

"Um." She put her arms around his neck. "I should think it'd be pretty obvious, *love*."

His smile was sweet, but a little wry. "Come on now, Mag. I know you better than that. You're upset, and you shouldn't be. Her being here means it's almost over. And the sooner it's over, the sooner we can go back to living a normal life."

She hugged him close and the tears spilled. "Living with you will never be what I'd call normal, but I want to go on doing it, Mick. If this should go sour and something happens to you, I—"

"Ho! Wait a minute. Back up. Did I hear you say you wanted to go on living with me?"

"No, you idiot!" She scrubbed the tears away. "I've been cooking and cleaning, washing a ton of rock dust out of your clothes every evening, for a lark. Mick, you are the only man besides my father for whom I've done these things. It seems right and good to me, and I don't want anything to take it away."

"Then nothing will." He touched her face tenderly. "Just a little while longer. Trust me. I'm really not taking any risks."

"Oh, right! Stuck down there in that hole all day. I was in it, remember? You could be trapped down there like a rat. No risk?"

"Darlin', I've got allies you wouldn't believe if I told you about them."

She broke away and walked to the other end of the living room. "You mean the aborigines? I've met some, and they are a fascinating and gentle people. Fierce as they look, I didn't detect—"

"Maggie," he said, his tone patient. "You're in a different world here. I doubt if you could detect your way clearly out of a paper bag. Would you ever have trusted a man looking like Nigel in the States?"

She had to smile in spite of her inner turmoil. "Nigel would make a perfect Hell's Angel. No, you're right. I would have run screaming in the other direction if he'd approached me at home—or, at least, the polite equivalent of running and screaming. Nigel is not a man one should willingly offend."

"But you trust him."

"Sure, but—"

"Case in point. Now come on, let's see if I can do justice to that bit of temptation you're supposedly wearing." He crossed the space between them so quickly she had no time to reply. Then she was in his arms, being kissed and carried to the bedroom. After that, discussion was limited to the immediate present....

IN THE MORNING Mick was gone when she woke. Two sentences into the note he had left for her, Maggie knew the horrible extent of her folly in allowing him to romance her out of the previous night's discussion-argument. "My dearest love," it said. "I don't know when I'll be back. My plan is to lure my enemy into the bush, where I'll have the advantage." He wrote on telling her to stay home and wait. He would be fine, and she was safe. Their future together depended on that.

Maggie crumpled the note in a rage. Stay home and wait? The hell she would! She grabbed clothes, pulling them on while cursing his male narrow-mindedness. She wasn't dumb enough to think she could make it out in that god-forsaken wilderness he called the bush, but there certainly were things she could do.

And hooking onto Darlene Turner was the first of them.

This proved less difficult than she had thought it might. Relieved to see her lumbering bodyguard nowhere in sight, Maggie packed up some jewelry samples and hiked through town to the hotel. At the front desk, she slapped the leather case down on the counter in front of the startled day manager, who was also the owner. "Have I got a deal for you, Archie," she said, smiling. Fifteen minutes later, she was set up in the lobby, peddling her wares to tourists.

Darlene Turner came down from her room close to noon. Every dyed blond hair was in place, but the woman still looked the worse for wear. Her lips, painted carefully, were swollen and her eyes looked bloodshot. Either she'd been slapping herself in the mouth half the night and drinking, Maggie figured, or she'd had some help with that puffy look. While helping an Italian couple make a selection from her case, she kept one ear out for what Turner was saying to Archie.

"...truck and driver to go out into the desert," the woman said. "My... husband's doing some exploring and I'm supposed to meet him." Archie gave her directions to a garage that specialized in hauling sightseers. Maggie noted the location, but didn't try to follow when Turner left the hotel. Fear for Mick's safety made her cautious and more clever than she had ever been in her life.

She waited until Darlene returned, looking extremely hot and sweaty after being out in the noonday heat. Closing up the now almost-empty jewel case, she jumped to her feet and waylaid the woman just as she was about to start up the stairs. "Hey there," Maggie chirped. "You're American, too, aren't you?"

Darlene Turner looked as if she was going to jump right out of her skin. Maggie kept a silly smile on her face. "I'm from the States," she went on. "Stuck out here in the middle of nowhere because of my boyfriend. He's an Aussie. Say, can I buy you a beer, honey? You sure look like you need one."

"Um," said Darlene.

"Oh, come on." Maggie hooked her arm in Darlene's elbow and pulled. "I don't see Americans that often out here. What do you do? I make jewelry."

She managed to get the jewel thief out of the lobby and into the pub, sat her down at a table and ordered beer for both of them. Frightened and startled at first, Darlene soon recovered and played the part she had been given with remarkable aplomb, considering that she was talking with the close friend of a potential victim. Maggie kept her temper in check only by reminding herself she had far more to lose at this point by blowing things than by waiting. Darlene seemed to believe her disguise was adequate. After all, Maggie had only seen her briefly in the past and that had been months ago.

But pry as she might, Maggie couldn't get one iota of useful information from the woman. Knowing it was useless to push too far and make her quarry suspicious, she concentrated on disarming the other woman by chattering like a magpie. Several hours and a number of mugs of beer passed by and when the sun began to set, turning the sky and land rosy, she finally ran out of things to talk about. Darlene had uttered maybe one hundred words to her ten thousand, and Maggie was getting desperate. It was her one opportunity to help Mick, and nothing had come of it.

Then an angel walked into the pub, looking for Darlene. Nigel caught Maggie's eye briefly, and the warning in his glance was unmistakable. Then he ignored her. Lifting a chair in one huge hand, he set it down next to Darlene and began discussing the arrangements they had made for travel the next morning. Maggie left the scene as soon as she could exit gracefully.

The combination of too much beer and no success left her weary and in the mood to sit down and cry. She walked slowly back home, wondering how such a good idea as latching on to Darlene had just been shot, smoking, from the sky. Well, at least it wasn't a total loss, she reminded herself. She knew the woman was off to rendezvous with the man who had killed Ian and who was probably going to try to kill—

Ice swept through her veins, stunning her into stillness. Mick was in terrible danger. She knew it just as surely as she knew she was slightly drunk. Her head cleared then, and she was totally aware. She smelled dust and felt the burning heat of the setting sun on her face and hands. A searing pain lanced through her side and she cried out, stumbling toward the entrance to the house.

"Miss Wellington?" A massive black shape rose out of the shadows, causing her to yelp in surprise and fear. "It's all right," the man said, stepping into the dying sunlight. "I'm come from Mick." The aborigine studied her for a moment. "Are you all right, miss?"

"No." She gasped for breath, leaning on the door for support. "But I don't think it's me. I think it's Mick who's hurt." The feeling of pain and danger fled as suddenly as it had come, and she straightened, looking at the newcomer. "I'm sorry," she said. "I don't know what happened just then. I've had a bit too much to drink."

The man smiled, but he was watching her intently. "My name's Davis," he said. "Ran into Mick out there." He waved vaguely in the direction of the wilds. "He asked me to come and see if you were doing all right. Are you, miss?"

"I . . . I don't know." She opened the door. "Come in, Davis. Tell me where he was and how he was when you saw him."

She made tea, finding that she wasn't really drunk at all, just shaken up by the strange experience. The smells and feelings and the pain had been so intense, it now seemed as if it couldn't actually have happened. But she knew it had.

Davis sat and drank his tea, explaining that he had met Mick quite a ways out and Mick had asked if he would look in on her. Maggie arched an eyebrow at that, but made no comment. Davis looked a bit uncomfortable, then.

"Look, Miss Wellington," he said, his broad, dark features registering concern.

"Maggie."

"Maggie, then. Mick O'Shay and I go back a long, long way, and if he asked me to . . . What's the matter?"

"I don't know!" Her vision began to blur and she felt a terrible thirst. The stabbing pain hit her again. The last thing she saw was a bright orange disk rising over a flat, black horizon.

MICK DRAGGED HIMSELF behind the escarpment of rock. Though the wind was blowing, hiding the small sounds he was making, the moon was rising and Midler would be able to spot him soon if he didn't find better cover. John Midler. That was the murdering bastard's name. He'd actually introduced himself. Just before he fired the shot that had torn into Mick's side, he had laughingly admitted killing Ian and had boasted he would do the same to Mick. Only he planned on taking his time about it—enjoying the process.

Enjoying the hunt.

Mick bit back a groan of pain. He was letting the wound bother him far too much. It wasn't that serious, only painful. He'd been through much worse in his time.

Only now he had far more to live for. Tad needed a father who wasn't off chasing after revenge. Maggie needed a man, a husband who would put her love where it belonged: at the forefront of his life. He damned the pride that had led him to believe he could take on Midler alone and triumph. *Mick O'Shay*, he told himself, *you are no longer a one-man show.* He should have taken his friends up on their offers of help.

But hindsight wasn't always clearest. He was out here alone with nothing but his wits between himself and death. His gun was lying at the bottom of the shaft back at the dummy mine he'd been pretending to explore when Midler had caught him entirely unaware. The man had to have been part snake to sneak up on him like that!

"O'Shay!"

Mick pulled his lips back in a snarl as the hated voice sounded over the freshening wind. He still had most of his strength and his bare hands. He was tempted to stalk the man and try rushing at him. Slitting his eyes against the increasingly thick dust in the air, he rolled onto his back and tightened the pressure bandage he'd made from his bandanna and belt over the wound in his side. The dust storm would act in his favor if he wanted to try a hunt of his own. It was better than cowering under some boulder, waiting like a rabbit to be flushed out.

Committing himself and the two people he loved to God, he moved out from his shelter to open ground. The dust storm was now heavy enough to protect him unless he was a few feet from Midler. In fact, it was hard now to see more than a few feet. Standing cautiously, he tried sensing where his enemy was. Another mocking shout from the man, and Mick knew. His first step took him toward the killer.

His second sent him plunging to the bottom of a mine shaft.

MAGGIE CAME TO and found herself surrounded by worried-looking dark faces. She was lying on the sofa in Mick's living room. Davis, kneeling beside her, raised her head and offered her some water. "You fainted, miss," he explained, "but I think perhaps it wasn't a faint. I think you saw a vision. These are the elders of my tribe. Can you tell us what happened?"

Maggie sat up. She had a terrible headache and her right arm throbbed with pain. "I don't know," she said. "First, while I was outside, I felt bad—a pain in my side. Then in here, while we were talking, I got so thirsty, and I saw the moon. It was big and orange. It didn't look normal. Now my head and arm hurt, too." She paused while the men murmured to each other and nodded. Her side twinged a bit and she grimaced, then the pain faded.

"You have touched his mind," a particularly wrinkled and dusty-colored old man said. "Your spirits are joined, and you feel his pain."

Maggie gave a cry and started to stand. Davis put a hand on her shoulder. "There's a bad storm," he said. "You stay here. We'll search for Mick."

For the first time, she heard the howl of the wind. It sounded no worse than a blizzard at home. "The hell with that! Tell me what to do, but I'm going with you. No argument!" She glared at Davis, then at the others.

MICK STRUGGLED BACK to consciousness. The world was dark as midnight and roared like a mortally wounded beast. Sand and dust covered him like a shroud, but no wind buffeted him. Reaching out, he felt cool stone. A mine. He'd fallen into a damn mine! He tried sitting up and nearly screamed out loud. His arm. His goddam arm was broken! He was trapped and helpless as a baby. His only hope was that Midler would lose his way in the storm—maybe fall down another shaft.

But if he didn't, when the weather cleared, Mick was a sitting duck. His plan had been simple—confront Midler, capture him and wait until Nigel drove out with the Turner woman. He had been sure he could get a confession by playing the two against each other. Nigel's word as a witness would never be doubted by those in authority. But now, Mick was really on his own. Nigel would never risk taking a woman out into a storm like this. Davis and his aboriginal friends would wait it out, too. They had better sense than to—

A small rock crashed down into the shaft, bouncing near his feet. He thought he heard his name being called over the howling wind. This was it! Midler had found him. Mick struggled to the rear of the shaft where it was wide enough for him to stand erect. Ignoring the agonizing pain in his side and arm, he stood, taking the chunk of rock in his left hand. He prepared to die fighting, Maggie's name on his lips.

"HE'S DOWN THERE," Maggie yelled, her lips an inch from Davis's ear and her voice muffled by the mask she was wearing as protection against the driving dust and sand. "I know it. But I have to be the one to go to him."

"Miss . . . Maggie, it might be the other man. I can't let you." Davis turned from her and shouted instructions to his fellow tribesmen and Nigel, who had insisted on coming with them when he'd shown up at Mick's home and had been apprised of the situation. Maggie watched through her goggles while the men conferred, ignoring her. A thick rope was produced, and one of the aborigines went to look for a rock to tie it to.

Maggie looked down the hole. The beam of her flashlight showed scrapes along the side that could have been foot and hand holds. They were small—too small for any of the men—but big enough for her. She quickly memo-

rized the pattern, switched off her light, slung her rifle over
her shoulder and was over the side and starting down before anyone could stop her.

In the dark, Mick waited. The beam of torch light had
galvanized his strength, pulled it from regions he didn't
know existed in his soul. He was not going to die! He had
to live, and not for himself. Midler had killed and would
kill again. He had to be stopped, because if Mick died at his
hand the man was sure to go after Maggie. Her danger had
come to him only in the last few seconds. He sensed that she
was in terrible jeopardy right at this moment—impossible,
of course, because of the protectors he'd sent to her. What
Nigel couldn't handle, Davis could. And Davis would call
on his entire tribe if need be.

Midler's descent into the mine was causing a shower of
rock and gravel to fall, and Mick readied himself to strike
the moment the man hit the bottom of the shaft. Midler's
attention would be on getting his weapon ready and turning on the torch. He'd never see the blow that would end his
existence! Silent as death, Mick moved toward the front of
the mine.

MAGGIE LANDED ON her feet and dragged off her goggles,
mask and scarf. The dust caused her to cough, keeping her
from using the flashlight for a moment. She bent over,
covering her mouth with her hands.

A rush of air was all that warned her of the missile that
had been sent toward her head. It missed and crashed into
the wall behind her. Maggie screamed, dragged her rifle off
of her shoulder and fumbled for the light.

"Maggie?" Mick's voice was hoarse, almost unrecog-
nizable. "Oh, my God! Maggie!" He stumbled forward
and fell into her arms, crying her name again before passing out in her embrace.

Morning found the group of seven—Nigel, Maggie, Davis, his three brothers and Mick—huddled toward the back of the mine. During the long night, Maggie had tended to her injured lover's hurts and when sunlight streamed down the shaft he was awake and in only moderate pain—physically, not emotionally. Emotionally, he was in agony.

Over and over he kept thinking about how he had come within a hairbreadth of killing her. Of destroying the woman he would love for all his lifetime. No amount of reassurance would soothe him, and she knew he was still struggling with his feelings of hatred and need for revenge.

Nigel passed around a canteen, and when they had all sipped at it he rose to his feet. "No sense waiting here," he said. "Davis, let's you, me and the men go trackin'. See what kind of reptiles the storm left for us."

"This is my fight, Nige," Mick said, his voice only a croaking whisper. "You get her back to town. We'll take care of any cleaning up needs doing."

"I do not believe this!" Maggie looked around at the stoical male faces. No one seemed to disagree with Mick. "He's been shot and he has a broken arm. He's not going anywhere but to a hospital."

"Maggie." Nigel's voice was kind, but firm. "If he leaves it like this, Midler's just gonna come after him again. And he might not have friends with him next time."

She lost what little remained of her temper. "The man *shot* him! Can't the police arrest him for that? What is this? 'A man's gotta do what a man's gotta do?' I won't let you people go on with this insanity!" She continued to rave, scarcely noticing when Davis and one of his brothers slipped out of the mine and disappeared up the shaft. "Mick," she pleaded. "You had a very close call. Can't you see you mustn't stay?"

Mick shut his eyes, wishing he could shut his ears. She was right, of course. He had no business being anywhere but in an emergency room. But a terrible sense of foreboding kept him from saying so. It wasn't finished, and it had to be or he would know no peace for the rest of his life.

He wasn't doing any killing, though. His near miss with her had taught him well and instantly. That she had found him was a miracle; that he had missed was one also. He opened his eyes and regarded her with all the love he felt in his heart and soul. "Look at me, love," he said. "And believe. I'm staying here until John Midler is hunted down and captured. Then he'll be turned over to the authorities. There will be no more killing. But I have to be—" Shouts from above ground interrupted him.

Maggie, still holding his hand tightly, nodded, indicating she had heard and understood him. Then she turned in time to see Davis almost falling down the shaft in his hurry to get to them.

"The land has worked," he shouted. "It took revenge for Ian! It took revenge for you!" He pointed at Mick, and Maggie's spine tingled while the hair on the back of her head seemed to rise. "The land!" Davis repeated reverently.

"What the bloody hell...?" Nigel looked at Davis, then at Mick. The big man's eyes were wide.

Mick stared at Davis. Then he nodded. "Where is it?" he asked.

"Near. Very near."

Mick started to struggle to his feet. Relief sent him strength. It was over. At last. All over. Maggie, her face a study in puzzlement and worry, helped him up. She understood, he was sure, with her heart, if not her mind. She would see. She would see. A powerful feeling of gratitude to his native soil flooded through him and he swayed into her arms.

"Oh, this is crazy," she fussed, but the fire was out of her voice. "You should lie here until they can send a helicopter for you. What is so important that you have to crawl out of here now?"

He straightened, his arm still around her neck. "The man who killed Ian is dead, Maggie. No one had to kill him. The land did it."

"What?" She stared, seeing something different and new and good in his eyes. His demons were gone, she suddenly realized. Mick O'Shay was a whole man again, a man without hatred.

"I have to see it, though," he said gently. "I hope you understand, love."

"She must see it, too," Davis said. "She is bonded to the land through you, Mick."

Mick looked at his friend. Through the night the story of how Maggie had felt his pain and led the party almost directly to where he had lain had unfolded. Mick believed, though he found it almost too fantastic to accept that she had grown so close to him she would experience that same mystical bonding he'd shared with Ian and Tad. He knew he would view Midler's corpse with a sense of justice done, but he didn't want her subjected to a horrible sight. "I'll tell her—" he began.

"No, you won't." Maggie straightened under the weight of his arm. "I'll see for myself. I don't know about all this 'land' stuff, but I will not be shielded just because I'm a woman. I have a right."

Davis nodded solemnly. "She does."

"I do," she repeated.

Mick looked at her, then smiled. "Then, let's go."

With Nigel's help they reached the end of the tunnel and stood at the shaft. Davis's brother was still at the top, and he lowered a rope with knots tied in it to make climbing easier. Maggie eyed Mick's injuries anxiously. He smiled again. "Don't worry, love," he said. I've climbed out of worse places in worse shape than this." He wrapped the rope around his good arm.

Then he stopped. "This should go up with us," he said, bending down slowly and picking up the chunk of rock he'd almost brained her with. "A reminder to me," he added, stuffing it inside his shirt. Returning to the rope, he started up with Davis close behind to help him. When Maggie got to the top, he was lying on the ground, the most peaceful expression she'd ever seen on his face. "We have to marry now, love," he said. She said nothing. Part of her wanted to shout "Yes!," but part of her still remained unsure.

The landscape was serene, a new layer of reddish dust and sand covering the harsh-angled rocks. The sky was a blue that rivaled the finest turquoise. They walked in a line, with Mick resting his good arm across Maggie's shoulders. Davis led the group; Nigel flanked it. They were, she thought, not unlike soldiers, weary after a battle, but victorious.

They did not have far to go. They were so near to the mine shaft, in fact, it made Maggie break out in a cold sweat to realize how close the line between life and death had been for Mick. Davis stopped and pointed. Mick drew her closer, and she heard a soft sigh escape his lips. The sight of Midler's body wasn't so bad. His hand clutched his chest, but his eyes were closed. Sand and dust covered most of him.

"Bloody right," Nigel said from behind them. "Bloody right."

The aborigines said nothing, but she could see in their eyes that they agreed with the earth's rough justice.

Mick looked for a moment longer, then turned and his knees gave out. He dropped to the sand and Maggie sank down beside him, crying out in alarm. Nigel strode over and lifted him up in his massive arms. "Time to head

home, lads and lasses," Mick said weakly. Maggie looked
as worried as he'd ever seen her. "Don't fret, love," he
said. "I'm just relaxed." He reached out to her, and the
piece of rock he'd hidden in his shirt fell onto the ground.

Davis, who was standing near, bent to pick it up. Maggie heard him utter an exclamation in a language she didn't
understand, but she saw Mick's eyes widen. Then Davis
showed him the stone. "It can't be!" her lover said, awe in
his voice. He laughed. "It just can't be!" She tried to see
what it was that excited him so, but he hid the rock inside
his shirt again, and no amount of teasing or nagging would
get him to show it to her.

CHAPTER EIGHTEEN

"HE DIED OF heart failure, Mick. Simple heart failure. The coroner's investigators, or whatever they're called over here, said they found medication in a small bottle buried in the sand not five feet from the body." Maggie massaged Mick's hand. "He must have gotten overwrought looking for you, taken out his pills and dropped them. Nature did the rest."

"Call it what you like," he said, easing himself around to a more comfortable position on the hospital bed. "With Turner now on her way back to the States in custody, it's all done. I feel as if I've been freed."

"You look it, too." She smoothed back a stray lock of hair from his forehead. Lines had disappeared from his face and he looked his age instead of years older. Not even the weathering caused by the sun and storms could erase the freshness she saw. And nothing could erase the love she felt. "In fact," she added softly, "you look wonderful."

He grinned. "So, have you set the date yet, love? I'm not feeling real patient, and they say I'll be out of here in a day or so."

"Mick, I do love you. More than ever. But we need to talk seriously about this marriage thing." She carried his hand to her breast and pressed it against her heart. "This has been an extremely intense and emotional time. But are we sure we—"

"Of course we're sure!" He sat bolt upright, a scowl on his face. "How much surer can two people be?"

"We had an unusual experience. That's true—some sort of miraculous mental contact during a terrible crisis, just like what you and Tad had during the avalanche. But is it enough to base a lifetime—"

"I'm not even thinking about what happened in the mine!" He grabbed her, managing to jerk her onto his lap with one arm. "I'm thinking about the way we worked together in your shop. The way we loved and fought and loved again, even when we couldn't live together." His green eyes took on a brilliant intensity. "I'm thinking about the home we established in Coober Pedy. How I could come home at the end of a hard day and find you waiting with food and love and caring. How you worked on your jewelry while I mined. Neither of us took anything away from the other's profession. In fact, I think we helped one another. Maggie, open your eyes. We've already started our life together, even without being married. I only want to make it official."

"Mick, let me down. If one of those linebackers you people call nurses comes in, we're both in deep trouble!"

He grabbed her chin with his left hand, roughly. "What's the matter with you? I don't understand! We've been through heaven and hell together. Why should you care if anyone sees us?"

"I'm..." She pushed away from him and got down from the bed. The window blinds were open, and she went over to stare out at the city. "I don't know, Mick. But I do know I need to do a lot of thinking before I give you an answer about marriage."

"Thinking? That's a damn lame excuse!"

She didn't turn and answer. Silence, deep and uncomfortable, filled the room. Mick tried to ponder the situation objectively. It was not easy.

After the rescue, Mick had been shipped to Adelaide for treatment of his injuries and Maggie's love and concern had kept her glued to his side. Once his recovery had been assured, however, she had seemed to drift away. Now that the excitement, uncertainty and danger was past, had she fallen out of love? The idea hurt more intensely than any physical injury he had suffered. "Talk to me, Maggie," he said, anger and anguish making his voice harsh. "Don't you love me?"

She continued to look out the window. "I said I do, and I meant it. I believe whatever happens, I'll always love you. But..."

Mick waited, his heart pounding.

She turned, her arms folded tightly across her chest, her own anguish obvious. "But we've been on such a roller coaster, Mick. Such highs and lows. I grew up seeing marriages that worked based on serene daily lives, on security and normal—"

"Normal!" The word exploded from him and he was out of bed before she could stop him. He captured the back of her neck and twisted his fingers in her hair so that she couldn't escape. "Nothing about us has ever been normal, Maggie Wellington! What we have is special—a very great gift!" He glared at her for a moment, then pulled her to him for a kiss that was passionate, demanding and punishing.

Maggie didn't resist. She didn't want to. No doubts could prevent her from desiring him. As his lips caressed her desperately, roughly, she cried, knowing her love would force her to let him go, let him return to the wild, free life he had known before meeting her. She would return to the quiet, sensible existence she had known previously....

"Maggie." He broke the kiss, but not his hold on her. "We've shared things few people ever will. Can you deny that your heart, your *soul* touched mine? That we experienced a dimension of oneness unique to most couples?" His eyes burned as if he had a high fever.

"No, I can't." She met his gaze steadily. "And I'm not afraid of that."

"Then of living in a cave the rest of your life? We won't. I told you a long time ago I wasn't going to mine for a living any more. I'll—"

"You'll what, Mick?" She put her hands on his chest and pushed. It did no good. "You'll come live in Sullivan Springs and just vegetate? Watch me work? Help Tad with his homework until he goes to college? Who are you? You're a miner, Mick O'Shay, and mining is what you ought to be doing. You need the hunt, the excitement, the highs of finding treasures, the—"

"I need *you*! The rest will work out. I know it!"

"I don't. I—"

"Mr. O'Shay!" The deep female voice made them both start and turn. A heavyset, red-haired nurse stood, frowning, in the doorway. "You've a nice arse, lad," she said, pointedly noting the open back of his gown, "but if it isn't back in that bed in one second, it's liable to suffer. Miss Wellington, perhaps you'd better leave."

"I . . . I was just going." She moved away from him. "Mick, I can't marry you."

"Get out." His expression was bleak, bitter and he clearly meant her, not the nurse.

"I love you."

"For all the good it does me." He went back to the bed and got in. "Maggie, get out. Leave me and don't come back unless you find your heart. I think you must have set it in gold somewhere along the line and stuck it in the back of your goddamn safe. I don't want a wife without a heart. I had that once, remember?" He closed his eyes.

Maggie hesitated, then bolted past the nurse. She kept her pace steady until she got outside. Then she ran and ran, heedless of the stares her headlong pace caused. She was free! He had given her freedom. Now what was she going to do with it? Was it a gift, one she could use to find the truth for herself? Or was it a curse, dooming her to spend the rest of her life regretting the words she had spoken? There had to be something she could do to find out! *Think, Margaret Wellington,* she commanded herself. *Think and find out what your heart and soul really want!*

"YOU JUST LEFT her there?" Patrick's fist slammed down on the table. "My God, man! Where were your brains? Where was your heart, damn you!"

"I didn't leave her. She left me!" Mick leaned forward, just as mad as the older man was. Madder, perhaps. He'd had days to nurse his fear and anger. "She all but told me to kiss off, then up and disappeared. I checked out of the hospital just hours after she left, and when I got to her hotel room, she was gone. Only this time, she's not traipsing around in the woods behind her house. She's truly lost, Patrick. Lost. I thought—"

"You thought she'd come home." Patrick sagged back on his chair. "Home. Mick, she doesn't have a home with me any more. Whether she thinks so or not, her home's with you."

"I know." The starch of indignation went out of him, and Mick sagged, too. The strain of leaving the hospital too soon had taken a toll on him. The agony of not knowing if his love was safe had nearly finished him.

The two men were seated in Patrick's kitchen. Less than an hour ago, Mick had burst into the older man's home, intent on surprising Maggie and dragging her off to the nearest altar, bound and gagged, if necessary. When he'd found she wasn't there and no one knew where she was, he had almost lost his control. Only the arrival of Davey and Tad from school had caused him to maintain an edge of sanity. After spending some time with his son, telling the boy everything and allowing the others to listen in, he'd asked for some time to talk to Patrick. A war counsel, he had said, was needed. Nell volunteered to take the boys out. It was the next to last day of school before summer vacation, and they would drive over to Sullivan Springs and celebrate by getting ice cream and attending a movie. After they left, the war really began.

"You didn't go back to Coober Pedy?" Patrick asked. "Why?"

"She hates it. It's the last place in the world she'd go. She doesn't fit the life. She's afraid she—"

"My daughter's many things, O'Shay. But she isn't afraid of anything. If she's shown fear, it's for you. Fear she'd do something to hurt or harm you. Did you tell her you wanted to live there?"

"No. In fact, I made the point I wasn't planning to mine. She didn't believe me."

"I don't believe you, either." The older man got up and refilled his coffee mug. "You got shot, broke your arm and maybe your heart, but you look better than you ever did when you lived here. You're a desert rat, Mick—meant for the mines, not the mountains."

Mick uttered a curse word quietly.

"What about that stone you found after Midler died?" Patrick sat back down. "I heard you tell Tad it was the opal to end all opals. The treasure of a lifetime. When he asked about the seam you found it in, I saw a gleam in your eyes. You're dying to get back and search for more like it, aren't you?"

"There can't be more like it. One of a kind, it is. I left it in San Francisco with the jeweler Maggie admires so much—the one who beat her out for first prize at the Exposition. He's making it into a wedding ring."

"For Maggie?"

"If she won't wear it, no woman will!"

"My God, but the two of you are stubborn idiots! You really do deserve each other. No other human should have to put up with you. You say the cops won't look for her in Adelaide?"

"They have a witness who heard me tell her to nick off— a nurse who was none too taken with me to start with. Maggie checked out of her hotel room herself, and the clerk said she was in good spirits. The cops see no reason why they should chase after a sheila who seems to know her own mind and whose lover was enough of a mug to—"

"I get the picture." Patrick stood again and started pacing. "And your friends in Coober Pedy?"

"She'd not go—"

"Damn it, man! You're a hunter. Don't you know to check every possible lead?"

"I did!" Mick stood now, regalvanized by anger. "I checked in San Francisco. Jeff put me on to all her old mates. No one has seen her since April. Jeff hasn't heard from her, and she used to write him when we lived—"

"In Coober Pedy. I know. He talked to me from time to time, and he said what she was writing made the place sound intriguing enough to make him want to visit. I can say the same. Her letters to me were all positive. She worried about you, but not the place."

"Then she must have lied to make you think she was all right." Mick turned and stared out the window. Spring had come to the mountains while they had been gone. There was no more snow except at the highest elevations. The grass was emerald green, the sky softly aquamarine and the air was clear as the sound of a crystal bell. In the corner of the yard and bordering the house, Nell's flowers were blooming in jewellike colors. It was beautiful. "She loves it here, Patrick," he said. "This is her home. I can't ask her to leave it. Wherever she is, she must know that. Her home—"

"Her home's where you are, you silly bastard." Patrick went over to the phone. "How the hell do you call that place long distance? It's a damn good thing you're a miner. You don't know beans about digging through facts, only rocks." His tone was harsh, but there was a decidedly humorous twinkle in his eyes.

MAGGIE WIPED DUSTY SWEAT from her face and the back of her neck with a handkerchief that was already rust-colored from previous wipings. Following the advice of her new friends, she had staked a claim on the mine where Mick had lain and as often as she could, she spent time down in the shaft, chipping away at the rock. Not many women mined, she had been told repeatedly by Trev, Nigel and Davis, but she was the claim holder, so work she had to.

It was certainly different from anything else she had ever done, but she had found, after her body had stopped screaming at her with newfound sore muscles at night, that the undertaking did have its rewards. The stones she'd dug so far were of high quality and she had already earned enough from selling her jewelry to maintain a comfortable standard of living here. Each week, however, she carefully set a generous amount aside for rent on Mick's cave. Someday he and Tad would come back. She would deed the mine over to him and pay him back for the time she'd spent in his home.

She moved her hand up on the small pickax and chipped at a likely looking section of rock. Over the noise she made, she could hear the soft murmuring of two of Davis's brothers talking. She had long since given up trying to get off to work by herself. She literally went nowhere without an escort, overt or covert. Mick's mates believed he would skin them alive if they allowed her to come to any harm, and no amount of talk could dissuade them. He was coming for her as soon as he could. That was the accepted wisdom.

Only why, Maggie wondered at least a hundred times a day, hadn't he come yet?

She had spent long hours examining her mind and heart before deciding to come back. Without Mick around to make her crazy or angry, her thoughts had finally come clear. She loved him with every fiber of her being, but if she was going to marry him, she had to know if she could be the wife he needed—if she could stand his life the way his first wife had not been able to. This was the biggest gamble she would ever take with her life, but she had to take it. She had checked out of the hotel without a word to him, thinking he would know she had gone home—not to her home, but to his. If she could learn to make it in his environment, maybe they did have a chance for happiness.

But weeks had gone by, and there was no sign of Mick. Maggie chipped away, dispiritedly. She had been cautious about giving out her location to anyone, not writing her dad or Jeff at all during this time. She wanted Mick to turn up one day and find her living his kind of life. Then, they could talk about marriage. Then, she could offer herself as a wife who would—

The pickax clinked instead of clunked. Maggie perked up and turned her light on the seam. An edge of opal winked out at her. Using the very tip of the tool, she worked until the precious stone fell into her hand.

"Good on yer, Mag," a familiar young voice said from right behind her. "Thatn's gonna have a lot of fire."

"Tad!" Maggie managed to stay in her skin, but only just barely. "Where did you come from?"

"Up there." The boy pointed toward the mine opening. "The lads let me come on down."

"I ... I mean, what are you doing here? In Coober Pedy?" Excitement ran like hot ice through her veins. "Is Mick ... ?"

"Oh, I'm here for a weddin'. Da said it was all right if I came. You know, school's out now in the States. We're all on summer holiday," Tad replied casually. "Mind if I look at the stone?"

She handed it over with fingers that shook. "Whose wedding, Tad? Where is your father?"

"Last I saw, with yours." He studied the opal. "Gonna be a good one when it's shaped and polished."

"Tad!"

His grin reminded her achingly of his father. "Oh, don't you worry. I ain't gonna keep it." He held out the stone. "Here."

"That's not what I mean, and you know it!" She curled his fingers back around the opal. "WHERE IS YOUR FATHER!"

"Up there."

"Ohmigod!" Maggie shot past the boy and scrambled up the rope ladder to the mouth of the shaft. Mick, her father, Nigel, Trev and Davis and his brothers were sitting in the shade of a rock outcropping, doing serious damage to a case of beer. She paused, half in and half out of the hole, not able to believe her eyes. Her heart, however, believed, and rejoiced.

Mick looked in her direction, tipped back his hat and smiled. "Hello, Mag. Want a wet, cold one?"

TWO HOURS LATER, the lovers lay entwined on the bed in the cool darkness of Mick's cave. Maggie had taken a while to properly greet the entourage from America, which included Nell and Davey as well as Jeff, and then had begged some time to discuss the imminent future with Mick. They had left the hotel where everyone else, including Tad, was staying and had walked hand in hand, without talking, to Mick's home. Before any conversation, Maggie had insisted on showering and showering had led to other things. Deprived for so long, they had fallen onto each other in a loving frenzy and had made up for the lost weeks with a vengeance. Not even the cast still on Mick's arm had stood in the way of their expressions of passion and love. Finally, however, they'd become sated.

"What's this about a wedding?" she asked, stroking a finger lazily across his chest. "Tad said that's why you're all here."

"Don't play dumb, Mag." He lifted her hand and kissed her palm. "It doesn't fit your image."

"Well, then. Why do you think I'd be willing to marry you now?" In the darkness she couldn't see his expression, but she knew he was smiling.

"Maggie, my love, whether you marry me or not, we're mated for life. We're just like the wolves or eagles or any other animal that has one love, one mate for all time. Try as we might to lose each other, we'd only end up sharing everything, including our thoughts and feelings."

"You took so long to find me, though." She rested her head on his shoulder. "I didn't know if you'd ever come— and when you did, if you'd want me."

"I thought you'd gone home." He twined his fingers in her hair. "I was so mad, I was nearly deranged. I was ready to drag you off by this silky stuff." His chest rose and fell as he took a deep breath. "I would have, too, if I'd found you hiding out in your little shop and workroom."

She raised herself up on her elbow. "You'd have been hard put to do so, Tarzan. If I hadn't wanted to be dragged, you'd have had a fight to end all fights on your hands."

"It would have been worth it." His hands cradled her face, and he kissed her.

Later, after Maggie had thrown on a robe and was fixing tea, she confessed, "I don't know that I really thought logically about coming here. It just seemed the right thing to do. It's your home, and if I was to be with you I thought I ought to learn to live here."

Mick, wearing only jeans, leaned against the counter and asked, "Why?"

"Because." She regarded him. His half-closed eyes were still smoldering with sexuality. "It's your home."

"Home is where the heart is," he quoted. "I went to find you in Sullivan Springs, where I thought your home was. Your dad opened my eyes in a hurry. He's a wise man at times. I believe his exact words were: Her home's where you are, you silly bastard."

She burst into peals of laughter, nearly spilling the hot water.

"So we figured you'd be where you'd figure I would be," he went on, ignoring her mirth. "And there you were, burrowing in the rock just like a proper mole. By the way, the opal you gave Tad is worth a small fortune. That's a rich, rich vein you've struck."

"Not as rich as the one I struck here." She set the mugs of tea down and walked into his arms. "If you're still interested, Mick O'Shay, I'll marry you and live here with you for the rest—"

"No, you won't."

His kiss cut off her unhappy protest, and as he kissed her, she couldn't understand why he was refusing marriage now that she was ready—and after he had apparently primed everyone to expect it. There was far too much joy and love in his caress for refusal.

"No, you won't," he repeated softly when the kiss ended. "Because we're going to live in Sullivan Springs for the rest of our lives. Your work is too important for you to be buried out here. You need to be where people can see the incredible charm and beauty behind your creations. I've applied for the papers to open a business there, Maggie. The mines in the mountains have enough treasures hidden for a man like me to spend forever exploring them. And I plan to set up the safest ones as tourist places. I could lead people into them and show them how to dig for the gold and stones. It could be an exciting life!''

"But only in the summer. Oh, Mick. I can't ask you to give this up. What would you do during the winter? Oh, we could come here then!''

"But—''

"Oh, don't you see? It could work—part of the year at the Springs, part of it here. And Tad could have the best of both worlds. He could choose if he wanted to go with us or stay with Nell and Davey and Dad. I think that would please him, don't you?''

His arms locked around her waist. "You'd do that for me? Live part of your life here?''

"You'd do it for me. Why not?'' Her arms went around his neck.

A slow smile, the happiest one she'd ever seen Mick O'Shay wear, spread over his face. "Then, Mrs. O'Shay-to-be, I expect we'd better plan on two weddin's. One for here, one for there. So no one's disappointed.''

"You're reading my mind again.''

He looked at her and drank in her beauty. It wasn't confined to her delicate features or the pale skin now reddened from exposure to the sun and heat. For him, her loveliness ran as deep as the farthest reaches of her spirit— as far as eternity, which was how long he intended to be with the future Mrs. O'Shay.

Maggie felt the power of his love as she gazed into his green eyes, remembering how their emerald fire had been the first part of him that had caused her heart to beat with excitement. Her love for him was as true as the purest gold and would stand all the pressure and pleasures and pains of time. They were meant to be together, after all!

THE WEDDING was to be held a week and three days later. Many of the miners and merchants who had befriended Maggie would take part in a jubilant outdoor celebration. It would be a far cry from a predictable, formal marriage.

Nigel produced and set up a huge tent and secured it against any but the strongest gusts of wind. Fortunately, the pleasant weather was bringing only balmy breezes, so the canvas structure was in no immediate danger. Acting as supply chief, with Jeff, Trev and Georgie as general factotums, he also arranged for food and enough beer to float a small navy. They even managed to scare up some flowers.

Nell bullied Maggie gently into a quick trip down to Adelaide for a proper dress. Perfectly content to be wed in jeans, Maggie protested, declaring that a fancy dress was hardly appropriate for the setting and situation. "I'm not a virgin, Nell," she said. "The whole community knows we've been living together."

"So?" Nell's expression showed she was determined. "This is the second most important day of your life. The first was when you were born. No matter what happens after this, you and Mick will be joined as one. Don't you think he'd appreciate it if you looked like a bride?"

"I suppose so." Actually, she doubted Mick would care if she came naked to the altar, just so long as she came.

She felt the same way about him.

A clergyman who traveled the Outback communities administering marriages, funerals and baptisms was rounded up to perform the official aspect of the event. Named only Reverend Ralph as far as Maggie could tell, he was a florid-faced man of indeterminate age who enjoyed the festive nature of the ceremony. He visited the couple the day before the wedding and asked, "Just how married do you two want to be?"

"Very," they replied in unison.

Ralph regarded them speculatively for a moment, then nodded and finished the beer Mick had given him in one gulp. "Done," he said, then burped.

Tad and Davey weren't much help, spending most of their time exploring and hanging out with Tad's old chums. They had rigged a sand sled for Davey so he could go places where the chair would have bogged down, and after a bit, both Nell and Maggie gave up worrying or fussing. The boys were young, healthy and inventive. They would be fine.

And Tad had started calling Maggie Mum.

Patrick, with Jeff's assistance, went about arranging the official, legal details, so no question of the veracity of the marriage could ever be raised: the Australian wedding would be the real one—the one in America only taking place for the benefit of those who hadn't been able to attend at Coober Pedy. They also made friends with Davis and his people, learning daily about a society so ancient it made their own culture look like one newly born.

In short, the time spent before the wedding day was fascinating and fruitful for all.

Maggie bowed to Nell's recommendation that she spend the night before the wedding at the hotel and stay out of Mick's sight until the actual ceremony. Her future husband surprised her by agreeing to the arrangement without argument. He and Tad, he said, were going to put their heads together and figure out where to dig another couple of rooms in the cave—a project that would commence once the honeymoon and trip back to the States was finished. Maggie suspected this was just an excuse for Mick to go off and have a bachelor bash, but she trusted his hand would be steady and his head clear in the morning.

Her new mother spent the evening lovingly helping Maggie prepare to look her best the next day. The affection between the two was further cemented as Nell confided how happy she was with Patrick and how confident they were that the future would bring fresh joys and challenges for them to face together as a couple and as a family. "It isn't everyone, you know," Nell said, as she prepared to set Maggie's hair, "who gets related suddenly to so many wonderful people. And just by falling in love with a man who has a rich heart. I love loving him and I love fighting with him. It's the way a strong marriage goes. I think you and Mick can look forward to the same."

Maggie laughed. Loving and fighting? They were already experts at both.

But it was comforting to hear from an older and wiser woman that life could be good with those two aspects of a relationship in balance. Maggie slept well.

At dawn, Nell woke her and preparations began. Because of the heat, the ceremony was scheduled for nine in the morning. Maggie tried to remain serene, but by the time she left the hotel on Patrick's arm, her heart was doing an entire gymnastics routine every three seconds.

"I've never been prouder," Patrick said as they settled into the back seat of the closed sedan someone had offered to drive the bride to the pavilion. "Happier, yes—when I married your mother and when Nell came into my life. But, honey, you have been such a fine daughter to me. Sacrificing and giving up so much for me when—"

"I didn't give up anything, Dad." She squeezed his hand. "Caring and loving don't call for sacrifice. I wanted to do what I did."

Patrick grinned, although his eyes were moist with emotion. "You're a good person, Maggie. I only pray Mick

O'Shay really knows what kind of woman he's going to be honored to have as his wife.''

Maggie said nothing. Her heart added a few intriguing twists to its athletic endeavors.

FINIS

MICK WAS STANDING under the pavilion, sweating bullets. It wasn't the heat getting to him, although the weight of the tuxedo he'd bought down in Adelaide was many times what he would ordinarily have worn on a day like this. And the high collar and bow tie was cutting painfully into his neck.

He was worried sick about Maggie. So often they had seemed close to uniting in harmony forever, only to be blown apart by their own tempers or unforeseen circumstances. Would the same thing happen today, now that they had agreed to take the final step?

He looked around at the assembly of his friends and family. Tad, his best man, had refused to wear a smaller version of his father's formal getup, but had yielded to a smartly styled suit that made him look at least eighteen. Several young ladies in the congregation were eyeing him with interest. Mick almost smiled. Maggie's crew were dressed up to the nines, and a surprising number of townsfolk had put on their Sunday best for the occasion. Nigel wore a clean outfit of safari tan, and his massive face had been freshly shaved. Davis and his brothers, honored guests, honored Mick and Maggie by their traditional attire. *Now,* Mick thought, sweating more heavily, *wouldn't it be a pretty pickle if she decided to duck this.* If she did, he decided, hunting the horizon for the dust cloud that would proclaim her approach, he really was going to go after her like a caveman!

"Relax, Da," Tad whispered. "Maggie's not gonna let you down."

"It's the clothes," Mick lied. "They itch."

"Yeah," his son said. Then the boy blushed as he caught the eye of a flaxen-haired sixteen-year-old lovely sitting near the front.

Mick sighed softly and thought how soon it might be that he would stand in Tad's place for him. Seventeen wasn't so far away for the boy, but Mick prayed his son would have better sense than to marry so young—better sense to wait for a woman like Maggie, one whose love and fire could complete his life, not burn it up. His feelings for her welled up from deep within, and he almost shouted aloud for joy when he saw the plume of dust that heralded the arrival of his bride.

Maggie was almost faint with nervousness by the time the car pulled up at the front of the pavilion. Patrick patted her hand, kissed her cheek and tried to hide it when he brushed tears away. She looked at him, tears in her own eyes, and nodded, understanding his unspoken words and unable to say a thing herself. He got out and came around to open her door.

Gathering the skirt of her wedding dress, Maggie stepped out onto the reddish, dusty ground and immediately, her nervousness vanished. She was home!

Meanwhile, Mick waited, resisting the urge to crane his neck and stare like most of the congregation. He'd see her soon enough, he told himself. *Be patient and have some dignity.*

Then the small band that had volunteered to play for the ceremony struck up a jazzy version of *Here Comes the Bride*, and Mick stared along with the rest of the people.

She was Beauty walking! He felt like going down on his knees and worshiping her, she was so lovely. Her hair, curled and glossy black, framed her face, the veil accent-

ing the sable silk. She looked straight at him with such love
in her eyes that he almost ran down the aisle and into her
arms. Her dress, a white confection of satin and lace, embraced her body and made him long to do the same. Soon
enough, he would!

Maggie forced herself to walk slowly and with proper
dignity by her father's side. Mick had never looked hand-
somer to her, standing there, waiting for her. She hadn't
believed her eyes when she had first seen him in a tuxedo,
but his dressing elegantly for this most important occasion
endeared him even more to her, if that was possible. When
she reached his side and left Patrick for Mick O'Shay, she
knew her heart had chosen the right path.

The wedding ceremony was everything Ralph had
promised. He quoted from the Scriptures, led the assembly in song and preached a short but eloquent sermon on
the joys and responsibilities of matrimony. Maggie absorbed every word, just as she absorbed the sensations
being so near Mick brought to her heart and body.

Ralph finally reached the part about the rings. Mick
grasped her left hand and took something from Tad. Maggie watched, entranced, as he slipped a ring onto her finger. The opal, surrounded by diamonds, blazed like a small
fire against her skin. Maggie had never seen the like of the
stone, but when she looked into Mick's eyes, she knew
where it had come from.

"The rock I nearly hit you with," he whispered, caressing her hand. "This was lodged in it. Now you'll wear it
always, so we can both be reminded that out of trouble,
happiness can come."

"I love you."

"I love and treasure you!"

Ralph cleared his throat. "Can we get on with it, please?
You've forever to talk to each other."

"Forever and a day!" Mick said. His arm went around Maggie's shoulders.

Minutes later, they were married. The assembly erupted into applause when Mick kissed her, but Maggie only heard the words her husband whispered: "Our forever will always be special, Mrs. O'Shay. Special and treasured. Don't you agree?"

She showed him she did, and the applause sounded like thunder.

Harlequin Superromance

COMING NEXT MONTH

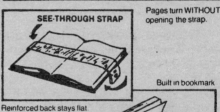